I9634660

ONE MISTAKE TOO LATE

A HAUNTING LOVE NOVEL
BOOK 3

AMANDA SIEGRIST

Copyright © 2025 Amanda Siegrist
All Rights Reserved.

This material may not be re-produced, re-formatted, or copied in any
format for sale or personal use unless given permission by the publisher.

NO AI TRAINING: No part of this material may be used in any AI training
of any kind. Without in any way limiting the Author's exclusive rights
under copyright, any use of this publication to "train" generative artificial
intelligence (AI) technologies to generate text is expressly prohibited. The
Author reserves all rights to license any and all use of this work for
generative AI training and development of machine learning language
models.

Every part of this material was human created, including all written words
and the cover.

All characters in this book are a product of the author's imagination. Places,
events, and locations mentioned either are created to help inspire the story
or are real and used in a fictitious manner.

Cover Designer: Amanda Siegrist
Photo Provided by: depositedhar/muntenesa.gmail.-
com/leolintang/depositphotos.com
Edited By: Editing Done Write

McCord Family Novel

Protecting You

Trust in Love

Deserving You

Always Kind of Love

Finding You

Dare You to Love

Mona & Mason

The Paranormal Chronicles, Volume 1

Perfect For You Novel

The Wrong Brother

The Right Time

The Easy Part

The Hard Choice

Psychic Love Novel

Exploding Love

Captured Love

Slaying Love Novel

Won't Let You Go

Doomed Love

Deadly Crazy

Evidence of Sin

Finding Redemption

Obsessed Hope

Short Stories

Paint By Murder

Follow Me, Sweet Darling

Sleighville Novel

Dashing Through the Fear

Here Comes Chaos

The Last Noel

Standalone Novel

The Danger with Love

Conquering Fear Novel

CO-WRITTEN WITH JANE BLYTHE

Drowning in You

Out of the Darkness

Closing In

1

He RAMMED *his shoulder into the door again, determined to get inside. Nothing would keep him out.*

"Stop it! Please stop!"

Nothing penetrated his mind other than getting inside the room. His senses were on high alert. The smell of blood. The pounding of her veins. Her erratic heartbeat.

Predator instincts were activated the moment he stepped into the house. That first whiff of blood. The initial beat of her heart. He'd gone from the front door to the bedroom in a second. The sole thing that stopped him from draining every last ounce of blood from her beautiful neck was a locked door.

Every time he hit the door with a hard thump, the loud echo of it filtered into the air. He didn't feel any pain. He didn't feel anything anymore. No warmth. No coldness. Nothing mattered but the need for blood.

"Open." Whack! "The." Whack! "Door." Whack!

He would get in one way or another. Why didn't she understand that? He would have her blood. The wonderful aroma filled his senses, urging him on in the intense blood lust he'd found himself in.

One more hit to the door, and the frame finally cracked. He paused, staring through the small opening to see his wife crouching in the corner.

He smiled, revealing his long fangs. Oh, sweet victory was near.

"Why are you doing this, Donnie?!" she shrieked as the door toppled to the ground with one last strike.

HE BOLTED UPRIGHT IN BED, shivering from the nightmare. The room was plunged in darkness, though if he opened the curtains he knew the sun would be shining brightly. Not that he could see the bright glow. It would kill him.

A glance at his clock on the wall told him he had another few hours before the sun would set. No time like the present to get up.

The first thing he and his friends had done when they purchased the house and property had been to vampire-proof it. Tinted windows, so that if the curtains failed them during the day, sunlight still would not penetrate inside. The last thing they needed was to be burned alive in their own home. On some rare days, though, he thought about removing that barrier and letting the sun fry him alive. The memories were...too much.

They had a top-of-the-line security system surrounding the property. Cameras all around the perimeter, along with a steel fence that was also charged with electricity to keep anyone out. Visitors had to stop at a gate and be buzzed in. Not that they had many visitors. Mason and Mona and the rest of the gang on occasion. But there were hunters out there they had to avoid. If one of them found them, they'd do everything in their power to get inside. To stake them through the heart. Or chop their head off. Being secure was a necessity for survival. Mona had also put a few protective spells on the property. They were as safe as they could be.

Their home was their escape, their safe haven from the world and everyone in it. Donnie hadn't felt truly safe in a very long time.

They were considered the enemy. Predators. Evil beings that needed to be eradicated from the earth.

He wouldn't disagree.

He'd done things in his life he was not proud of.

Of course, he'd had a master that tried to wield him into something he despised. It had taken too many years to escape, and another too many years to find redemption.

He was still seeking that.

It didn't take long to shower, dress, and ready himself for the evening. Joe was already in the kitchen when he strolled in.

"You look like shit," Joe said, eyeing him a little longer than he liked. "Another nightmare?"

He knew Joe wasn't wrong because he felt like it. He didn't need the obvious thrown in his face. Not even the nice suit concealed how horrible he looked. Not that that had been the reason he put one on. He always wore a suit with a vest. Dressing with confidence portrayed confidence. Some days he lacked that trait, so he needed to fake it as much as he could.

Ignoring Joe's prying, he headed for the fridge and grabbed a bag of blood.

"Donnie?"

He trembled at the sound of his name. The lone reason he reacted that way was the nightmare still echoing in the far corners of his mind. His wife screaming his name, begging him to stop.

Startled by the hand on his shoulder, he nearly dropped the bag in his hand. How had he not heard Joe approach? Well, to be fair, as vampires, they were light on their feet. No heartbeat to detect. Could move at the speed of light. Vampires could sneak up on another vampire with them unaware until it was too late.

"Talk to me. It's already bad enough Peter moved out—four months and counting. I don't want something coming between us too."

Yeah, that had been unfortunate when Peter moved back in with Mona and Mason. But he didn't argue. He didn't fight one of his best friends. They had a disagreement, and it wouldn't be solved until one of them caved. Currently, it was more in their favor than Peter's. Three against one. While he didn't like fighting with the three men he'd come to look upon as brothers, sometimes it was inevitable.

He was the oldest of the three. Maybe that's why they looked at him as their unofficial leader. But they'd been together for close to two hundred years and there was bound to be arguments every now and again.

He shook off Joe's hand, shut the fridge door—though he had wanted to slam it—and grabbed a glass from the cupboard. They might be vampires and survive solely off blood, but he'd be damned if he'd turn into an animal and drink it straight out of the bag. They used glasses or mugs as often as they could. To feel normal. To pretend they weren't monsters.

"Donnie—"

"Yes, Joe," he stated evenly, "I had another nightmare. I do not want to talk about it."

It was the same song and dance they played every time a nightmare hit him. He'd never give in, and Joe would never stop inquiring. Though the nightmares were not as frequent as they had been many years ago, they still popped up without warning.

"I talked to Mason. He wants our help on a case later tonight. Something to do with a hoard of goblins."

He took a large swallow before replying. The dark, heavy liquid filled his veins and soothed the ache he had every second of every day. It would maintain the urge for a while, but then he'd need another drink, another bag to tide him over. It was a never-ending battle resisting the urge that filled him up.

It had gotten easier as time went on. Compared to when he'd been turned, no one would be able to tell he even struggled. He was *that* good at hiding the pain he lived with daily. While Joe and the other guys didn't talk about their thirst either, he knew they struggled as much as he did. It was the way of life for a vampire. He doubted any vampire didn't grapple with the urge.

"I didn't realize there were goblins in the area."

"Well, it is a preliminary report from Bailey based on a sighting from Kade and Mason. They took a picture before they had to leave the area. She researched what she could. You know Bailey. She's gotten it wrong before, but she tries so hard."

Bailey was wonderful. A hundred-year-old ghost recently turned human, she had an adjustment going back to the living world. Especially when she'd been tied to one house for the entire duration of her spectral life. So many things had changed in the world for her to catch up on. She deserved a grace period.

But Joe wasn't wrong. She embraced the line of work Kade, her husband, had decided to jump into and enjoyed helping. Except she didn't always get things right. Last month they walked into a den full of lycans who weren't happy to have their land trespassed upon. She had told them the property was vacant. While the lycans didn't attack, it had been a tense-filled visit. Thankfully, Mason and Kade were the only ones who had stepped on the property. If a vampire had been with, he had no doubt an all-out war would've started. He didn't enjoy fighting other creatures unless there was no other choice. And killing another creature—well, he avoided that all costs.

His killing days were over.

"Maybe while we're at Mason's we can have another chat with Peter."

He drained the rest of his glass and set it in the sink. "Peter is not going to change his mind and neither are we."

"Look, maybe he's sort of right."

Wow. Donnie did not see that coming.

The argument all started when they left Mona's house one night. They all had felt the presence. The evil rising from the basement. Of course, evil lived down there. Mona had imprisoned her aunt, who had tried to kill her. Her aunt Marcella was a very powerful witch.

Peter wanted to vanquish her aunt once and for all.

Donnie, Joe, and George wanted to leave it alone. At least for now. When the time came, it would be Mona's decision how she dealt with her aunt.

Peter then suggested they should talk to her. Tell her about the evil they could feel. While Donnie wanted to do that, so much had been going on lately to even broach the subject. Not to mention—and his big reasoning for not doing so—Mona was already walking a tight line with her emotions. Struggling with being a witch and expecting too much of herself. One wrong word and she could go over the edge.

Hell, she'd stopped wanting to practice witchcraft after

the entire incident with Charly and a demon trying to kill her. Mona blamed herself that the demon had gotten so close to Charly. She had been the one to open the portal when they were searching for the person who had killed Kade's second wife. She hadn't closed it properly, which allowed Thomas—the man who had killed Bailey over a hundred years ago—to escape. To inhabit a druggie. Who then latched onto Charly, wanting to kill her. It had been a chaotic mess, and Donnie was grateful everyone came out of it unscathed.

While Mona had gotten over her fright at being a witch and was back to doing spells and learning everything she could, one wrong move and she could go backwards into a dark pit of despair.

Since they couldn't come to an agreement, Peter moved out and in with Mona and Mason. Peter agreed not to say anything to Mona—yet—but he refused to leave her alone in a house where evil was on the precipice of escaping. Donnie couldn't fault him for that. It had been a good idea. Someone—other than Mason—needed to be there to protect Mona. He'd informed Peter he agreed with that. Though Peter was still very upset with the three of them for not siding with him.

He wanted to tell Mason what was going on, yet he knew Mason wouldn't be able to keep it from Mona. Or if he did tell Mason and she found out he knew, she'd get angry at him for keeping secrets from her. It was an impossible situation, and Donnie hated being in the middle of it. He cared for Mona. Like an older brother looking out for his sister. He'd known her mother, and while he hadn't sworn to protect Mona, he'd took it upon himself to do so anyway when she rammed into their lives. Sometimes making decisions that affected someone in his family was the toughest thing he had ever faced. But, as the unofficial leader, he was tasked with making those difficult decisions.

"Donnie?"

Why did they always expect him to be the voice of reason? As if he knew better than all of them. More often than not, he felt like he failed at such a role.

Joe wanted his blessing to talk to Peter.

Donnie couldn't give it to him. Hell, it shouldn't be his decision whether Joe spoke to him or not.

"Maybe you should move in with them like Peter did. One more protector couldn't hurt."

"Marcella could escape and kill Mona."

And the notion Mona had to kill her own aunt could send Mona into a spiral they might not be able to get her out of. It was a rock meeting a very hard place.

Donnie knew Mona would never be able to harm her aunt. It's why she imprisoned her instead of killing her when she attacked. That would leave it up to them to take care of her aunt.

He despised killing another creature—or human. Not to mention, Marcella was a very powerful witch. She wouldn't be easy to kill. Not that he doubted his abilities. But he also couldn't guarantee everyone would come out of it unharmed.

"I'm not your keeper, Joe. You do what you have to do."

Then he walked out of the kitchen, done with the conversation. He was halfway up the stairs, on the other side of the house, when he heard Joe clear as day, even though he hadn't left the kitchen.

"I'm worried about Peter, but I can't leave you, Donnie. You can deny it all you want, but you're struggling. You've had that nightmare way too much in the past few months. You know that's not normal."

He wouldn't deny it. Wrestling with his nightmares had become more regular than he liked.

Of course, they started when the mess with Peter did.

Damn.

Fix one problem, and it would solve the other one.

Joe was right, and he hated to admit it.

Max: How's work?

Stella: Same as the last time you texted. <eye roll emoji>

Max: Attitude not necessary.

Stella: Neither is the worry.

YET, it never mattered where they ventured to, the worry always stayed. As did the attitude. Stella couldn't help herself. Of course, neither could Max.

"What's that?"

Stella set her phone facedown and looked up to see Detective Holstrom by her desk, eyeing one of her files. She flipped the folder closed, shielding his view.

No matter the precinct, no matter the city, all detectives were the same. All *male* detectives. Nosy damn busybodies who thought they could handle any situation better than a female. It irked her like nothing else.

"What that is, is none of your business."

A muscle in his cheek twitched, though he didn't say anything. Surprising, for a man. Usually they couldn't hold back, especially when she put them in their place.

She moved around a lot. Too much. But it was safer that way. Not to mention, she and her friends had work to do all over the world. People needed help everywhere, and staying in one place for too long was never wise.

Everywhere they went, she had to deal with assholes like the one before her. Meddling where they didn't belong. And she never held back.

"I'm sorry, Detective Waters. I didn't mean to pry. It's..." He eyed the folder. She could see a vein pop out in his neck, as if he were struggling with the urge not to flip it back open. "The marks on the body are...strange."

Yes, two tiny holes on a neck were strange. It had baffled the medical examiner. Though cause of death had been easily determined. Massive blood loss.

Because that's what vampires did. They sucked the blood of their victims until every last drop was gone. Which also created two tiny holes on the neck. From their very long fangs.

Of course, she didn't divulge her knowledge to the medical examiner, and she wasn't about to do so with Holstrom either. Most humans couldn't handle learning they weren't alone in the world. That creatures from movies and books were real and living amongst them.

"What's even stranger is the fact you're still standing in front of my desk like I'm going to continue this conversation."

He flinched, taken off guard.

Yeah, she had that effect on people. She never held back. And hesitating for even a moment could mean life or death. So being sharp with her tongue was a necessity. As were her skills in protecting herself.

"I apologize again." Then he walked away with his tail between his legs.

Or at least she envisioned it happening. She was new to the precinct, so she didn't know everyone very well—yet.

She always made it a point to figure everyone out. Who was her enemy. Who could be considered an ally. Holstrom had been a hard one to pin down. He worked alone as far as she could see. Didn't take shit from other people and expected people to do as he asked. He had also struck her as someone who didn't poach on another detective's work, so for him to stroll over to her desk and do so shocked her.

She knew this town had acquired some new residents they wouldn't like having in their midst. A coven of vampires. How many, she wasn't sure yet. But she'd find out. The easiest way to do that most of the time was to be right in the middle of things. Being a cop always put a person in the middle. She'd gotten good at solving crimes, even the non-creature kind. Something that made her proud to admit.

The case Holstrom had been spying on had just landed on her desk today. The crime scene hadn't yielded much. Other than a dead body. Vampires never left a trace. Even if they did—like DNA or a fingerprint—it would never show up in the system. They were dead. They didn't exist as people anymore. Some vampires were very skilled at hacking the system and creating new identities and wiping out old ones.

Most broke into places without leaving a mark. Unless they were a newly turned vampire, then they could make a huge mess. But most of the time, whoever turned them— their master—kept a close eye until they could be trusted to be on their own.

Her first victim, Laura Bertum, thirty-one years old, was found by her husband after coming home from a night shift. She'd been discovered on the kitchen floor as if she had gotten up in the middle of the night for a drink of water and had been surprised by a visitor. Or so it appeared.

The husband, Daniel, though he didn't say anything

about it, his expression had been leery about her state of dress. A negligee. Which gave Stella the impression his wife didn't wear those kind of things for him. Suggesting she had someone else over while he was at work. Stella couldn't determine if Laura had been alone when she was attacked or if her mystery guest had witnessed it and fled the scene. Even if the vampire had been alone, it wasn't an improbable situation. He would have focused on Laura and let the mystery guest get away. And the vampire could've gone after the person when they were done with Laura. All a vampire needed was a decent scent to hunt something down.

All in all, she didn't have much to go on. But it was a start. A sign a new coven of vampires had arrived in this town. All it took was a start for her to begin her quest.

Her phone pinged.

> Max: Are you visiting the crime scene again? I want to come with.

> Stella: Maybe.

> Max: <annoyed emoji>

Stella chuckled. Her non-committal response irritated him. Well, his constant texting all day long bothered her. He worried like an overprotective parent.

While he had good reason—something she didn't want to think about—she needed him to stop coddling her. She could handle herself.

Of course, as Max was a lycan, it would be useful to bring him with to the crime scene. He'd be able to pick up a scent as well as a vampire could. Both had a strong sense of smell. She loved to tease Max that he had an overly large nose even when not in wolf form. He hated when she brought it up.

Honestly, she didn't know if she would visit the crime scene tonight. At least, not right now. Going at night was risky. Sometimes, vampires circled back. Some liked the thrill of watching humans search for a culprit. Some assumed they'd get another meal out of all the activity. They weren't wrong. She'd seen too many cops get killed while working a murder scene. It was one reason she picked the occupation she did to hunt vampires. She could be in the mix of things and also protect the people trying to solve the crimes.

Violent creatures—like vampires—would classify her as a hunter. She didn't disagree with the terminology. Except she wasn't like the average hunter. Her sole purpose in life wasn't to vanquish every vampire on the earth—though it was a good one to have. Her purpose was to save as many humans as she could. It didn't matter what kind of predator she was stalking. Nasty warlock. Evil witch. Rogue lycan. If they hurt a human, she stopped them, and sometimes she had to kill them. As a detective, it made it easier to do so a lot of times. While humans were ignorant of the world they lived in, they helped more than they realized in tracking the monsters down.

First things first, she was hungry. Whatever she decided to do, eating would happen before anything else. Then she'd decide if a visit to the crime scene was next. If so, she'd tell Max to meet her there.

Her stomach grumbled.

Duly noted.

Commence eating now.

She packed up the files she'd work on at home. One unfortunate part of the job, in order to maintain appearances, was she had to work all cases, including non-creature kind. While it was good to get a normal criminal off the street, her time would be better spent focusing on the creatures themselves. But it was what she signed up for when she decided to hunt via the detective route.

Making sure her desk was clutter-free and everything out of nosy hands, she walked out of the office. Cool, fresh air hit her face the moment she stepped outside. A bit chilly for the middle of May, but the weather was always finicky in her eyes, no matter the city, state, or country she happened to be in.

She took a step forward and froze. Her senses tingled as the hair on her arms stood at attention.

Turning her head to the left, her mind reeled at the picture before her.

A vampire.

Right here at the precinct. In plain sight.

Standing very, very close to Holstrom. And the vampire didn't look happy.

Shit.

2

"Wow. I didn't expect you to get here so fast."

Donnie forced the smile he wanted to produce to stay hidden. Detective Holstrom wouldn't take it kindly if he thought he was mocking him.

Nor would Donnie mention he'd been in the area so that's why it hadn't taken him long. He might be fast, move like a blur, but he wasn't as speedy as Holstrom thought. Why ruin the illusion?

"What's the problem? I do have to make it quick. There's a goblin issue we need to address."

Holstrom's eyes bulged out. "Goblins? Seriously?"

At his astonishment, it was impossible for Donnie to hold in a short laugh. "I know you're new to this...world, but there are many, many creatures out there."

Holstrom let out a heavy sigh. "Do I need to worry about running into a goblin? Are they dangerous?"

"They're mischievous creatures. They like to attach themselves to a household. Create chaos and revel in it. Some even believe they are there to help parents discipline their children. Reward them when they behave well and provide punishment when they are disobedient."

Donnie swallowed another laugh that wanted to break through at the way Holstrom's eyes continued to bug out.

"And how do they pick the house they want to...create chaos in?"

Donnie shrugged. "I've never asked one before." Then he revealed a friendly expression. At least he hoped it bestowed the friendliness he meant to portray. While they didn't always get along, he wasn't the enemy. He didn't want Holstrom to believe that. "There was a reason you called, detective."

Holstrom jerked his head as if clearing the disturbing thoughts that had entered. "I think there's another issue we need to address. A..." He swallowed hard, his Adam's apple bobbing. His heart rate even sped up.

Though, it didn't take a vampire to know the man was nervous. All the obvious signs were displayed clear as day for a normal person to see.

"Yes? A, what? Please continue."

"A vampire problem."

Donnie cocked a brow, surprised, yet not. He wasn't naive enough to think all vampires were good. In fact, he knew most were monsters that ripped apart humans without blinking an eye. It was just the way of the world.

Vampires were predators.

Humans were prey.

Even he, at one time, had fed on humans. When he gained control of his impulses, he turned to animals. Then times changed and he was able to avoid hunting at all costs and buy bags of blood. Like a civilized...person.

"Do go on, Holstrom." He waved his hand for him to continue. Suspense wasn't something he was fond of.

"There's a dead body."

Anger erupted like a volcano. His hands fisted, his lips curling in disgust, which also displayed his protracted fangs in full view.

Holstrom backed up a step.

He knew his eyes glowed a bright red as well. That's what happened when his vampire senses went on full alert. He wasn't angry at Holstrom, though the man thought otherwise. His heartbeat that had been thumping increased its pace so much that if he didn't calm down he'd give himself a heart attack.

No, it wasn't Holstrom that upset him. It always set him on fire when another vampire stepped into his territory and thought they could hurt anyone. The humans he lived around might not be aware he existed, but he tried to keep them safe as best as he could. Somehow, he had failed.

"Detective Holstrom, do you have a moment?"

Donnie froze at the sound of the melodic voice coming from his left and let out an even breath to get his equilibrium back to normal.

Then he turned to the woman next to them, hoping he'd calmed down enough that his eyes weren't glowing. She didn't flinch once when their eyes met.

There weren't many times in life when he was caught by surprise. A handful he could recollect. This moment could be added to the short list.

She was a vision of beauty.

Long blonde hair, though it was up in a ponytail, so he wasn't sure of the true length. He could already imagine his hands running through the luscious locks as she was spread out on his bed. Not a picture he normally envisioned when he came across human women. They were off-limits. By a long shot. Nothing good ever came from lusting after a human. Which made his sex life not very active. Most times vampire women were too much trouble. So he rarely dabbled with them either.

Green eyes, so big and beautiful they sparkled like a precious gem even in the still of the night.

Wide, red lips that didn't display an ounce of warmth, at least not in his direction. But they looked kissable nonetheless. He couldn't stop imagining what it would be like to touch his lips to hers.

A curvy body with breasts that he knew would fit perfectly in his hands. He only needed to reach out to see how well.

And the scent of her blood. It filled his senses like an aphrodisiac. It was a fragrance he'd never inhaled before in his entire vampire life.

While that one thing should've surprised him all by itself, it was her heartbeat that also gave him pause.

Steady. Normal. A smooth rhythm.

He could tell she was pissed—not sure what about—but her heartbeat didn't betray her in the slightest that her fight mode had been activated. He would've thought she knew he was a vampire, except she was human. No detection of a creature of any kind lit up his senses. So why was she upset? And why was the anger directed toward him?

Holstrom cleared his throat, which pulled Donnie out of the long stare he'd been ensnared in.

"Of course, Detective Waters. Yes, of course."

Donnie chuckled at Holstrom's obvious nerves. Was the man afraid of him, or the woman?

"What's so amusing?" she spat in his direction, never even looking at Holstrom.

Not many people called him out, especially for something so trivial. It did nothing but make her even more attractive. Confidence was a huge turn on.

He despised when people were afraid of him. It confirmed what kind of monster he was.

"You have Detective Holstrom rattled. The man never repeats himself. I find that humorous. Or maybe I rattled him." Donnie glanced at Holstrom, winking. "I do apologize, my friend."

Holstrom snorted. "Why don't I believe that apology?"

Donnie feigned indignation by placing a hand on his chest. "It was from the bottom of my heart. Might I point out, you don't believe my apology, but you didn't say a word about me calling you a friend. I feel like we're making headway in this relationship."

Holstrom let out a huge breath, shaking his head. "I guess we are. I mean, I called you, didn't I? You came without issue."

Donnie inclined his head. Nothing else needed to be said. And not in front of the strange woman that, if his heart still beat, he knew it would be flying off the rails with energy.

"So all is well?"

Donnie turned to the woman—Detective Waters, he believed he heard Holstrom call her.

"Of course," Holstrom replied without hesitation.

Interesting. She'd come over to protect Holstrom.

From him.

She'd seen his anger and stepped into action. The one question he wanted to know was did she know what he was? That he could tear them both apart in under ten seconds.

"Was there something you needed, Detective Waters?"

If Donnie could hear the annoyance in Holstrom's voice,

then so could she. He'd better tread with care. She didn't appear to be a woman one should mess with.

She ignored the question and kept her full attention on him. Her beautiful emerald eyes mesmerized him. Damn near was putting him in a trance. One word and he'd do her bidding.

Which was odd!

Foreign!

Nothing—and nobody—controlled him.

"How do you know, Detective Holstrom?"

He glanced at the man to get his control back. When he returned his gaze toward her, the power she wielded came back in full force.

"I believe we established we're friends. Before we made that distinction, I'd say acquaintances via mutual friends. Mason Stewart and Mona Cordero. They run a private investigation company, and I help them on occasion. As does Detective Holstrom."

"Oh, so he called you about a case."

She didn't phrase it as a question, but he didn't want to respond regardless. He sensed whatever he said would be the wrong answer.

Holstrom cleared his throat. "Yes. Yes, I called him about a case. Mason needs help on one of his cases."

Smooth. Not lying, but also not telling the full truth. Neither were related.

"Well, I'll leave you two be." Then she turned her penetrating stare at Holstrom. "Let me repeat myself, Detective Holstrom. Because I think I need to. Don't step on any of *my* cases."

Before he could respond, she swiveled around and stalked off. Donnie couldn't tear his eyes off her. Her scent lingered in the air even when she pulled out of the parking lot.

A snap of fingers made him flinch.

Him.

Flinch.

At a tiny sound.

What had the woman done to him?

"I have never seen you so..."

Donnie's entire body went rigid, and he knew his eyes glowed red once again. While Holstrom stiffened himself, he didn't retreat.

"Do go on? So, what?"

"Befuddled by a woman."

Thundering laughter filled the cool, night air. "Such fancy words, detective, for such a stern man."

"Me thinks you protest too much."

His smile vanished.

Holstrom retreated that time by one step.

"Why do I sense the dead body you were talking about before we were interrupted is not your case?"

"You're very smart."

For a vampire were the words Holstrom left off that sentence. He'd let it slide. This time.

"It's Detective Waters's case. I saw a picture of the deceased woman while passing her desk. Two tiny holes on the neck. She shooed me away right away without even letting me ask one question. She might not like me, but I won't let one of my co-workers walk into a deathtrap. If it's a vampire who's the perp, then I need to help her. We need to take care of the problem."

Rage boiled inside, his gut clenching at the mere thought of her getting injured, especially by a vampire. If any vampire would suck her blood, it would be him!

No!

No, his days of doing that were done.

That wasn't what he meant to think. At all.

"Very well. I agree. This is either a sign there is a rogue vampire in the area, or we have a coven on our hands."

"Why does coven sound horrible? Like, a big swarm of vampires?"

Donnie chuckled. "A rogue vampire would be much easier to deal with."

"And how do we deal with this?"

Donnie inhaled, shivering at the way the remaining scent of her still filled the air. He needed to see her again.

But first, yes, they needed to deal with this issue.

"How do we get the location of the crime scene? Detective Waters—what is her name? Her first name?"

He wanted to wipe the stupid grin off Holstrom's face. "Stella."

Stella.

An exquisite name for such a dynamic woman. He'd never been flooded with so many emotions before when it came to a woman. He had no idea why he was now. And a human woman, no less.

"I imagine Stella didn't leave her case files in the building. She strikes me as the kind to keep things close to her." Too close, if he had to guess.

"This isn't the dinosaur ages anymore, Donnie. Everything is also digital."

His eyes narrowed and Holstrom got the hint he didn't appreciate his sarcasm. "I'll call Mason and tell him he's on his own with the goblins. You get an address. We have a vampire to track."

THE DOOR SLAMMED as she entered the house. The noise, despite being the one to create it, made her jump.

Max was in her face before she could even set her bag down on the small bench in the foyer.

"What's wrong?"

A wry smile appeared. "Everything is peachy keen. Now why would anything be wrong?"

"Umm, you slammed the door." Max threw a hand toward said device.

Yes, a tactical error on her part. Max could be like a dog searching for a bone when he wanted to be.

Relentless.

"The wind did it."

But she wasn't going to admit she did it on purpose. No way!

Max rolled his eyes as he followed her to the kitchen. She rummaged through the fridge, trying to ignore the intense stare on her back. He wouldn't give in until she addressed the issue. All she wanted to do was eat, relax, and go to bed. The most she could hope for was the eating part.

"Stella..."

She huffed because she could and it garnered another eye roll out of Max, which she took extreme satisfaction out of.

"Same old shit, Max. Other detectives trying to poach my work. Men!" This time she didn't care she slammed the microwave door. That should give him a message he couldn't misinterpret.

Men needed to mind their own business.

When she turned back toward the island that separated them, setting her plate of leftover roast beef meal down, Max had the grace to wince. His features softened, and she could see the apology in his eyes before he spoke it.

"I'm sorry. I didn't mean to jump in your face the minute you got home."

Her brow rose, pointing a meaningful glare in his direction.

"Okay." He offered a meek smile. "I didn't mean to bother you all day either with text after text. I hate not having anything to do."

That wasn't true and he knew it.

They all had a part to play in their endeavors.

She worked as a detective, getting as much information as she could on any crimes that screamed it was creature related.

Giselle handled the technological side, creating new identities for them when necessary. Hacking into systems when the need arose. Keeping them safe in their home with a top-of-the-line security system. It also helped she was a witch, preparing potions and casting spells like a pro.

And Max was the muscle. The bodyguard. The man who sniffed out trouble without breaking a sweat. Being a lycan helped him in so many ways to fulfill his role in their tight-knit group. For the past week, since they had arrived in town, he'd been doing patrols, searching for anything out of the ordinary.

Case in point: the new murder that landed on her desk today.

She knew it bothered him he hadn't found the coven's doorstep before an innocent human had been killed. But he wasn't a god. He couldn't prevent every death. None of them could.

"We will go to the crime scene together. I promise," she said between bites.

"Tonight."

Stella never took orders well. Especially from men.

While Max was more like a brother than anything else, it still irked her when he tried to exert any sort of control over her. He had a knack for doing it often.

"Not tonight."

He crossed his arms. "Yes."

Her fork clanged to the plate, only half of it consumed. She'd lost her appetite. Just like that.

"I need to take a shower. By the time I get out, hopefully you're over," she waved a hand in front of him, "whatever this is."

She stalked out of the room, not even sure why she was arguing about something so small. They *did* need to visit the crime scene together. The sooner, the better. Losing the scent of the vampire was not something that she wanted to happen.

Yet, she couldn't understand why she was balking at the idea.

She sensed tonight wasn't a good time to go. And when her senses pinged like they were, she always listened to them.

The hot water felt like heaven as the first spray hit her. It hadn't been a necessity to shower, but sometimes to avoid an argument, she ran straight to the shower. It was as good excuse as any.

She didn't need to wash her hair, though she did lather her body with soap. Then, when all done, she stood there, letting the water soothe her rattled emotions.

The longer she stood there, the more it made her mind veer to the vampire she'd met tonight.

A vampire whose name she didn't know.

It occurred to her in the brief exchange they had, he never offered his name, Detective Holstrom didn't provide it, and she never asked. It bothered the hell out of her. She wanted to know his name.

She hadn't known what would happen when she interrupted them, but what had entailed surprised her. He had seemed...friendly. For a vampire.

In truth, she had never stopped to chat with one before. It was either killing them or ignoring them because they weren't deemed a threat. Though the latter rarely happened. Not many vampires were good. They killed people because they needed the blood to survive.

But the vampire tonight...well, he seemed...good.

She shivered at the thought. Under the spray of hot water.

Holstrom hadn't appeared frightened by the vampire. Did he even know he had been talking to one?

Her hand paused on the faucet.

Maybe he had.

He'd made a point to stop at her desk and ask about the one file she cared about. The one where a vampire killed a woman. Was it possible Holstrom knew they existed? That he was friends with one? That he knew what had killed the woman?

Drying off, the thoughts swirled through her mind. So many she nearly fell stepping out of the shower.

She needed more information. She had to get to the bottom of this. How much did Holstrom know? What part did the vampire play in all of this?

His name!

She needed his name more than anything. It was an obsession she could feel building in her veins. She'd go crazy if she didn't know it soon.

That annoyed her. She never let anything distract her, and that's what this vampire was doing.

Distracting her!

In all the ways. Not just not knowing his name.

The way he stared at her. The way his dark-green eyes saw more than what stood in front of him, as if he glanced all the way to her soul. Saw all her secrets. Saw all her desires.

He had affected her in a way she couldn't remember ever feeling.

It disturbed her.

Instead of putting back on the nice pantsuit she wore to work, she dressed in an old comfy pair of dark jeans and a black T-shirt. A black hoodie went over it. To round out the wardrobe, she threw on a pair of black tennis shoes. The theme for tonight was black—to match her mood. Deciding she didn't want to waste time drying her hair, she threw it into a ponytail. Of course, she used a black pony holder as well.

Then she grabbed her keys and phone and nearly made it out of the house when a stern voice stopped her.

"Where the hell are you going?"

She turned around. "I'll text you the address to the crime scene. Take Giselle with you and see if you can track the vampire. I have something else I need to check out."

Max crossed his arms. His usual stance when he didn't like something she said. "And what would that something else be?"

"None of your business."

Then she slammed the door for extra measure.

3

———

DESPITE TRYING HIS HARDEST, he couldn't hold back his smile at times. Holstrom was a conundrum. Determined to follow him every step of the way as he tracked the scent of the vampire. But also scared shitless. His rapid heartbeat was a dead giveaway. Donnie was astounded by his bravery, but it wasn't necessary for Holstrom to join him. If he did come across the culprit, Holstrom would be useless. In fact, he'd be a distraction. While he didn't point that out, he should've. Charly would never forgive him if something happened to Holstrom.

And he'd never forgive himself.

They might not be friends—though he considered Holstrom one—but he was a part of their group. That meant Donnie would protect him with his life. He'd protect all of them to the death.

The husband of the victim had been home when they knocked on the door. Which had been a very good thing. As a vampire, he needed permission to enter someone's home. Otherwise, nothing on this planet would allow him to enter. Not even a spell. The distraught husband barely looked them in the eye as he waved them in. There hadn't been much to examine in the house. The crime scene crew had done their job well. That wasn't the reason they had come either. He was there to hunt.

He detected one vampire scent. That didn't necessarily mean anything. Not until he found the vampire. When Holstrom asked Donnie if the woman had been alone that night, no other humans with her, he hadn't been able to give a concrete answer. With the amount of police that had entered the house, it was impossible to know. Too many scents. Thankfully, creatures carried a different aroma than humans, so he was able to pinpoint the vampire's movements. They didn't stay long and followed the path the vampire fled that night.

It brought them to an abandoned warehouse not more than twenty minutes from the victim's house.

But no vampire.

The scent had disappeared.

"Why would he come here?"

Donnie shrugged. He couldn't read minds. Though he kept that sarcastic comment to himself. Just because he was a vampire didn't mean he knew how all of them operated. His species were like humans. So different in every way, each having their own personality.

"It doesn't look like anyone lives here or has been hiding out here." Holstrom walked around the area, his expression one of defeat. "I don't get it. What else do you smell?"

A lot of nasty shit. Too much.

"It's an abandoned warehouse, detective. I smell a lot. Homeless come and go. Too many scents to differentiate from another. I have a strong sense of smell, but I'm not perfect."

Holstrom's entire posture fell, as if the weight that had been crushing him finally took him down.

In that moment, he wanted to be perfect. He wanted to give Holstrom the answers he sought. He wanted to be a hero.

"Damn it!"

Yes, he felt that sentiment. Down to his bones.

Perhaps they—

He froze, his ears perking as he strained to listen. He knew his eyes glowed red as well. Especially when Holstrom backed up a step.

Now was not the time for the man to be terrified of him. He'd gone on full alert because he'd heard a car stop near the door they'd entered. Then he heard the car door shut with a quiet click.

It was the familiar aroma that had him relaxing before the door to the warehouse even opened.

"Detective Waters is here."

Holstrom frowned and before he could respond, the door opened.

Donnie knew he shouldn't look in her direction, knowing whatever spell she had over him would hold him captivated, but he couldn't stop himself.

They made eye contact. He couldn't tear his eyes away. For a brief moment, neither could she.

Then Holstrom broke the spell.

"Detective Waters, what are you doing here?"

She pinned Holstrom with a strong glare. "I'd like to ask you the same thing."

Holstrom's brows drew even lower, the confusion clear in his eyes. "Why?"

"Are you going to play dumb with me? As if you didn't listen to me? I told you to stay away from my case." Then she whipped her gaze toward him. "In case it wasn't clear back at the precinct, that includes you."

The last thing he wanted to do was upset her further. He felt like he was walking in a mine field. One wrong word and he would explode.

"My apologies." He bowed his head in sorrow.

She flinched as if surprised he apologized. It had also been an admission they were stepping on her case. He didn't want to lie to her. He might be a monster, not of his choosing, but he had principles he lived by. One was to always be honest, even in the face of death. This moment felt like a life-or-death situation. He couldn't figure out why he sensed that, but he did.

"What makes you think we're here because of your case?" Holstrom asked.

Oh, the poor detective. The man didn't know when he'd entered quicksand. He was about to sink and would go down fast.

"Your *friend* admitted as much. He was wise enough to admit his mistake. Yet, you're not."

"Look, Detective Waters, I—" Holstrom stopped speaking when she stalked to him, stopping inches from his face.

"You know what I don't like? I hate men who think they can solve anything. I hate men who think they're stronger, they're smarter, they know better. I could knock you to your knees in less than a second and you'd be at my mercy, Detective Holstrom. Would you like to see that happen?"

He was in love.

This woman had not only captivated him in ways he couldn't understand, she'd made him fall in love without even trying.

The dominance she displayed.

The confidence.

The beauty that flushed across her face as she threat-ened—and would follow through—was utterly attractive.

And with a solid, steady heartbeat.

There was no fear in any part of her body. She knew what she was capable of and she would deliver.

"No, I would not." Holstrom swallowed hard, his heart racing even faster than when they tracked the vampire to this place. Smart man, giving in.

"Can I say one thing?"

Or not.

Holstrom had a death sentence. He was trying to die tonight.

"Please?"

Stella's lips twisted upward, as if enjoying the way he begged. Then she nodded.

"You're going to think I'm crazy."

"I already think a lot of things about you and none of them are good. Crazy won't faze me."

Holstrom glanced at him, and Donnie knew in that moment things were going to turn even worse. He tensed, but forced himself not to go into vampire mode. If she saw his red eyes or fangs...

"I think your victim was killed..."

Do not do it!

"By a vampire."

Welcome to crazy town.

Not many humans could handle the knowledge of the paranormal world. Holstrom might've jumped in with both feet, barely causing a splash, but the man had his moments. It had taken him months to even say the word vampire or witch, always trying to avoid speaking such a simple word. At times, Holstrom still struggled with some of things they came across. Stella seemed like the type of person—

"Yeah, I know. And your friend is one as well."

She turned in his direction. They stared at one another. Her heartbeat was still steady and normal.

He thought he had her pegged, yet she had shocked him once again.

Holstrom stepped around her, coming closer to him. "He didn't do it."

Stella frowned.

Well, that was a surprise. Holstrom was coming to his defense. Maybe they were friends. Of course, he didn't think the man would turn on him. This wasn't the first time they'd worked together on a case. He figured Holstrom had to trust him a little bit.

"Not all of them are bad. He's helping me find the vampire who did this."

Donnie knew he should say something, but for once in his life, he was speechless. He didn't know what to say. He was still walking through the mine field. They were everywhere. He didn't want to explode. Part of it was Stella and the other part was Holstrom shocking him.

"I'm sorry for stepping on your case. I am. But when I saw those marks on that woman, I called Donnie. I would never let one of my co-workers get hurt or killed by a monster like that." Holstrom tensed. He felt Holstrom's eyes on him, but he couldn't drag his gaze away from Stella. "Not that I think you're a monster, Donnie. I didn't mean it in that way, indicating you're one too. I meant—you know what? I'm going to stop talking."

Wise, wise man.

The hole he started to dig would've gotten larger. He knew what Holstrom was trying to say. It didn't negate the fact he *was* a monster. There was no way to get around that. He had killed and, if provoked enough, would kill again.

A distinct odor wafted under his nose. It was the only thing that could've tore his gaze from hers.

"Get behind me." He shoved Holstrom toward Stella and blocked them both.

What he wouldn't give to have Joe, George, or Peter with him. While Holstrom and Stella both had their weapons, creatures usually required more than just human tools to take them down.

He put his arms out as if needing to show them the invisible line they shouldn't cross. As long as they stayed behind him, all should be well. When the moment was right, he'd give the order for them to run.

The door opened.

A lycan and a witch stepped over the threshold.

His eyes glowed red as his fangs lowered.

Stella was beyond words.

This vampire...

One she didn't even know and had been nothing but aggressive with stepped in front of her to protect her.

Against her friends.

She wanted to laugh out loud at the picture before her.

Though she stood behind him, she knew his eyes glowed red and his fangs were at the ready.

Max stood next to Giselle, not having stepped far into the building when they noticed them. She knew Max was seconds from morphing into his wolf form. He would attack and chaos would ensue.

She couldn't allow that to happen. As much as it pained

her, they were on the same side. She saw that now. While she didn't like people butting into her cases, she appreciated Holstrom's need to keep her safe. If she hadn't been aware that vampires existed, he would've been a lifesaver. Literally.

"Come closer and you die," Donnie growled, his hands still out wide.

Oh, and to know his name. When Holstrom had mentioned it so casually, warmth filled the pit of her stomach. Such a ridiculous thing, but it brought immense joy. It suited him. A strong, solid name, but old-fashioned. It made her wonder if it was short for something. The nice suit he had on with a dark-blue vest gave him that old-fashioned vibe. Not many men wore that kind of suit any longer. Sure, the jacket. But not the vest.

"Vamp, you will not live to see another sunrise," Max spat back.

Shit!

Things were about to hit the fan.

"Everyone, stop!"

Donnie's posture didn't relax but she saw him twitch at her bellow. Max couldn't see her as Donnie stood in her way, but she knew he would listen to her directions.

Hopefully.

They hadn't exactly parted ways this evening on the best of terms.

She reached out and touched Donnie's hand. A flash of desire hit her fingertips. Like a lightning bolt came out of nowhere. Instead of snatching it away like her instincts told her to, she pushed down. Guiding his hand to his side.

Then she let go and stepped forward so she was even with him.

"Stand down, Max. They're...on our side." She nearly said friends, but she didn't consider Holstrom her friend.

And a vampire? No, she'd never been friends with one of them either.

Max's left eye twitched, but he didn't soften his stance. If anything, he bolstered it. He was still seconds away from turning.

"Get away from him, Stella," Max said with clenched teeth. "I tracked his scent from the crime scene."

Holstrom moved around Donnie as well, forming a line with them. "Well, because that's where we started to track the actual vampire who killed that woman. Of course you would track it here because that's where we tracked the original vampire to." Then Holstrom leaned forward and looked at her. "How did you find us?"

That wasn't a secret she was ready to share.

She felt Donnie relax next to her. The move surprised her, especially when Max still looked ready to fight to the death.

"You appear to be Stella's friends. I mean no harm to you. We are on the same side." Donnie's smooth tone washed over her like a light breeze on a warm sunny day. And the way he said her name. Intoned with such tenderness. Who was this vampire? Why did he affect her so?

Max didn't relent.

Stella rolled her eyes as she took a few steps forward. "You better calm the hell down right now, Maxwell. I've had enough of your attitude today. I told you to stand down and you will listen to me."

Giselle snorted. "Oh my gosh, the tizzy he was in this morning. Save me from man babies. Like seriously."

Max glared at Giselle. "I'll have you know—"

Giselle threw a hand up in his face, shutting him down. "Go take a lap around the joint until you've calmed down. We're over your bullshit. Stella said it's cool, then it's cool."

"I'm supposed to leave both of you alone with a vampire?"

Giselle turned with such slow precision, Stella feared for Max's safety. He was in trouble now.

"Are you saying Stella and I couldn't handle him? Are you saying we're incapable women who can't defend ourselves? Because if that's what you're saying, you better start running for your life."

Max opened his mouth, but then shut it. "I'm going to go take a lap."

"You go do that."

Then he left the building, and the tension that had swarmed the place evaporated.

She loved Max like a brother, but he could be overbearing at times. So overprotective that she felt suffocated more often than not. He had good reason for being that way, but it didn't mean it made it any easier dealing with it.

Giselle came closer, until she was within arm's reach, and grabbed a hug. It wasn't necessary, but she understood the sentiment behind it. They both worried way too much about her. While they didn't know Donnie was a good vampire, they did have a moment of fright. She'd been less than a foot away from what they thought was imminent death.

After she let her go, they both turned toward the men. "So, someone care to explain a bit more what's going on?" The pointed glare Giselle sent her indicated she better do a lot of explaining. Especially why she left the house without them to meet up with a vampire.

Well, confront was more like it.

"This is Detective Holstrom," Stella said, pointing at her co-worker she decided she'd lump in the friend's territory. He earned it with his display of chivalry. "He works at the same precinct as me and saw my latest case. He knew it was caused by a vampire, so he called a friend who happens to be one to help him. You know I don't like people messing with my cases, so I left to tell him to leave it the hell alone. Again. Imagine my surprise that he knows all about the world we live in."

"Mm-hm, mm-hm," Giselle muttered while bobbing her head up and down. "And the part where you left knowing this one was a vampire and came anyway on your own? Not going to expand on any of that?"

Stella crossed her arms. She hated when they coddled her like a child. Since their last assignment, which had gotten a little hairy at the end, their behavior had gotten worse.

But she understood why they treated her like this. They'd been together since childhood. Max came into her life when she was five and he was seven. His entire pack had been wiped out by a coven of vampires. One major reason he hated the creatures. Her mother had taken him in as if he were her own. Giselle came into their lives a year later, the same age as Stella. Her parents had died in a plane crash. Non-magical related. A freak accident that took their lives. They'd grown up together as siblings. They'd learned Stella's history and why she had to be protected at all costs. She loved them for it, but sometimes, it was so suffocating, she hated it.

"No, I am not."

"Stella."

"Giselle."

Her friend tore her gaze away from her and toward the men. "Well, what did you two find out?"

"Not much. Donnie tracked the perp to this warehouse

and that's it. It ended here. Then Stella showed up and you're up to speed."

She looked around for the first time. Took her time to get a clear picture of everything. "It looks like it's been abandoned for a long time. I'm sure a lot of people have come and gone here. I want to know who owns it. When's the last time it was used? Anything and everything about this place."

Giselle pulled the strap of the bag she had slung across her shoulder off and pulled out a computer. Then she sat down on a crate, typing furiously away.

"On it." Her fingers stopped midstream. "You're not off the hook, by the way. Still in deep shit for leaving without us."

"Okay, Mom. I'll do better next time."

Then Stella walked away before her sarcasm turned into viciousness.

"I'm going to look around. I don't care what anyone else does."

She had taken two steps before Holstrom spoke.

"Does that mean we're working together now?"

4

FOR SUCH A SMART MAN, he could be so stupid sometimes. Donnie knew when it was inappropriate to laugh, but he wanted to let loose with a boisterous laugh at Holstrom. The man didn't know when to leave well enough alone. Or at least retreat for a moment.

While he wanted to step back and let Stella and her friends handle this case, he knew he couldn't.

One reason was because of her. The pull she had on him was so strong, he felt it to his very bones he'd do anything for her. The thought alone should frighten him. Yet, it didn't.

He waited with bated breath for her to answer Holstrom's question. Were they now working together?

Please say yes.

Because he wasn't positive how he'd react if she said no. That should also frighten him. And it did. He hadn't lost control in a very long time.

She flinched, glancing at him before turning her attention back to Holstrom.

Odd. What was that about?

Her heart rate was still normal, but something had jolted her senses for a moment.

"My friends and I can handle it."

Damn.

Not the answer he wanted to hear.

With a lycan in the mix, it would be hard to watch over her. His protective instincts were the highest they had ever been. He would rather die than see her get hurt.

"But it would be silly to say no to extra help."

Donnie let out a sigh of relief.

More audible than he intended because she glanced at him again. He held her stare, unable to look away. She was the first to break it—again.

Then she continued on her way, leaving the building.

"Hmm. You're engaged to a psychic. I'd love to meet her. How powerful is she?"

Donnie looked at the woman sitting on the crate. Giselle, he thought he heard Stella call her.

"Excuse me?" Holstrom asked, taking a step closer to her. "What are you talking about?"

"Charly Yarrow. Your fiancée."

"How do you know any of that?"

Giselle rolled her eyes. "It's my job to know everything."

"I thought you were looking up information about this building." Holstrom's jaw was locked tight, the anger seething through his teeth.

More laughter wanted to filter out. Did Holstrom think he could win a battle against a witch? The man needed to settle down.

Donnie understood what she was doing. She was protecting her friends. Knowing everything about new people stepping into their lives was a smart thing to do. She wouldn't find anything about him, but he figured she'd try anyway.

"I am. I can multi-task. This building and the surrounding ones are owned by a corporation. It's been vacant for the past year. Several police reports for vagrants, assaults, and even an arson in one of the other buildings on the property."

Impressive.

She'd gotten all that information and started digging into Holstrom within a few minutes.

Her gaze whipped from Holstrom to his. "You're next. Care to make my job easier and supply your last name?"

Donnie grinned. He had nothing to hide.

Except his livelihood. He didn't know these people. While they were working together on this case, he couldn't trust they wouldn't divulge his whereabouts to any hunter. He'd rather not die in the next few days.

"I will have to regretfully decline." He half-bowed to add to his sincere apology. If he knew he could trust them, he would tell them everything. But he didn't know anything about them. Something he'd rectify as soon as he got home. He'd do his research as Giselle was.

Her brow rose slowly as her lips formed a firm line, indicating she wasn't happy with his decision. He just added another layer of distrust between them. It couldn't be helped.

"Come, Holstrom, we should look around ourselves. The vampire came here for a reason."

Holstrom nodded and followed him. Giselle didn't argue about their departure.

Both Stella and the lycan had left the building, so he found it prudent to search the area where they were at.

They walked through aisles of half-empty shelves. Holstrom even opened a few boxes to see what was hidden inside. Dolls. Odd, to leave such merchandise lying around. They walked through several doors, connecting one building to another before a distinct scent hit him.

He stopped, holding out his hand.

"What? Is it the vampire?" Holstrom whispered.

A slow grin emerged. "No, but if it was, they'd still be able to hear you even in a whisper."

Holstrom blinked a few times, then jerked his head once that he agreed. "Makes sense."

"I smell blood." He exhaled. "And death. I don't think your victim was alone that night."

"Shit. How can you tell that? Maybe it's someone else."

He shook his head. "I can smell her too." Then he walked forward a few feet and rounded a shelving unit. Sprawled on the floor with his eyes open and vacant, lay a man. He wore no shirt and a pair of faded blue jeans. His neck bore two tiny holes. A midnight tryst with a woman and it led to his death.

"Well, crap. How do we explain how we found this body? And that it's related to the other victim?"

Donnie tossed a lazy shoulder up. "Does it matter? You're not arresting the individual who committed the crime. You can't."

Holstrom looked dazed for a moment, as if that thought had never occurred. "Right. Of course."

"What do we have here?"

Holstrom jumped at the voice behind them, twirling around in agitation.

Donnie moved with ease, meeting the lycan's furious expression. He had heard the man approaching and smelled the disgusting odor coming their way. He could've warned Holstrom of his approach.

"A second victim. From the same house as the woman," Donnie replied as kindhearted as he could.

He'd never in his life been on good terms with a lycan. While he didn't want to be right now either, he wanted to try. For Stella.

"Why should I believe you? Maybe you killed him."

Donnie stepped back, sweeping an arm toward the dead man. "By all means, see for yourself. I am not the enemy here."

"You're a vampire. So yeah, you're the enemy." Max brushed past him, glaring, though he made sure not to make actual contact with him.

Donnie wasn't sure how he would've reacted if he had. The lycan was making it easy to dislike him. He wanted to throw him clear across the room to show him he could. That he was stronger than him. That he shouldn't provoke him.

"What did you find?"

He flinched—again in one night—at the sound of Stella's voice. That's how riled inside the lycan had made him. He hadn't even sensed Stella approaching. So very odd and unlike him.

"Second victim, unfortunately." He stepped away even more so Stella could have a closer look.

Unlike Max, when she brushed by him, her arm grazed his shoulder. The jolt of electricity that sizzled up his spine was far from anything he'd ever felt before.

Stella didn't stop in her movements, so it must've been one-sided.

It had been the same thrill that had hit him when she touched his hand earlier.

"Same vampire as from the house," Max grumbled. Interesting. He never mentioned earlier he had smelled two vampire scents. Good to know his senses worked though. That he knew Donnie wasn't the only one in that house.

No doubt Max had wanted to smell him on the victim and have a reason to kill him.

"He ran while the vampire attacked the woman. Probably didn't take long to drain her, so he went after the guy. Chased him to this place and finished the job." Stella placed her hands on her hips as she stared at the body. "Did you smell any other scents?"

"No. Everything else is clear around here. Can't tell where the vampire took off to from here either. Too many damn smells to differentiate."

Stella turned toward him. "How about you?"

Oh, how he wished he had a better answer than Max. To one-up the guy and to make her happy.

"I have not either. It appears to be a dead end."

"Ha!" Max scoffed. "You clearly don't know how to investigate anything. I saw a few security cameras Giselle can hack into. We'll find this vamp, and we'll kill it."

Max stared hard at him, his furious glare telling him he'd kill him as well. Eventually.

"Well, I'll leave you to it." Donnie acquiesced with a short dip of his head.

"We're done here?" Holstrom asked, surprised.

"For now. At least, I am. You don't need me here while you call in the calvary."

"Of course. Yep."

Donnie wasn't sure what was making Holstrom more flustered than normal. Him, or the newcomers? But he'd have to guess a combination of both. It wasn't often the detective called him for help. Actually, Donnie couldn't remember another time he had. This would be a first. They were together when the whole group was involved, but not one on one like this.

"Max, you and Giselle can head out too. Holstrom and I can take it from here."

The man looked like he wanted to argue, but stood up and left. But not before giving him the evil eye as he walked past him.

"Thanks for coming, Donnie. I'll call you if I need you again."

"Please do, Detective Holstrom. I'm your partner now. I'll do some digging on my end as well."

"I don't do partners."

Donnie cocked a brow, surprised Holstrom wanted to argue semantics. He didn't mean forever and for other cases. Only this one.

"Detective, do you think you could take me on and win?"

Holstrom took a step back.

He even felt Stella tense, though he didn't look in her direction. The last thing he wanted to do was make her nervous, but he was trying to make a point here.

"I mean, we both know the answer to that." Holstrom coughed and then cleared his throat.

Donnie smiled, because yes, it was a very obvious answer.

"Then, for this case, I am your partner. Because you can't take on a vampire as much as I'm sure you wish you could. But I can." And he'd kill the monster without even blinking because this was his territory and no other vampire would step in his space killing humans. "Someone needs to protect you. Charly would be very upset and distraught if something happened to you. I would never wish that kind of pain on her."

"You're right. Thank you."

"I usually am right. As much as it pains everyone else." He turned to Stella, bowing. "I am at your service for whatever you may need."

Then he left in a flash, needing space from the temptation that had overwhelmed him to the point of pain.

That woman would be the death of him if he couldn't control his urges.

Oh, boy. That vampire was intense. More so than any other person or creature she had come into contact with.

For the briefest of moments, she was disappointed he left. Then she shook the foolish emotion away and got down to business.

Holstrom called in reinforcements while she had a quick word with Giselle. They had a starting point of information about the location. Not that Stella thought it would be that helpful. The building had been a random place to commit a murder. It simply happened to be the area the poor victim had fled. She doubted it mattered in the grand scheme of things.

When forensics arrived, she barked orders as if she'd been working at the precinct for years and could do so without pissing anyone off. Of course, they didn't appreciate her attitude, and she couldn't have stopped it even if she would've tried.

She and Holstrom looked around the property, even knowing they wouldn't find anything else. Max would've found something if there was something to be found. And though she didn't know Donnie well, she figured he would've too.

It was well past two in the morning by the time they walked to their cars.

"Do you want me to follow you home?"

The blank stare she gave Holstrom had him wincing and looking bashful.

"That was a stupid question. I see that now. Strong, capable woman. I know." He shrugged. "You look nothing like my fiancée besides you're both blonde, and your hair is way blonder than Charly's, but she popped in my head and my protective instincts came out. I meant no offense."

For that reason alone, she appreciated his concern. Living with two other individuals who worried way more than they should took a toll on her. To the point she wanted to run away and hide from them. Live her life the way she wanted—without fear. Of course, even if she ditched her friends for some peace, the fear would remain. It was the way of life for her. And they acted that way out of love.

While she knew Holstrom didn't love her, barely liked her, his offer was an act of kindness.

"No offense taken. I appreciate the offer. I'll be in the office early. Seven o'clock. I doubt I'll sleep much. I'll update you with anything we've found."

"Sounds good." Holstrom opened his car door, resting his forearm on the top frame. "I know you have...you know," —he looked around the area as if to see if anyone else was around—"friends with unique talents."

She chuckled. That was one way to put it.

"Besides Donnie, I do too. He's not the only one of his kind. There's four in total, and Mona, who's a witch," he said the last word in a whisper, even though no one else was in the vicinity. Then he continued in a whisper, "Donnie mentioned it could either be a rogue vampire or a coven. So it can't hurt to have as many people helping on this as possible."

Four vampires.

Holy shit.

She was still trying to come to terms with one affable vampire. Could they all be friendly and on their side?

Holstrom's eyes filled with panic when she didn't respond. "This whole....other world is still new to me. I get the sense it's old news to you. I also sense that vampires are usually not on your side."

Understatement of the year. She hadn't met one she hadn't killed. Because it was either kill or be killed. There was never another option.

"I first met Donnie when Charly was in danger. He scared the shit out of me. I mean, the way he moved so fast, the way his eyes glowed red. The way he threatened me if I made Charly cry. Well, it was that particular thing that scared me, but made me realize he wasn't going to hurt me for no reason. Only if I did something to hurt someone he cares about. His friends are the same way. They help us. I mean, this is the first time I've asked for help on a case, but he helps Mona and Mason, who run a paranormal investigation company. They help people and creatures and whatnot. What I'm trying to say is they're good people—vampires. I don't know what we're up against, but the more help on our side, I'd say is better."

He made a good point.

As much as it pained her to admit.

She wasn't ready to involve a slew of people, though. Not yet. Not until she knew who they were and what she was up against.

"I'm not saying yes, but I'm not saying no. I will accept

Donnie's help, but that's all I'm willing to allow. Because make no mistake, Detective Holstrom, this is still my case, and you won't run roughshod over me."

"As long as you know the option is there. Just wanted to throw that out there."

"Thank you."

She left it at that. He got into his vehicle, and she slid into hers.

Going home would be the smart thing to do. She could get an update from Max on if he found anything else. She knew he had patrolled the city, looking for more signs of vampires or the scent of the vampire who had already killed. Once a scent was identified, he never forgot it.

Giselle would have more information on the security cameras in the area. No doubt she took the original files for them, but then erased and replaced it with something else for forensics. If something paranormal was caught on camera, no need to cause panic for the ignorant. Sometimes ignorance was bliss. She liked to keep humans in the dark for as long as possible.

But not only would they give her updates, they'd grill her on her behavior. Why she confronted the detective and his vampire friend on her own when she didn't know if they were friend or foe.

She wasn't in the mood for that.

No, her mood was on the edge. Of what? She couldn't quite figure out. But going home wasn't an option.

And she sensed danger. The town was in trouble from a vampire. But this was a different kind of danger. Something else was brewing in the air, and she didn't like it.

She withdrew the necklace she wore at all times from underneath her shirt. Heart-shaped with an intricate design of swoops and swirls. It looked like a chaotic mess, but if one stared and concentrated, it was one big line connected from end to end. An infinity symbol multiplied by a hundred. No end, no beginning.

Her hand tightened around it as she pictured the one thing that would calm her mood. That would, perhaps, make sense of it.

Donnie.

5

DONNIE POURED himself another glass of blood, drinking it in one large swallow. It was the fourth glass he'd had since returning home. Talk about overindulgence.

He normally didn't need so much blood to sustain himself. Not that he ever lost control on the small amount he had every day, but he didn't like to drink more than was necessary. Their supply of blood was plentiful, but getting complacent could be their downfall. It was never wise to let one's guard down. He had learned that too many times in his last three hundred years of life.

After washing, rinsing, and drying his glass, he made his way to the living room. He'd relax for a few hours before he'd venture to bed. Not that he'd sleep well, if at all.

One, the nightmare would return. Since luck was not on his side lately.

Two, a human woman had grabbed ahold of his thoughts and refused to leave.

He'd stayed in the shadows until the police arrived, watching as they did their jobs with the efficiency he knew they possessed. But nothing in this world would bring them to the doorstep of their killer. It was all for naught.

He'd caught glimpses of Stella here and there, but not enough to satisfy his appetite.

So he left.

Before he did something idiotic.

He'd never bite her. Never drain her blood. But more like stupidly rush to her side to protect her from everything. This need. This intense urge to keep her safe assaulted him every time he laid eyes on her, every time his mind even thought her beautiful name. He couldn't figure out why. She was just another human.

Not being able to figure out this pull toward her was driving him insane. That had been one of the reasons for drinking an over excessive amount of blood. He needed full control over his senses. Instead of starting his own search for the vampire who killed two innocent people, he came home to get his head back on straight.

When he walked into the living room, he wanted to turn around and walk back out. Dealing with Joe was not on his to-do list for the remainder of the evening. George was still with Mona and Mason dealing with the goblin issue. He figured Joe would've helped as well, but when he returned home, he didn't ask why he was here. It would prompt Joe to ask him the same question. And to add where he'd been all night. Not that helping Holstrom should be a secret. But it felt like he had to keep it to himself. At least for the time being.

"What happened tonight? You've had too much blood."

Leave it to Joe to notice. And to question him.

"Nothing. Merely helped Holstrom with a case."

Joe narrowed his eyes, crossing his arms. "Partly true, I can sense, but not the entire story."

"Why are you on my case, Joe? Have you decided to take the role as my father or something?"

Joe laughed, rolling his eyes. "Dodging and deflecting will not stop me from getting the truth."

No, but it would give him time to gather his thoughts. How much did he want to tell Joe?

"There's another vampire in the area. Not sure yet if they're alone. But it's killed two people so far. Holstrom was wise in contacting me about it."

A heavy sigh echoed between them as Joe ran a hand through his hair. "We've been lucky to have this area to ourselves. This isn't good, Donnie. Activity like that will bring in hunters. We could be found. Be forced to move again."

Yes, that was a possibility he'd also thought. Not that he'd shared it with Holstrom. The detective already had enough on his plate to worry about. The last thing any of them wanted to do was move again. They'd been moving way too much in the last few years. Hunters becoming more adept at locating them. Trying to kill them.

He was exhausted from it all.

He understood why they hunted vampires. Most were killers. Took a human life without thought or care. Which made it unfortunate for him and his friends because they were lumped into the same category.

"Why didn't you call me?"

"The need wasn't warranted."

Joe zoomed closer to him in a blur, getting inches from his face. "We cannot allow more vampires to enter our territory. The need was definitely warranted. It's not like Holstrom would be much help to you."

Here they were again—fighting.

That was exhausting too.

He didn't even want to mention Stella and her friends. That would open up the argument into a dangerous territory.

A beeping sound had them both turning their heads toward the monitors on the bookshelf. Thanks to excellent vision, neither had to move closer to the screen to see they had a visitor at the gate.

"I don't recognize the car," Joe said, squinting his eyes as if that would help to see the person in the driver's seat. Their eyesight was excellent, but even they had their limitations.

Donnie didn't need to see who it was. He knew. Because he recognized the car.

Stella had found him.

Again.

This wasn't good. Joe was already on edge after what he'd told him.

She opened her window and pressed the call button.

"I'll handle this."

Joe put a hand to his chest as if it would stop him. But he remained in place because he didn't want to fight any more.

"You know who it is."

He gave a tight nod.

"What is going on, Donnie?"

He moved around Joe using his vampire speed and opened the gate for her. There was no getting out of this visit.

They stood several feet apart, but it felt like miles as he stared at his oldest friend.

"The case isn't Holstrom's. It's another detective's. Her name is Stella. I already know you won't like her friends. Can't say I'm a fan either. But in this instance, we need to work together."

"And who are her friends?" Joe grounded out.

Sometimes it was better to rip the Band-Aid off than doing it slowly.

"A witch and a lycan."

"A lycan!"

Yes, they had no issues with witches. More times than not they kept their distance from them. Sometimes, like with Mona, they were amiable. Mona was the first witch they had ever befriended so well—besides her mother. He considered her family, they were so close.

But he knew hearing a lycan was also in the mix wouldn't go over well.

"And Stella? What the hell is she?"

To his battered heart, human. Because nothing could ever become of them. He wouldn't be able to watch her live and die. Nor would he ever be able to turn her into a monster like him. A doomed relationship.

"The detective on the case. Also human."

A knock sounded on the door.

He moved in a flash, grabbing Joe's arm before he could answer the door. "You will treat her with respect and kindness." *Or you'll answer to me.*

Joe blinked twice, frowning. "There's an unspoken threat laced within that. Did you just threaten me?"

Out loud, no. Tinged in his tone of voice. A resounding yes. He couldn't have stopped it if he tried, which he hadn't.

He didn't answer Joe's question. The moment he let go of his arm, they both rushed to the door. He was older—in vampire years—by twenty-one years. Maybe that's why he beat him to the door. Or maybe it was the exuberant need to protect her that made him win.

Joe crossed his arms, scowling as he opened the door.

Steady heartbeat. Cool expression. Beautiful as always.

She didn't seem the least disturbed that she'd infiltrated a vampire's house.

"Stella, I feel like I should ask how you found me, but I sense you won't tell me as you didn't before."

She smiled. "You're such an astute man."

"To what do I owe this pleasure?"

"May I come in?"

He had no issue allowing her entry. But he needed to block her from Joe. Not that he thought Joe would attack her. He would never. But the irrational thought wouldn't disappear.

"I'm sorry if I—"

Apologies were not acceptable. She hadn't done anything wrong.

"Please, forgive me for my rudeness." He stepped back, sweeping an arm for her to enter. He closed the door behind her with a quiet click and sent Joe a stern look to be on his best behavior.

And yes, the look had a small threat hidden in it.

"Allow me to introduce you to my friend Joe." Donnie met Joe's hard gaze. "This is Stella. She works with Holstrom as I mentioned before."

"Yes, you also mentioned she's friends with a witch and a lycan. Have they graced our doorstep as well?"

Donnie took a step closer toward Joe to put himself between the two. "Uncalled for."

"Are we really going to do this?"

"If you insist."

"Uh, no, you seem to be insisting it, Donnie." Joe tapped him hard on the shoulder. "Our livelihood has been compromised. And I never expected it to happen because of you."

"I seem to have come at a bad time. I didn't—"

"Can't figure out why you'd come at all," Joe snapped at her.

"Do not raise your voice at her." This time Donnie did step in front of him, blocking her.

"We don't know her. We can't trust her. For all we know, there are hunters right behind her."

All possibilities. Donnie couldn't deny it. But it didn't feel right. He wouldn't believe it until he saw it happen.

"And my point is being made. Another car is coming up the driveway." Joe's eyes went red as he focused in on the distant sound.

Donnie's did as well. He wasn't sure if it was because he was preparing to fight Joe if he went after Stella or because of the threat coming up the driveway.

"Nobody let them in." Donnie pulled his phone out of his pocket, pulling up the security cameras via the app. "It's Mason."

"Maybe he can talk some sense into you."

Donnie rolled his eyes before turning toward Stella. "I apologize for—"

"Don't apologize for me," Joe said, cutting him off. "I'm not sorry. She found us and is refusing to tell you how. We can't trust her."

"You're more than welcome to leave, Joe."

A haughty laugh escaped him. "Are you kicking me out? Over a human! A hunter, most likely!"

A loud banging reverberated around the foyer. Joe zoomed to the door, whipping it open.

The strong smell of blood hit his senses the moment it flung open. The breeze carried it to his nose with ease.

"Shit, Mason!" Joe gabbed Kade's limp body from Mason and dragged him inside.

Joe dashed into the living room, setting Kade on the

couch. Donnie followed with Mason and Stella joining them.

"What happened, Mason? Where's Bailey? Mona?" Donnie asked, tossing off his jacket. He handed it to Joe who pressed it on the large gash covering Kade's chest from the top of his right shoulder down to the left side of his stomach.

"She's at home with Emerson. She has no idea this happened. Mona's at home too."

Donnie gestured for him to continue. "And what happened?"

Mason shrugged, throwing his hands up in the air. "I don't know. I don't know. George and Peter came with us to handle the goblins. It went well. We got them to leave town with minimal fuss. Mona was on cloud nine how easy it went. Peter and George went their own way, not sure where. Mona started puttering in the kitchen on spells. Kade was about to go home when his friend Todd called. He was drunk. Spouting nonsense. He hates the guy, but he told him he'd pick him up from the bar. I offered to go with for something to do and moral support. We got there and..." Mason's eyes bugged out. Even odder, they were glowing a bright blue. "Todd wasn't there. This...thing...jumped out and attacked us." Mason lifted his arm to show them the deep gash. It was still bleeding, but not heavily. It would require stitches, but nothing as serious as Kade's wound. "Kade got the worst of it. Your house was closer than mine. I should've brought him to the hospital, but...Shit, Donnie, your house was still closer. Save him."

He held Mason's gaze for the longest time, then looked at Joe. His expression told him Kade didn't have much longer left in him. He'd lost a lot of blood.

"He's lost a lot of blood, Mason. The wound is massive."

"What am I supposed to tell, Bailey?" Mason's voice cracked as his eyes filled with tears. Eyes that were still glowing brightly. Why were they glowing?

"I can tell her for you." It wouldn't be an easy conversation, but Donnie would do his best to take the burden off his friend. "But if you came here thinking I'd turn him, I won't."

Mason didn't say a word, as if that was what he had expected.

"Death is always better than hell." And his life had been hell more times than not. The life of a vampire wasn't an easy one. "Nor is not having the choice to choose. Perhaps if he was conscious...but he's not. I would never make that decision for someone. I know what it's like for it to be taken out of your hands. So does Joe. He won't turn him either." Donnie didn't even need to ask his friend. The four of them had decided as a group they would never turn a human. Never.

"Bailey and Emerson..." Mason choked out. But then he nodded as if agreeing it was wrong to turn Kade into a vampire without his consent.

"His pulse is weakening," Joe murmured. "We could give him a transfusion of blood. I could try stitching up his chest. I'm no doctor, but I've seen enough to try."

And it would be a useless effort. The gash was too large. Doubtful even a hospital could've saved him.

A warm hand touched his shoulder. The zing he always felt when Stella touched him attacked his senses.

"I can help, Donnie."

IF GISELLE or Max were here, they'd force her out of the

house and out of town. They'd be so against what she was about to do.

But she couldn't let an innocent man die.

She couldn't let the heartbreak she saw enveloping Donnie continue any longer.

This man—this human meant a lot to him.

The fact he refused to turn him meant a lot to *her*. He had principles. A good moral compass deep in his heart. He might be a vampire, but he wasn't a bad one. Most, if not all, would've finished the man off by draining the rest of his blood. While Donnie's friend Joe seemed to hate her, he hadn't touched the man either.

Both good vampires.

What a refreshing change for once.

"Are you a doctor?" Joe asked.

His question pulled her out of the trance she'd been stuck in when she laid a hand on Donnie. Touching him had thrown her attention off without effort.

"No." Then she knelt by Kade, eyeing Joe. "Back away, please."

He narrowed his eyes. "You said you're not a doctor, so how can you help him?"

"You're about to find out, if you would step away."

By the obstinate look in his eyes, she worried she was making a colossal mistake. Exposing herself like this.

"Move already, Joe. I trust her."

Then the worry washed away. She barely knew Donnie, but she knew without a doubt having his trust was a precious thing. She sensed if it ever came to it, he'd protect her with his life. Even against his friend.

She removed the jacket to reveal the massive gash across his chest. Inhaling a large breath, she took out her necklace, squeezing it with a death grip in her left hand. What she was about to do didn't require her necklace. Most of the things she performed rarely did. But feeling its power, knowing it was in the palm of her hand always helped center her. It had been her mother's.

She made brief eye contact with Donnie, noting the trust in his eyes, then withdrew first, closing her eyes. Raising her right hand over Kade, she let loose the power she guarded like a princess locked in a faraway tower.

"Holy shit."

Joe's excited cry did not stop her. She felt the power flow through her fingers and down into the chest of a man she didn't even know.

She even heard Donnie's sharp intake of breath, but otherwise no other shock verbalized. And the other unknown man, Mason, was quiet but eliciting heavy breaths as she worked her magic.

The power filled her up everywhere. It was always a heady feeling. It made her feel invisible. As if nothing could touch her. Half the time, she hated that feeling. She never wanted the power to go to her head. She never wanted to get to the point where she thought she was untouchable.

Because that was a lie.

A deadly lie.

If she were untouchable, then so would've been her mother. And her mother before that. And so on and so forth.

"I can't believe this. Donnie!"

She still didn't open her eyes, nor hear Donnie's reply as he didn't vocalize one. But she knew he made some sort of gesture for his friend to stop.

Maybe it was not utilizing her power all the time. Or

perhaps it was the extent of the wound, but she felt her energy waning. Of course, that was the thing about what she was doing. To heal a wound, she had to absorb some of it.

She dropped her hand and opened her eyes. Kade's eyes were open and staring at her like a lost child. Then his gaze slid down to his chest. The gash had shrunk quite spectacularly, but there was still a line cut along his chest. It would need to be stitched. However, on a good note, the bleeding had stopped.

She stood up and backed away, stumbling a bit. She doubted she would've fallen back down, but a strong pair of arms caught her. The urge to re-close her eyes and enjoy the sensations of Donnie holding her nearly won.

"I would still give a transfusion of blood, and you may now use your doctoring skills to close the wound. I need to use the restroom."

She tore out of Donnie's arms and fled the room. Of course, she knew she got away because he allowed her to. His strength would outmatch hers. Well, without her powers he would. And using those again so soon wasn't an option. She'd used up too much healing Kade.

She had no idea where the bathroom was, but she opened and closed a few doors before she came across it and plopped down on the toilet seat.

A few deep breaths did nothing to calm the racing of her heart.

No doubt about it now, Giselle and Max would kill her.

After getting her breath back, she stood up, pulling off her shirt. A bright red line slashed across her chest. Thankfully, not open or she would've required Joe's skills on her as well. She'd removed most of the gash from Kade, but not enough to give her the full wound. A tiny smile brightened her face. She was getting better at it. Not absorbing the full wound.

But there would be no hiding the scar. It would remain on her skin for the rest of her life. A reminder of the life she had saved.

The door opened before she could do anything but turn from the sink. Donnie stepped inside, closed the door, and was inches from her before she could even blink. The man was fast on his feet. Normally, she had a better reaction when dealing with a vampire. She could be fast when she needed to be.

He looked pained as he stared at her chest. She figured she should feel self-conscious that she only had a bra on, but she didn't. His stare didn't unnerve her in that sense. No. It unnerved her at the intensity of it. As if he were in pain as well. As if he could feel her pain. Because although she had no open wound, it felt as if her chest had been sliced open. Whatever Kade was feeling in the living room, she felt the same.

He reached up, hesitant at first, but then he followed through, tracing the line with a light brush of his finger.

"This is the first time tonight that your heart is racing. I could hear it all the way from the living room."

Yes, well, she exposed herself to two vampires and two humans she didn't know. Nothing good ever came from revealing who she was.

"You have a scar. The same I imagine Kade will have."

He was stating the obvious. She didn't think it required a response.

"You saved his life. I know he will be forever grateful. I know his wife Bailey will too." Donnie's finger brushed the line once more. "I know I am. I know what you did was not something you wanted to do. But you did anyway."

She did.

And she still didn't know why.

"You're a witch."

Yes, she was. A very powerful one. She knew he understood that by the hesitant gleam in his eyes.

6

SHOCK DIDN'T BEGIN to cover anything coursing through his mind.

A witch!

So powerful she could disguise it. He'd never come across a witch so formidable. But he had heard of ones like her.

A cosmic witch. So potent they had become extinct. Or so he thought. Every creature in the world was frightened by a cosmic witch. They had vast powers that no one even knew how much they were capable of.

When he'd first been turned, he'd heard of stories. Brutal, devastating destruction caused by such witches. It had taken many creatures together to defeat them.

Yet, one lived and breathed right before him.

And he didn't fear her.

He feared *for* her!

"What do you need?"

She blinked rapidly as if confused by his question.

"Are you in pain?" He found himself tracing the scar

again, unable to believe what she had done in the living room.

The scar itself was proof she had healed Kade to the point of saving his life, but she'd absorbed the wound itself. Her heart still raced, and he hated hearing the speedy sound. He didn't want her frightened of him. He'd never hurt her. Ever. So if he could stop the sound and bring it back to an even keel, he'd do everything in his power to do so.

"Stella?" He stopped tracing the scar and brushed her cheek, holding his hand there. He liked touching her way too much. The feel of her soft skin. The way her eyes dilated with pleasure. Brief, but he swore it was there. "Are you in pain?"

"Yes, but I'm sure it's not as bad as your friend. I'll be fine."

He swallowed hard. Would she be fine? The wound had been life-ending. The pain had to be excruciating. And her heart still pounded with intensity.

"Your heart is still racing. Why?"

She held his stare, but didn't answer him. Sure, the question put her on the spot, but he needed to know if it was him that was causing it. It was unacceptable if so.

"I would never hurt you."

The way her eyes narrowed said she didn't quite believe that.

"You saved my friend Kade's life. That puts me in your debt. Despite that, I would still never hurt you."

She let out a soft sigh. "I think I believe that."

Good. They were on the right path. To what? He wasn't sure yet, but he needed her to trust him. To know he'd never lay a hand on her. He'd die for her. He imagined she wouldn't believe that if he uttered such a crazy thing.

"But I don't believe that about your friend Joe."

His hand tightened on her cheek. Then loosened when he felt her tense. With a delicate touch, he brushed his fingers down her arm until he reached her hand, clasping it within his. Then he lifted it and placed a tender kiss upon the top of it.

"He would never harm you either. We may have been arguing, but that's what brothers do on occasion."

He had to trust in that. Because he couldn't fathom killing one of his oldest friends he thought of as his true brother.

"I am on your side, Stella. Your secret is safe with me. With my friends."

"It's a pretty big secret, Donnie. I might be able to believe you, but the other people in your circle? I doubt that."

How did he convince her? Because he sensed if he didn't, she'd disappear from his life. The thought of that...it was unthinkable.

"Your friends, Max and Giselle, they obviously know. It's why they were so protective of you."

"Yes."

"We can be trusted the same as them."

The way she cocked her brow said she still thought it doubtful.

"Please don't leave town, Stella. Don't run from me."

"I don't even know you, Donnie."

"For reasons I can't even fathom, I feel a pull toward you. This intense, uncontrollable pull that has me linked to you. I fear that if you leave, I will follow."

"I know how to disappear. You wouldn't find me."

"I would. Stella, I would."

She inhaled a sharp breath, yet her heart rate had

settled. Not even his promise—not a threat—to follow her had ramped it back up.

"I have no plans to leave until I solve my current case. But my intentions were never to remain in this town. My friends and I don't stay in one place for long. We help people and we move on. I will eventually leave."

And he would follow.

The burning need to do so wouldn't evaporate. He knew deep in the pit of his stomach he would follow. Perhaps it was because she was a cosmic witch. His desire to keep her safe. Being what she was, she needed all the help she could get to remain in hiding and safe from every single creature out there who could learn the truth. Because he knew his friends were of a rare breed of creatures who didn't hurt others based on fear.

Maybe that's why he had such a strong pull toward her. For what she was. Did that mean she was causing him to feel this way?

No. He didn't think she would force anyone to do something they didn't wish to do.

Donnie placed another kiss upon her hand. "Joe's finished stitching up Kade and giving him some blood." She didn't even question how he knew that. Excellent hearing, something she knew he possessed. "He's now helping Mason. I'll let you get dressed. Meet us in the living room. Something hurt my friend and perhaps you'd like to help with this case as well."

There was a moment of silence.

"Of course."

Though she had agreed, she had hesitated at first.

Donnie left her before he did something stupid. Like kiss her.

Kade was sitting up on the couch when he returned. Joe

was treating Mason who sat in the recliner across from the couch.

"How are you, my friend?" Donnie asked as he sat down next to Kade, who looked dazed.

"Joe gave me some painkillers, but the pain is still pretty intense. Joe couldn't tell me much about that woman. Who is she? I owe her my life."

"She's a detective. She works at the same precinct with Holstrom. I'm helping them with a case that involves a vampire killing people."

"I don't know how to thank her."

"No thanks necessary."

Donnie glanced behind the couch to see Stella walking into the room. He stood and moved away from the couch to allow her to sit instead. She chose to stand.

Kade even stood, though looked in tremendous pain as he did so.

"I owe you a debt of gratitude. Thank you."

She inclined her head with a smile. "You're welcome. You should sit back down. I know you're in a lot of pain. Trust me. I feel it."

Kade's eyes widened. "You literally feel it?"

"Yes," she said, as she put a hand on his shoulder to guide him to sit. Kade obeyed. "It's impossible to heal someone else's wound without absorbing some of it. Rest. Take it easy. You need it."

"What I need is to find out why my ex-friend wanted to kill me," Kade mumbled as he laid back down.

Joe backed away from Mason, setting the first-aid kit on the small coffee table next to the chair. "I doubt that was Todd."

"Seriously," Kade groaned. "It sounded like him."

Joe grinned. "Many creatures can mimic people or

things. Could've been a changeling or a shapeshifter. Who'd you piss off, Kade?"

"Well, tonight a bunch of goblins."

Mason chuckled. "They were a feisty bunch, but I don't think they had anything to do with this." Then Mason lost his cheeriness and stood up. His arm had a long, jagged stitch along his right forearm. It would heal but likely leave a scar.

"Your eyes aren't glowing any longer, Mason," Donnie commented. Odd how they had glowed when he arrived and now they were not.

"I didn't even notice they had glowed," Joe added.

Because his focus had been on Kade.

Mason shrugged, as if he had no idea as well. Donnie glanced at Stella.

"I wonder if it's because of Stella. She was blocking us from knowing she is a witch, but your senses still picked up on it."

Joe tensed. "His eyes glow when danger is near."

They did, that was true. Somehow, Mason sensed danger around him and his eyes glowed. But Donnie would never believe Stella was a bad witch. She saved Kade's life.

No. It wasn't true.

The tension in the room rose. Mason looked at Stella. "Thank you for saving my friend."

"Again, thanks aren't necessary."

"So, you're a witch. As we all saw, especially with the weird blue light that emanated out of your hands. But Joe tells me you're a powerful witch."

"Is this leading to a point?"

Mason flinched at her sharp tone. His Stella never beat around the bush.

His? Not quite, but he feared he wished it were true.

Joe straightened his stance, his body taut and gearing up for fight mode. Even more so since Donnie had stupidly pointed out that Mason's eyes glowed because of Stella.

Donnie tensed, prepared to fight his friend if need be.

Tensions in the room flared to epic proportions. More so than when she had first entered the house.

When the man didn't respond, she glanced at Donnie. His eyes were red and his fangs were visible. Knowing he was a vampire and seeing it were two separate things. His friend Joe even had his fangs out, his eyes a deep red.

The looks should've frightened her, yet not an ounce of fear hit her veins. She never got scared of a vampire. There hadn't been one she'd gone against and lost, so what was there to be scared about?

Donnie wasn't preparing to hurt her. He was getting ready to defend her. How she knew that, she didn't know, but there was no doubt in her mind.

The last thing she wanted was for him to be fighting with his own friends. Especially because of her.

"I'm a rare witch. I'm known as a cosmic witch. One of the most powerful beings in the world. Which scares everyone. And I'm rare because what scares people makes them lash out. My mother was killed right in front of me. Only because she trained me well did I come out unscathed. I hid, invisible to all there, until they left. Until they were hundreds of miles away. I was ten. My family has lived in hiding and fear our whole lives. We always survived until one person found out the truth. Then it always went downhill from there. It's not impossible to kill us, but it is pretty damn hard."

She focused her gaze on Joe on the last bit of her speech.

He didn't tear his eyes away from her. He didn't react in any way.

Mason winced, then shook his head. "You misunderstood me. I don't blame you because I wasn't being clear. I'm not your enemy. I never will be. I know my eyes were glowing, and the guys are right when they say they glow when danger is near. But they don't just glow for that." Mason glanced between the two vampires. "When we first came upon you guys, my eyes were glowing too. And you all turned out to be friendly. So I wouldn't say they only glow when danger is near."

A bit of the tension relaxed in the room.

Mason continued. "My wife is a witch. I love her so much it hurts sometimes." Water gathered in his eyes, confusing her. "She didn't even know she was a witch until recently. Her mother kept it from her. Her aunt tried to kill her, steal her powers. She's struggling, and I want to help her in any way I can. I thought...you obviously know what you're doing." Mason threw a lazy hand toward Kade. "I thought having another witch to talk to would help her. That's all."

She sensed the sincerity in the man. Not an ounce of fear or hatred toward her. While she never revealed her secret, she had tonight. She didn't want to admit it, even to herself, but it all had to do because of Donnie. She did it for him. If they should be thanking anyone, it should be him.

Like Donnie had confessed to having a strong pull toward her, she felt the same toward him. It was why she had used her powers to locate him. She'd sensed danger coming his way and wanted to help. If she hadn't followed her gut, his friend would be dead right now.

Max and Giselle had been with her since childhood.

Since before her mother died. That was the sole reason she trusted them both explicitly. While she still had so many reservations with these people, she would give them the benefit of the doubt. Of course, she'd have to confess to Max and Giselle everything that happened tonight. They'd have her back if anything went sideways.

"Yeah, maybe you could help with the evil aunt issue too," Joe added. His eyes had returned to normal and his fangs were gone.

"What?" Mason looked at him.

"Joe," Donnie said through gritted teeth.

"Enough is enough, Donnie."

"You're putting Mason in a tight spot."

Mason held his arms out, wincing from the pain in his arm. "Stop arguing. I don't know what's going on with you two, but I get the feeling this isn't the first time you've had a similar conversation. Bring me in the loop."

"Why do you think Peter has been living with you two?" Joe asked, crossing his arms.

"Because you guys have been arguing about..." Mason's expression revealed it all clicking into place. "About Mona and her aunt secured in the basement. You know something we don't, and you're worried about Mona and her fragile state. Which you should be. But don't tell her I said that out loud. You also didn't want to bring me in the mix because I wouldn't be able to keep it from her, and if I did, and she found out, it puts me in the doghouse. How far off am I?"

"Spot on," Joe answered. "We can feel the evil filling up the house. Her aunt might be locked up, but she's still a pretty powerful witch. I can tell you not as powerful as Stella here. Not with her being a cosmic witch. Peter is there for your protection, if she would escape. And she will at some point, Mason. It has to be dealt with."

Mason tore his gaze off Joe and toward Donnie. "What are your thoughts on this, Donnie?"

"That Joe should've kept his damn mouth shut because now you're in that tight spot. I never wanted to put you there."

Mason stalked to Donnie, shoving a finger in his chest. "And I have a witch in the basement who wants to kill my wife. You would let that happen?"

"Do you really believe that of me, Mason?"

All the ire went out of Mason. "No, I don't. But I'm pissed you guys were fighting about us like this. Now I'm pissed I know why. Now I don't know what the hell to do." Mason pointed at Kade. "And now this. With Kade. Joe mentioned a vampire killing people. What the hell is going on here?"

It was a lot of chaos going on in this small town. Stella agreed.

But one thing at a time.

That was her motto. Because when you tried to focus on too much at once, nothing was ever solved. At least not efficiently.

"Okay, so we have several problems to address. The sun will be rising soon, so that leaves out Donnie and his friends to help for a while." Stella gestured toward Kade. "You need to go home and rest. There will be no arguments on that front." Then she looked at Mason. "You and your wife can visit the scene. Find out what kind of creature attacked your friend. If she needs the revealing spell to do so, let me know and I'll text it to you. It's not that hard of a spell. Max and Giselle will continue to look for our vampire killer and whether it's a rogue one or part of a coven. As will Holstrom and I. I already told him I'd meet him at the precinct at seven."

The fury in Joe's eyes that she'd have the audacity to

boss him around flamed with vengeance. "Oh, is that what we'll all be doing? And how about the evil witch in the basement? Or helping Mason and Mona with whatever creature attacked Kade? Once they know what kind attacked, they'll need backup. You going to leave them high and dry with that?"

"One step at a time. I've offered my help by sharing a spell. Of course I'll follow through with anything else. And as for the aunt, she's still locked up. Not an issue at the moment. Don't make it one."

"What I'm hearing is you won't help with it."

Why should she? She didn't know why the woman tried to kill her niece. Why she apparently was evil. She didn't know anything about any of these people.

Stella moved closer to Joe to show him she was not intimidated. Though her rock steady heartbeat should've told him that already. "What do you expect me to do? Kill a witch?"

"She's a threat to Mona as long as she's alive."

Stella had eliminated many creatures, but never another witch. Not even an evil one and she'd come across them a time or two. Her first instinct was never to kill. Of course, when it came to vampires, there was little other options there.

"Then we'll strip her of her powers."

"I've only ever heard of binding a witch's powers, not stripping them," Joe snapped. "I mean, I know Mona's aunt, Marcella, stole Mona's mom's powers because she killed her. You can strip a witch's powers without killing her?"

She could. Just because he had never heard of it didn't mean it wasn't possible. Because he had also never met a witch like her either. So there was that.

"I'm done speaking about this right now. We'll circle

back to it once we accomplish the other tasks. Again, one thing at a time. Otherwise, we're fighting chaos."

She turned around—the only time she'd ever turned her back on a vampire—and met Donnie's gaze. His eyes were still bright red, all the anger directed at his friend.

Moving with confident steps, she stopped in front of him. "The pull isn't one-sided."

That had his fight mode vanishing. His eyes returned to the dark green they usually were.

"I don't understand it either. I'm not sure I like it."

With those parting words, she left. Hating herself for admitting anything to him.

7

By the time Mason and Kade left and they had cleaned up the small mess in the living room, the sun rose. George hadn't made it back home, so Donnie assumed he was still at Mason's. Good. Maybe two vampires should stay on the premises until Mona's aunt was taken care of.

Donnie drained another glass of blood before heading for his bedroom. He wouldn't sleep much, but he planned to try.

"We should talk about her."

He paused outside his door. He'd nearly escaped this conversation.

"What is there to talk about? She saved Kade's life, and now she's helping with finding out who did it."

Joe crossed his arms. "She's a cosmic witch."

Donnie's eyes flashed red. A warning for Joe to tread carefully. Something he had never had to do toward his longtime friend. "She's not a threat."

"I heard you while you two were in the bathroom. She has a spell on you! Why can't you see that?"

No. He would never believe that.

The powerful pull he felt toward her was something else. Something otherworldly. Something that he had never felt in his life. The moment she had confessed to feeling the same, he knew she'd never felt anything like it either.

"It's not a spell. I don't know what it is, but she has no control over it any more than I do."

"We need to be careful around her."

Donnie fisted his hands, then relaxed them, letting out a slow breath. "Joe, as my oldest, dearest friend, I'm going to say this once, and with the utmost respect as I can. If you hurt her in any way, you will answer to me."

Joe flinched, backing up a step as if Donnie had delivered a huge blow to his gut. "I hope you're not wrong about her."

Then Joe was gone in a flash.

Donnie walked inside his room, closing the door and flipping the lock. It wouldn't keep Joe out if he wanted to gain entry. But it made him feel better.

Sleep would never come easily, so he decided to work out instead. Lifting weights that he had in the corner. Then turning to the small punching bag he had. Throwing punch after punch after punch. When tiredness still hadn't hit him, he hit the floor, doing pushups, sit-ups, and as many burpees as he could before he got bored of doing them.

His room had a connecting bathroom. As did Joe's, George's, and Peter's. They all liked their own space. While the house hadn't been equipped with all of that, they made sure to add it in as soon as they had purchased it.

A long, hot shower did nothing to settle him down. By the time he was finished and dried off, the bed still didn't look inviting.

He laid down anyway and closed his eyes.

For hours he laid there with his eyes shut but not sleeping. As a vampire, sleep wasn't necessary for him. But he enjoyed lying down every day because it was a normal human function. While he wasn't human any longer, anything that made him feel human was the goal. Because if he lost the last part of his humanity, he'd truly be nothing but a monster.

Around two o'clock in the afternoon, he gave up and completed another workout. He felt a bit rejuvenated after that, yet the shower added nothing to his energy. He was dressed and in the kitchen for another glass of blood by three thirty.

After downing three glasses—more than he normally had for breakfast—he called Mason. Something he should've done a while ago.

"What have you found out so far?" Donnie asked in lieu of a greeting.

"Well, the spell Stella sent Mona worked like a charm. Mona was so giddy about how easy it went. It was a lycan. It all happened so fast, I don't remember what the creature exactly looked like, but the extent of Kade's wounds suggest it's correct. A large claw could've caused it."

Donnie chose to ignore Mason doubting Stella's spell. That it could be wrong in its assessment.

"Could it be a lycan from last month when you two accidentally trespassed on their land?" Donnie prayed it wasn't that because Bailey would blame herself for everything. It had been her mess that brought them on the land in the first place.

"That's the same thing I thought. They lured us there somehow, using Todd as bait. And while I wanted to ask them about their whereabouts, I didn't want to go alone with Mona."

"They're not going to confess they attacked Kade."

"Yeah, I know, but I know when someone is lying to me. If I talk—"

"Absolutely not, Mason. Do not step foot on their land again."

"Well, how do we address this issue then? It was an honest mistake. We didn't even attack them when we were there. We figured out we were in the wrong place and left. There was no need for them to go to this level of violence. Kade could've died."

"I'll talk to them."

"Donnie..."

Yes, he knew the risks involved. Lycan and vampires were two creatures who had always been hated enemies.

And he didn't want to keep asking Stella for favors. They were already riding a delicate line with her.

Max wouldn't help them. If that man had his way, he'd kill them all.

"I'll request a meeting with their pack leader. I won't even step foot on their land until I have permission to do so. I don't want an all-out war with a lycan pack. As much as I hate it, we'll forgive and forget anything happened yesterday if they do as well. It's the only way to avoid further violence between us."

"Kade survived, so as much as I hate it too, I agree with that. I'm telling you right now, Donnie, if he had died, they would have a war on their hands."

Oh, he understood that. Donnie would've avenged his friend's death as well. There had been no need for the attack to begin with.

"Have you spoken to Holstrom? How is the vampire hunt going?"

"They're still looking. Trail seems to have gone cold."

Unfortunate to hear, but not surprising.

They'd need another victim to appear. As horrible as that sounded.

"Keep me updated. I'll be over as soon as the sun sets."

He hung up with Mason and called Kade to check on him. He was resting and doing well. Bailey was fussing and doting on him, but he knew Bailey. He knew she felt guilty. He'd also stop at their house and try to put her mind at ease.

When he finished the call with Kade, he set his phone down on the counter, thinking of what he'd do until he could leave.

Then Joe spoke from the living room.

"We have company. Your new friends are here."

Though he sounded aggrieved by the fact, Donnie couldn't wait to see Stella once again.

He'd pictured her in his mind more than anything else as he had tried to sleep.

But seeing Max and Giselle were another story.

How would they greet him this time? With him knowing who Stella really was?

He grabbed another bag of blood, drinking it straight from the plastic. Something he never did. But he needed sustenance for the incoming battle he was about to have.

He met Joe in the foyer, who had his hand on the door-knob. Getting into a physical fight with his friend was not on his to-do list. But he wanted to toss him across the room and far away from Stella.

They had built a porch around the front door. Instead of putting in screens, they put in windows that were tinted from the sun's harmful rays. So if they had visitors during the day, it wouldn't harm them to open the door.

When Joe opened the door, Stella wasn't standing there, deflating his heart. Giselle and Max were.

"May we come in?" Max asked with a jovial expression

as if he wasn't in front of two vampires, one whom looked ready to attack.

Donnie wouldn't mind if Joe got in a hit or two before he stopped him. Of course, Stella wouldn't be happy about that, so he figured he shouldn't let any fighting occur between them.

"Of course." Donnie zoomed to Joe's side, putting what looked like a relaxing hand on his shoulder when in reality it was filled with enough strength to tell his friend to back away.

Joe obliged.

They stood on one side of the foyer while the witch and lycan took a spot on the other.

"How can we help you?" Donnie knew they weren't here for help, but he'd try to maintain pleasantries as long as he could.

"I hear you and Stella had an eventful evening last night." Max still hadn't removed his smile, though the venom was clear in his eyes.

"Yes, it was quite unexpected to find our friend had been brutally attacked by a lycan." Max could do with that what he will. Donnie was losing his patience with the man.

Max's eyes flashed with fire.

Donnie knew Max wasn't the culprit, but it brought him immense joy to see the aggravation sweep across his face at the accusation.

"There will be repercussions for such an unprovoked attack," Joe seethed through gritted teeth.

Donnie had to give his friend credit. He was maintaining his composure rather well. Joe wanted to eliminate both the creatures standing before them. They knew it too.

Max was undeterred, stepping closer to Donnie,

ignoring Joe. He seemed to have gotten the full-blown ire of the man.

"Stay away from Stella. I won't say it again."

He was never one to take orders well, especially from a lycan. Even if he had the decency to follow his directive, he knew it would be impossible. The pull she had on him was too strong. Nothing would keep him away.

"She's helping us find the lycan who hurt our friend, and we're helping her find a rogue vampire. Your request is denied," Joe spat, surprising both him and Max.

He had never expected Joe to come to his defense. Not when he'd been as adamant he stay away from her as well.

But when push came to shove, Joe would always have his back.

Max shot a furious look at Joe. "It wasn't a damn request."

"Look, I get it," Joe said as if he wasn't talking to a lycan about to shift into wolf form, "we know she's a cosmic witch. You're protective of her, as you should be. I'm protective about my friends as well. So I get it. But we're not staying away if she doesn't tell us herself."

"I will end you—" Max stopped speaking when Giselle put her hand on his shoulder.

"You have quite the security system. And I'm impressed by the house itself. Not one ray of sunshine hit the foyer." Giselle displayed a brilliant smile. "You've been at this a long time."

They'd never admit how long. Donnie never shared his age with anyone. Charly had an inkling because of the past vision she had of him.

"Have you ever met a cosmic witch?"

"No." There wasn't much for Joe to add. This was a first for them.

But he thought he should dig a little deeper to keep the peace. "We've heard of stories. Of rumors. We've never come across one ourselves," Donnie said. "I won't pretend I've never killed anyone. I think we've all hurt people we wished we hadn't. But I don't hurt people anymore. Not unless it's a me or them situation. Unless it's the last resort. That includes creatures of any kind. Will I kill the lycan who hurt our friend? I want to. I want to rip them to shreds. Drain every last ounce of blood from their body."

Thinking about it had his vampire side flaring to life. His eyes flashed red as his fangs extended. It got his point across. Giselle tensed as did Max. Then he forced it down and returned to normal.

"But we have no intention of killing that lycan, even though they deserve it. I don't want a war with a lycan pack. It's the last thing I want." Donnie blew out a heavy breath. "I don't want a war with Stella's friends either. I'm telling you right now that I would lay down my life for her. You can choose to believe that or you can choose to fight us. I put it all in your hands."

She shoved her phone in her pocket, shaking her head. What was she going to do with her friends? On one hand, she wanted to throttle them until they begged her to stop. On the other hand, she wanted to hug them until they squirmed in her arms and begged her to let go. Bottom line, she wanted some begging to be had!

"Problem?"

She looked at Holstrom. The man was always butting into her business when she least expected it.

"Of course not."

Besides the fact her two best friends were so overprotective they chose to ignore her demands to leave Donnie and his friends alone. She knew it.

"You looked—"

"I'm fine, Detective Holstrom. No need to worry yourself over me."

She had enough of that already.

He blushed, and it produced a smile she couldn't stop. The emotion was so foreign on him. But cute.

"I'm done for the day." Holstrom looked at the watch strapped to his wrist. "Past the time I wanted to be done too. But if you need me, let me know."

In the grand scheme of things, Holstrom would be nothing but a deterrent in a fight against any creature. Being human had those disadvantages. But she appreciated his willingness to jump into the fray.

"We've done what we could to find..." She grinned, raising her brows in a you-know-what-I'm-talking-about gesture. "Any searching we might do tonight should be simple. But I'll call you if the need arises."

She grabbed her belongings, deciding she'd leave for the day as well. The sun would be setting soon, so she wanted to be ready for any vampire that might cross her path.

Foe.

Or friend.

They walked out of the precinct together. Holstrom followed her to her vehicle and she tried not to get irritated at his display of macho-ness. She understood he was trying to be nice, but if something jumped out to harm them, she'd be more prepared to fight them off than he would.

Did he even know she was a witch? Had Donnie and the other two relayed what happened last night? Holstrom hadn't mentioned anything about it, and considering it was one of his friends who had gotten hurt, she was surprised.

She opened her car door and turned toward Holstrom, who stood there staring at her with the oddest expression. One she hadn't witnessed from him before.

"I've been stewing on this all day and I don't know how to say it."

She would've never guessed he had been bothered by something. Well, yes, sure the vampire case they were working on wasn't pleasant. But besides that, she hadn't detected any underlying issue pressing on him.

"The best way is usually the honest way. Spit it out."

Holstrom gave a tight nod. "Thank you for saving Kade's life. When I first met him it was because he was suspected of killing his wife. He was nothing more than another perp to arrest. Now he's someone I consider a good friend. It would've been a hard loss to deal with. What I don't understand is why you didn't mention you were a witch?"

Her fingers tightened on the doorframe. How did one explain to a human—very new to the paranormal world—she was a witch hunted every day of her life.

"I was wondering if Mason or Donnie had mentioned what happened last night." More like earlier this morning, but that was semantics. She was running on two hours of sleep and she could feel it catching up to her.

"Honestly, I need to have a word with both of them because I didn't hear it from them. Bailey called Charly in tears and Charly told me on my lunch break. So all I have is secondhand information. Did you really heal his wounds with a touch of your hands?" He waved off the question. "Of course you did. What I want to know is why you didn't mention you were a witch?"

"Why does it matter?"

Would he have treated her differently? Because she didn't want that.

"Look, I know when it comes to all of this stuff, I'm at a great disadvantage. Huge! My gun might help me, but I'm not naive enough to think I have a fighting chance against a vampire or a lycan, or hell, a witch. But being forewarned is being forearmed."

"So you know whether to be on your toes that I might attack?"

Same thing, new person.

Everyone feared her.

Sometimes, she even felt Max and Giselle's fear ripple through her skin. As if she'd lash out and hurt them with her power when they irritated her. Of course, she'd never hurt them. Or anyone for that matter that didn't deserve it. She might wield immense power, but it didn't mean she wanted to use it.

"No! So I'm better prepared to help you in a fight! If I know you can handle yourself, I'm not going to be worrying about you as much as I thought I needed to. I mean, come on. Mona can produce fire in her hands. That woman doesn't need me stepping in the way to protect her despite my instinct wanting to."

Wow.

This man.

This human man.

"You would've tried to save me from a vampire with no regard to yourself?"

He nodded. "I still would. Though, with you being a witch, you're going to save me."

She giggled. "And that bugs you, doesn't it?"

"Forgive me for being a guy who wants to protect women."

Stella let go of the doorframe and touched his shoulder. Elation filled her up when he didn't flinch in the slightest. He wasn't lying. No fear enveloped him concerning her. "I appreciate your concern over my well-being. Truly, I do. You're a rare breed, Holstrom. Charly is a lucky woman."

"I think I'm the lucky one, but thank you."

Her hand dropped away. "I'm sorry I didn't tell you. Please don't take it personal. I don't tell anyone. I'm…" What did it matter what she told him? His friends knew the truth. He'd eventually find out. "I'm not a normal witch. I'm what they call a cosmic witch. Rare. To most, extinct. Powerful. So powerful, it scares the living shit out of anyone when they find out. I don't move around so much because I enjoy it. It's for survival. Staying in one place too long brings attention and that never turns out well. There's magic in these hands." Stella raised her hands, staring hard at them. Wishing the magic away. She didn't want it.

"I don't have power or, hell, even immense strength, but you can count on me to be on your side. Protecting you to the fullest extent that is possible."

Her gaze lifted, water welling in the corner of her eyes. "That is one of the nicest things someone has ever said to me. I didn't think I'd like you, Holstrom, but you're dousing out all the preconceived notions I had of you. I'm sorry for those."

"Your secret is safe with me."

She believed him. That was a rarity for her as well, trusting in others.

"You said if I needed anything to ask."

"We're partners on this case," he said with a tender grin.

"I like to think we're friends now too. So, yeah, if you need anything, let me know."

Stella felt her phone vibrate in her pocket again.

"I need a few hours of sleep. I'm so tired I don't even know if I can drive home."

"I can—"

She held up her hand to stop the offer of bringing her home. That's not what she wanted.

"You're very accepting of me and what I'm capable of. And maybe that's because of who you are. Or the lack of knowing about the paranormal world. But some of the others last night, they weren't as welcoming. That's put my friends on edge. Makes them hover and try to put me in a bubble. Something that I can't stand."

"Mason is married to a witch. I doubt he wants to hurt you."

A tired smile spread across her lips. "But notice you didn't mention Joe or Donnie." She didn't know why she clumped Donnie with his friend. She didn't fear any repercussions from Donnie. But Joe was a whole other matter.

"I haven't had as many interactions with them. For obvious reasons." His eyes bulged, then he chuckled. "I can't speak about Joe, as I haven't had that much interaction with him. But I have with Donnie. And I don't think he'd hurt you either."

It was nice to know he felt the same way she did.

"You want me to talk to them?"

She waved off his request, touched he'd fight on her behalf. "No. Nothing like that. They're going to think what they want and fear what they can't control. My friends are going to do what they feel they have to. I want to crawl into bed and catch a few Zzzzs. Do you have a spare room I can hide out in for a few hours?"

Holstrom laughed, the loud, boisterous sound filling the empty parking lot. "That is the last thing I expected to hear. But yes, I have a spare bed you can use. Hiding right under their noses. They'll never expect it."

She joined in the laughter with a wicked grin. "Exactly."

8

SOMETIMES WAITING for the sun to set was excruciating. Especially when he wanted to flee his own house.

After the tense moment with Stella's friends, Joe went right back on his case. To rid their lives of Stella.

Her friends had left peacefully. Of course, not without issuing one more warning to stay away from her. Then Joe went on a rant about how things would get ugly sooner rather than later. Here, Donnie thought he'd been on his side. For a moment, he had been. He wanted that back.

He drank a few more glasses of blood, hoping to dispel the ache in his gut. It did nothing to soothe him.

As soon as the last rays disappeared under the horizon, he was out of the door in a flash. Not a word of goodbye to his longtime friend. Joe didn't follow.

He should take care of the lycan problem. Request a meeting with the leader of the pack. Visit Mason and find out how things were going there. Stop in on Bailey and check on Kade.

Instead, Donnie found himself standing outside Holstrom's door. The one man he didn't need to see. Sure, he should've called him about the vampire hunt, but Mason had updated him already on the matter. Since Holstrom hadn't reached out to him, he hadn't found it necessary.

He knocked before he could change his mind. As he stood on the porch waiting for his knock to be answered, he knew he made the right choice. The scent in the air told him so.

Charly opened the door. The sweet smile she greeted him with helped part of the deep ache festering in his stomach to dissipate.

"Donnie, it's so good to see you. You look..." She frowned, while she searched for the right word. "Lost."

Not what he expected to hear, but it fit. Right here, in this moment, he felt lost. And like he was being pulled in a million different directions.

"Is everything okay?"

He produced a grin he knew she saw right through. "I wanted to check in with Holstrom about the current case he's working on." Something he could've done by phone. Yet, his instincts had driven him here and now he knew why.

"Yes, the vampire killer. I'm up to speed with everything that has happened. Including Kade." She glanced behind her shoulder, then leaned closer, though was careful not to touch him. Nothing good ever happened when she touched someone. Seeing a person's past was hard on her, and painful on the recipient, knowing their secrets were vulnerable. "Breck wasn't happy he had to hear about that from me. He thought he would've been told by you or Mason. I know you'd never hurt him, and deep down, he knows that too. But it took a lot for him to call you yesterday. He thought he was a part of the group. To be someone who would be notified that one of his friends was injured."

Well, he'd been thoroughly put in his place. And rightly so.

Donnie placed a hand upon his heart. "That was a huge mistake on my part, and not done in malice. To be honest with you, Charly, I've had a rough day. My mind has been everywhere it shouldn't be. I apologize. Something I shall do with Holstrom as well."

"No harm done, Donnie." The gentle smile told him she meant that. "Come on in."

He followed her inside, shutting the door. Then he inhaled, making sure the scent he'd detected outside hadn't been an anomaly.

Still there.

Charly moved toward the living room, and he figured he needed to as well, despite the urge to search the house. To follow the trail and where the scent ended that swirled under his nose, tempting him. Seducing him.

Holstrom walked in from the kitchen area, holding a beer bottle and a tired grin plastered on his face. "I'd offer you a beer, but…"

But he didn't drink such things.

"The thought is appreciated." He glanced at Charly, whose smile remained before sliding out of the room. "I want to say that I am sorry I did not call you about Kade. It wasn't my intention to keep such things from you."

Holstrom nodded, taking a large gulp as he sat down on the recliner. Donnie took a seat on the couch.

"I spoke to Stella about it. It was an enlightening conversation."

Donnie wanted to relax, but his body tensed at hearing her name spoken. "How so?"

"Well, knowing she's a witch is one thing. I mean, Mona is one. Not a big deal. But finding out she's this, like, rare powerful witch is something else. I'm not much help when it comes down to it, but I've got her back. Against anyone who would try to hurt her."

It was one of the reasons Donnie respected Holstrom in every way. The way he'd stepped up to the plate and protected Charly had been surprising. Then falling in love with her. Even more shocking. But hearing him now speaking about Stella in such a manner, not that startling anymore. It was who he was. A man who served and protected.

He didn't miss the subtle threat either. Holstrom was warning him that he had better not hurt Stella.

"I'm glad to hear that. She has nothing to fear from me either."

Holstrom sat up, leaning toward him with the beer bottle dangling between his fingers. "And Joe? The other... vampire friends of yours. How about them?"

"They will not touch her." Donnie gritted his teeth, feeling the tip of his fangs wanting to break free. Holstrom must've noticed it because his posture stiffened. Now he had to explain his reasoning. To an extent. "I find myself very protective of her. They won't hurt her, and not just because they know they'd answer to me. Because that's not who we are, Holstrom. We don't hurt other creatures because they might be more powerful than us."

Holstrom let out a long breath, jerking his head up and down. "That's what I thought. I've always prided myself on reading people well, and I didn't think I read any of you wrong. But you never know. I had to say something." He relaxed back in his chair. "So what brings you by? I didn't make much headway on the case today. I have a feeling it's going to be a hundred times harder finding a vampire killer than it is finding a human killer."

Donnie chuckled. Holstrom had no idea how much harder.

"I don't know why I came here. I started driving and this is where I ended up. Mason already relayed you had no new leads on the case. I do have the lycan pack I need to deal with for attacking Kade. I should also check on him. But instead, I found myself on your porch."

Holstrom frowned.

"I know she's here."

Holstrom's frown deepened, his fingers tightening on the bottle. His heart rate even sped up. All indicators Donnie was correct in his assessment. In the scent he'd detected from the moment he stepped on the porch. He hadn't known he'd find her here, but something had driven him to this place. Some instinct. He wasn't leaving until he saw her.

The detective leaned forward again, lowering his voice. "She wanted some peace and quiet. A place to grab a quick nap. With you all knowing the truth...her friends have not been kind in their learning about the events that transpired. They're worried about her, but she needed a safe space."

And she found one here.

Smart woman.

Holstrom would do everything in his power to keep her safe.

Maybe that's why he felt himself drawn to his house. Because he had felt her presence in the area. The pull she had on him was stronger than he imagined.

"I can't leave without seeing her."

A chuckle floated out of Holstrom's lips. "Are you asking for my permission to go check on her?"

"It is your home."

His eyes narrowed. "And if I said no, leave her be?"

Donnie glanced away, his eyes flashing red and his fangs

descending for a moment. Shielding Holstrom's view didn't stop the man from realizing he'd went into vampire-mode for a split second. The man's heartbeat ratcheted up a notch.

"I would respect your wishes."

"Even as it pains you to do so." The obstinate man laughed. "You like her."

Donnie whipped his gaze back at him.

The irritating man kept laughing. "You like her a lot."

"It doesn't matter how I feel. Nothing can come of it."

Holstrom's brows drew low. "Why?"

"In case you didn't realize it, I am immortal. Other beings are not."

Realization slapped the detective in the face. "Right. Of course. I knew that." All traces of humor fled. "She trusts me. I don't want to break that trust."

Donnie understood that sentiment. Trust was a precious thing. "I won't wake her. Don't ask me to explain it, but I need to see her. I need to see with my own eyes she is okay. She won't even know I'm there."

"One quick, quiet peek."

He bowed his head, then was gone in a flash. Holstrom's laughter reached his ears all the way upstairs, outside her room. Nice to know they'd gotten to a point in their odd friendship where he felt comfortable laughing around him. It hadn't been that way a few months ago.

Donnie gripped the doorknob hard and twisted, opening the door without a sound. Stella lay on her side, facing the door. She looked peaceful in her sleep. As if no worries touched her life when awake. And of course he knew that was the furthest thing from the truth.

He glided to the bed in a flash, standing so close he could feel her breath on his hand by his side.

The ache to touch her consumed him. Yet, he resisted.

He told Holstrom he wouldn't wake her and he didn't want to break his word.

He'd done what he came in here to do. Check on her and see she was unharmed. He twisted, ready to zoom out of the room in a flash, when a hand grasped his.

Her soft touch scorched his skin and filled his veins with longing.

"Donnie..."

SHE SENSED she wasn't alone a moment right before the door opened. She'd always been a light sleeper. Fearing for one's life did that to a person. The second the unknown person stepped inside, the instant terror that always hit her when someone snuck up on her vanished in a flash. She knew without even opening her eyes it was Donnie.

So she remained silent and still, her eyes closed, waiting to see what he did. Despite her friends' many objections and warnings, she didn't fear him. Not one tiny ounce of fear. His friends...well, they were another matter. But Donnie would never hurt her. Why she knew that, she could not say, but her gut told her to trust him. She always listened to her gut.

He was quiet, as if not wanting to wake her. When she knew without taking a peek he was about to leave, her hand shot out to stop him. Instincts screamed she couldn't let him leave. Not yet.

"Donnie..."

Words failed her. She couldn't explain even to herself why she stopped him from leaving. Hell, she still hadn't opened her eyes. What would she see in his near dark, murky green depths?

"I didn't mean to wake you. Go back to sleep, Stella."

A cold hand brushed her forehead. Before he could extract his hand from hers, she pulled on it. Not that she could match him in strength and force him to do anything, but he obeyed, sitting down on the bed.

Another brush against her forehead had her opening her eyes.

They stared at each other for the longest time. Her hand clutched his with such ferocity, it surprised her. If it shocked him, he didn't show it. His free hand kept sweeping light, tender caresses across the top of her head, as if fascinated by the fact she was allowing it. It was strange to let a vampire touch her so intimately. The notion surprised her as well.

"Why are you here?" Her voice sounded strained and unfamiliar, as if she hadn't spoken in ages.

It wasn't the first thing she wanted to say to break the silence. It made him snatch his hand away from her face. The loss of his touch sent a wave of sadness through her.

"Checking in with Holstrom. I hear you had an uneventful day. I'm sorry no progress has been made in your case."

"Me too."

But they both knew he could've called.

"How did you know I was here?"

A low chuckle slipped out of his lips. "What makes you think I came because of you?"

Because she knew he felt the same intense pull that she experienced.

"I didn't know you were here until I stepped on the porch. Your scent is very distinctive...and potent."

His eyes dilated with pleasure, a hint of red showing. His vampire side had wanted to break free, but he forced it down.

Or was she wrong and it wasn't pleasure she'd seen? More like craving something he could never have.

Her blood.

"I didn't mean to wake you. But I couldn't leave without seeing you."

"Why?" she whispered, afraid to even ask the simple question.

He leaned closer, his gaze intent—and deadly. "I don't know."

Then his lips were on hers, extracting the desire she'd tried to ignore she felt toward him. How could she pretend any longer when his hard, insistent lips were forcing it out? She couldn't. She let go, reveling in the hottest, most erotic kiss she'd ever had. He devoured her. The kiss ripped away barriers she'd erected to protect her from ever falling under anyone's spell. Her life was dependent on keeping people at arm's length.

Their tongues dueled and clashed, as if they were arguing instead of enjoying the meeting of lips.

Then her tongue graced a sharpened tooth and she flinched. Donnie rushed backward until he was in the door-frame. His eyes glowed red, but his mouth was clamped shut. It didn't matter. She knew his fangs had dropped. She'd felt one.

Before she could speak—not even sure what she'd say— he zoomed out of the room in a blur.

What the hell happened?

Her heart raced, a very uncommon occurrence for her. She'd trained herself to remain cool and calm in every situation. Because it was never a good sign to a creature like a vampire or lycan when one's heart rate sped up. It meant fear was emerging. They fed off fear. At least vampires did.

Taking her time to get up, laying there for far longer

than she should've, she finally found the courage to get out of bed. She needed her heart rate back at an even keel before she confronted Donnie downstairs. Not that she was naive. He'd heard the rapid pace.

When she ventured downstairs after using the bathroom, her heart fell to the floor.

Donnie wasn't there.

"Hey," Holstrom said, springing to his feet from the recliner. "You look well rested. I hope you slept okay. Would you like something to eat?"

"Where's Donnie?" Then she froze, realizing how rude that sounded. "I mean, yes, I slept well. I feel much better, thank you. I'm not hungry."

Holstrom laughed. "And all you want to know is where Donnie is. I'm not sure."

She looked around the room. "He didn't say goodbye?" Because he clearly left the house.

Holstrom shook his head, wincing. "Look, yell at me, not him, for disturbing you. I should've never let him go upstairs. You wanted to be left alone by everyone. I'm sorry. You trusted me and I broke that trust. It won't happen again."

That made her lips tilt upward. Holstrom thought he could've stopped Donnie from seeing her. What a comical man at times.

She had no intention of hollering at Donnie. They needed to talk about that kiss. Maybe do it again.

What?

No!

Thoughts like that were dangerous. Kissing a vampire was dangerous! What had she been thinking?

"Or maybe I should yell at Donnie. Did he do something?" Holstrom went from ashamed for messing with her peace to alert and lethal in an instant.

"No. He did nothing. It's fine. No need to yell at anyone. I appreciate you letting me use your spare room." She turned her attention to the other side of the room where Charly had walked in. "Thank you for your hospitality. I'm sorry for intruding."

"You're always welcome here. Are you sure you don't want something to eat? I can heat up the chicken meal we had."

The same meal she had skipped when she first arrived. She hadn't wanted to do anything but close her eyes.

"I'm fine. I should go, but thank you again."

They let it slide and wished her safe travels home. By the time she reached her house, her emotions were still out of whack.

The urge to call Donnie and demand he come to her was strong. She barely resisted.

Max was on her the moment she opened the door. A too common occurrence in recent weeks and she despised it.

"Where the hell have you been? Not answering your phone either! Giselle couldn't even locate you. How dare you block your location from us?"

Sometimes being a powerful witch came in handy, especially when she wanted some space from her overprotective friends.

This conversation would require a strong drink. Ignoring Max, she circled him and headed for the kitchen, where she grabbed the scotch and poured a generous glass.

"Seriously, Stella. That's the first thing you're going to do when you come from wherever the hell you were."

"To get through this tantrum, yes."

Max's eyes bulged at the insult. He looked ready to leap

into wolf form and attack her when a hand clamped his shoulder. Giselle made eye contact with him for several seconds before training her attention on her.

"We're worried about you. Is that so wrong, Stella? Your life is—"

"I'm in no danger from them." She would not allow this train of thought to go any further. Sure, she was somewhat leery of Joe's motives, but Donnie would never allow him to touch her. She knew it without an ounce of doubt.

Giselle let go of Max, crossing her arms. They stared hard at each other, neither conceding the battle. Until Giselle let out a huge huff.

"I will begrudgingly agree that I don't think you have anything to worry about from that Donnie fellow. But I don't have as much faith about the other one."

That statement confirmed her suspicions that her friends had gone behind her back and confronted them. Something they wouldn't admit earlier, and one of the reasons she hadn't wanted to come home right away. Because she knew this conversation would happen.

"Stay away from them. All of them! Even Detective Holstrom." Max still looked ready to change into wolf form.

Which would be silly. He knew she'd best him. Even when they spared in their makeshift gym downstairs, she kicked his ass every single time. And without using her witchy powers. When one wanted to hide what they were, they had to be stronger in other areas. She trained to fight every day, making herself as strong as she could be.

Despite that being solid advice—something she would've listened to in the past—she knew she wouldn't be able to stay away from Donnie.

She also didn't take orders well.

"Do you want to stomp your feet to go along with this tantrum? You're more than welcome to."

Max rolled his eyes, shaking his head as he looked at Giselle as if she could talk some sense into her.

"Calm down, Max," Giselle said in a soothing tone, as if comforting a child, which confirmed to Stella Giselle thought the same thing. He was acting like a petulant child.

"He's not wrong, Stella. We need to be careful around them."

Which was a more diplomatic way of saying stay the hell away from them.

"Look, I have a job to do. So does Holstrom, and I trust him. We find this vampire and eliminate it. Keep the citizens of this town safe. That's the main objective here. I can't effectively do my job if I'm also trying to avoid my friends."

"What has gotten into you?" Max turned away from her, running an aggravated hand through his hair. He spun back her way. "This isn't like you. Being reckless. Getting close to vampires. They're killers!"

The power flowed through her veins. She felt it making its way to the surface. The feeling was so foreign. To want to unleash it toward one of her closest friends. A man she'd always seen as a brother to her. Family.

"Okay, okay, we all need to take a breather here." Giselle stepped in front of Max, pushing him toward the exit. "Go calm down. Now. The way you're reacting isn't helping."

When Max stood there, the anger slicing up and down his body, Giselle pushed harder. He stumbled, which must've pulled him out of the dazed rage he'd been in. He stole a glance toward her, then back to Giselle, before turning and stomping out of the kitchen.

Giselle moved closer to her, enacting a protective bubble spell around them. Stella knew she wasn't worried about

Max coming back and attacking. He would never. But it would keep his acute hearing from eavesdropping on their conversation. Soundproof.

"Tell me what's going on."

Stella crossed her arms, her brows drawing low. She had no new information to share. "You know everything I know. I'm sorry I didn't come home. I needed space. I wanted to avoid what is happening right now for as long as possible. I needed a nap."

"That's not what I'm talking about." Giselle mimicked her stance. "I've never seen you this...defensive of a vampire before."

Stella couldn't answer that. She couldn't even explain it to herself why.

"He's the same way. When we warned him off. To leave you alone." Giselle's arms dropped to her sides, her expression intense. "Stella, I've never seen anyone but us act the way he did toward you. He said he'd die before he let something happen to you. He doesn't even know you. How can he be so protective of you?"

Stella shrugged.

"You feel the same way toward him, don't you?"

"I don't know what I feel. It's so..." She threw her hands up in the air. "Confusing. I feel this weird pull toward him. I can't explain it. His friend thinks I'm putting a spell on him. If I thought it were possible for a vampire to do such a thing, I'd think the same about him."

Giselle frowned. "What are you going to do about this?"

She wished she knew.

The first thing she intended to do was discuss the kiss. It had to be done. From there, she had no clue.

9

DONNIE LEFT Holstrom's house in such a hurry, he left his car there. He rushed throughout the city until his emotions settled down. Even then, his veins were thumping hard with desire.

He'd gone into vampire-mode kissing her! How could he have been so reckless? So far gone in his desire to nearly bite her.

Being a vampire made his sex life much more difficult than it had ever been as a human. Finding someone he wanted to sleep with wasn't easy. Humans required a delicate balance. He had to maintain control not to reveal himself. Though, he'd never lost control before. This was a first.

Walking aimlessly around town, his thoughts all over the place, it startled him when he heard his name.

"Yo, Donnie!"

Of all the people to run into.

Jock, Holstrom's brother, sat at a table outside a coffee shop, waving his hand with a ridiculous grin. He had accepted the paranormal world with ease, more so than

Holstrom had. It didn't bother him in the slightest he was waving and gesturing to a vampire—one on the edge of turning—to join him. Not that he knew the turmoil going on inside him.

"Jock, good evening to you."

"Care to join me?" He leaned in. "I mean, I know you won't have a cup of coffee, but feel free to sit and chat a bit."

Why the hell not?

He pulled out a chair and sat down.

"So, how's it going? Breck tells me he has a tough case right now."

Translated into Jock knew a vampire was out there killing people.

"No new leads yet. But we'll handle it."

"I never had a doubt. And that thing with Kade. So glad he's okay, man. Seriously."

He knew a lot more than Donnie realized.

Jock leaned forward again. "You know I'd never say anything about..." His brows raised high. "You know. Everything. You don't have to look like I'd spill all your secrets."

Normally, he could hide his expressions and how he was feeling. This proved he hadn't gotten his equilibrium back from that intense kiss.

"And I appreciate your discretion." Especially about Stella. Jock wouldn't reveal her secret either.

"You looked...lost. You okay?"

That was the second time today someone had told him he looked that way.

"I mean, I know it's none of my business. You don't have to tell me anything. But that's what friends are for. If you need an ear, I have one!" Jock laughed, relaxing into his seat.

It made Donnie chuckle. Not many humans would feel

free to laugh and joke with a vampire. Or coax them into talking about their feelings.

But maybe having a neutral ear was what he needed. He trusted Jock to be impartial about anything he might tell him.

"Have you ever had a past relationship that ended... badly?" There was no term that fit what happened between him and his wife.

The one woman he thought he'd live long years with and then die together. Except he'd been turned and she remained a human. He'd lost his freedom, his life, and the woman he loved with one bite.

Jock nodded. No surprise flickered in his features at the way the conversation turned. Donnie loved how Jock rolled with the punches. "I have. It was a pretty intense relationship. We fell for each other hard. When I wasn't working, I was with her, and vice versa. But her family hated me. I don't know why."

Donnie didn't understand that either. Jock was one of the nicest humans he'd met in a long time.

"We fought too much about it. I didn't want to fight about it either. Family is important. I would never ask her to choose between me or her family. I don't know how it all fell apart, but it did. Now when I see her around town, well, awkward doesn't begin to cover it." Jock took a sip of coffee, then grinned. "I'm assuming you have had one end badly."

He didn't speak of his wife. Ever. To anyone.

Sure, he had alluded to Bailey one time he had loved a human. But that was the most he'd ever uttered out loud about his wife. While Joe knew bits and pieces about his past, not even his oldest friend knew the entire story.

Yet, he was the one who brought up the question. Who started this chat. He could forge on.

"I was..."

Or flee.

"Married."

Jock blinked rapidly, then set his cup down. "Before..." He cleared his throat. "Before you never aged again and at an age where you look like you walked out of the cover of GQ."

Donnie chuckled. That was one way to describe it.

"Yes. Before all that. You can imagine how my marriage ended."

Jock's eyes rounded into large saucers. For the first time in all his interactions, a slice of fear entered Jock's eyes.

Donnie leaned forward, shaking his head. "I did not touch her. I didn't mean it ended that way."

That didn't mean he hadn't been close to it. The reoccurring nightmare he'd been having wasn't made up in his head. He'd damn near killed his own wife because of the blood lust he couldn't control.

"It also doesn't mean I didn't want to. In the beginning, it was impossible to control the urges. The ache in your gut. The need flowing through your veins. You can't possibly understand the struggle."

"No, you're right, I can't. I'm sorry you ever had to go through that."

Still go through it, but he didn't want to frighten the man even more.

"I had to leave. Go as far away from her as I could. The last image she had of me was one of violence. I hate that about myself. That I put her through that. She lived to be fifty-four years old. Staying away from her had been hard, but necessary. Watching her die had been devastating. I would take her being alive and unable to be near her over her death."

Jock wagged his head ceremoniously up and down. "So my story doesn't compare to yours in the slightest. You got me beat."

More laughter slipped out. Jock smiled at the sound. Perhaps that had been his goal. Yet, how could he know Donnie would laugh at such a statement? Maybe he would've been offended.

This was why he'd poured his heart out to Jock. He knew he wouldn't make a big deal about it. He'd listen and not judge.

Jock lifted his drink, sipping. "The first question was a prequel to another one."

Yes, it was. And now that they'd come this far, he didn't want to continue.

"You like someone. It's weighing on your mind. Your relationship ended badly, and we know why. Not your fault, by the way." Jock said that as if he knew he hadn't asked to be turned into a monster. "I get it. Once bitten, twice shy."

Donnie stared at him as his statement hung in the air. Jock had the grace to wince. "That did not come out intentionally."

Then they both burst out laughing.

"I never talk about my wife. Never. I'm glad I chose to do so with you."

A sly grin morphed on Jock's face as he puffed up his chest like he won a prize. "I have many talents." Then he turned serious. "But I'm right, aren't I? You like someone. It feels unattainable."

"It *is* unattainable. I'm a," Donnie cocked a brow, silently saying the word vampire, "and she's..." Well, a witch. But the main problem was it also made her human. Mortal. She would die like everyone else. While the years would keep passing him by. He'd never torture himself with such pain ever again. One time was enough.

He should've never kissed her.

Now the ache for her would grow stronger.

Jock hummed, jerking his head up and down as if he understood the dilemma. "An obstacle, for sure. I've never come across this kind of challenge before, but I do love a challenge. Let me think on it."

"There's nothing to think about, Jock. I would never turn someone. Never."

"Nope, I know." Such confidence on the matter. Amazing. "But I also know there's a solution somewhere. There has to be. You're supposed to live and live and live...alone?"

Yes.

Unfortunately.

"I got this. I love a challenge." The shit-eating grin said he couldn't wait to solve it.

But there was no solution, other than him to keep his distance from Stella before the pull became too much. Where he lost control and did something he'd regret.

"Holstrom!"

Donnie looked around when someone hollered the name. The detective had tried to find him and succeeded? That would be the last time he left his car somewhere. Why had the detective felt compelled to find him? What had Stella told him?

A man crossed the street, smiling and pointing at Jock.

"Hey, Benny!" Jock replied, pointing in return.

Wrong Holstrom. Donnie forgot the two were brothers, they were both so different in every single way.

Yet, Donnie tensed as the man got closer. Because it wasn't a normal human walking across the street.

It was a lycan.

A KNOCK on her door made her freeze. She'd managed to escape further inquiry from Giselle, but she knew it wouldn't be the end of it. Afterward she fled to the bathroom and took the world's longest shower. Now she stood in front of her closet wondering what to wear. It shouldn't matter what she threw on, but of course her brain had to put her in turmoil. What if she saw Donnie again?

Ugh!

It didn't matter what he thought of her.

Whoever was on the other side of the door wouldn't wait long. So she grabbed a random shirt from the closet and put it on before opening the door.

Max stood on the other side looking much calmer and more amenable to talk.

"I'm sorry. The thought of you getting hurt makes me... act a way I can't help."

It was a sentiment she appreciated because it meant he cared. She wrapped her arms around him, letting him know with the hug that she forgave him. Fighting with her friends was the last thing she wanted to do.

He held on, squeezing her tight.

The hug ended, yet she still felt a wide gap between them.

"I know you two talked when I left the room. Silence is always a dead giveaway I'm being blocked from the conversation."

And that's why the tension lingered.

"It wouldn't make you happy what we talked about. Let it go, Max."

He gave a quick jerk of his head. "I will. For you. But just know, I'll kill him if he hurts you. That includes your feelings."

Duly noted.

She wasn't planning on letting Donnie get that close to her. She didn't think she'd survive the attack on her emotions either.

"What's on the agenda this evening?"

Max shrugged. "Scour more of the city for the vamp. We didn't find anything today, but that doesn't mean shit. They can't come out to play during the day anyway. Maybe we'll pick up their scent tonight."

"Sounds like a plan."

She grabbed a jacket and threw it on, then slung her purse over her shoulder. Giselle met them by the front door. Obviously those two had a chat before Max came to see her.

They ventured around town with the window rolled down, so Max could detect the scent. Though nothing good hit his nose. If she had something of the vampire's, she could've done a location spell. It would've made things so much easier.

After driving around for more than an hour, she suggested something that brought the tension back.

A visit to Mona's house.

She wanted to meet the witch, who had a witch locked up in her basement. By the short conversation the men had last night, her aunt had tried to kill her and she managed to trap her. It wasn't easy to trap a witch, so that made Mona quite skilled. Yet, they had given the impression she wasn't.

The unknown always bothered Stella. Which was the case she made to her friends, who finally conceded.

Giselle found their address and they made it there a short time later.

Before she could knock on the door, it opened. Joe stood on the other side.

"What are you doing here?"

Max stood on her left, with Giselle on her right. She knew they were both ready to attack if need be. Stella had no worries it would come to that, despite his hostility.

"Well, we aren't here to visit you. Are the actual owners at home?"

A small woman with vibrant, flashy clothes on and long black hair pushed Joe to the side and smiled. "Hi, I'm Mona." She held out her hand. "You must be Stella. Mason described you to me, but he didn't say you were as beautiful as you are."

Joe huffed under his breath. "She's nothing compared to you, Mona."

Mona swatted his chest. "Be nice. Since when are you a crank pot? Go help Peter hang the shelf in the kitchen."

He glared at her and her friends before leaving.

"Sorry about him. He's been like that since he arrived. So moody. Come in, come in." Mona ushered them in and led them to the living room. "Can I get you anything to drink?"

They declined and took a seat on the couch while Mona sat on a white chair that looked rather uncomfortable. Then she pulled a piece of licorice out of her sweater pocket and started chewing.

Before Stella could strike up idle conversation and then bring up the real reason for their visit, a black cat and a large wolf walked into the room.

Meow.

Mona looked at the cat, chuckling. "Yes, Scatter, this is Stella and her friends." Then Mona looked admonished. "How rude of me. I didn't get your names."

"This is Max," Stella said, pointing to her left. "And this

is Giselle." She pointed to her right. Then she flicked her hand toward the animals. "You have not one, but two guardians. I've never heard of that."

Mona's hand dropped from her mouth, the piece of licorice falling to the floor. "I'm sorry, what?"

Did this woman truly not know what the animals were? Stella sensed what they were right away.

Joe appeared in the room in a blur. Mason rushed in after him. Once again, her friends tensed next to her.

Then two more vampires appeared and Stella had her first hint of unease. Three vampires and a witch against two witches and a lycan. A little uneven, but they would come out on top. They always did. It never did well to think of the alternative. Losing.

Plus, she might not possess the most physical strength in the room, but she was the most powerful. It would zap a lot of her energy—potentially even kill her—but one spell would eliminate them all. She'd never used that particular spell before, but she knew it in case she ever needed it. Dire situations were always possible.

Mona stood up when Mason stepped closer to her, wrapping his arm around her waist. "Mason, this is Stella. Which you know. Her friends are Max and Giselle." She beamed at them with a lively expression, before continuing. "You know Joe." Mona pointed in his direction, then flicked her wrist at the other two vampires. "That's Peter and George."

Stella stood up. Her friends followed suit. She felt on an even keel now. She imagined her friends did as well. They would follow her lead. They wouldn't attack unless she did first.

"What did you mean by she has two guardians?" Joe snapped.

Had the man never heard of them? She had assumed he was quite old. An old vampire who'd been around a long time would've heard of guardians. Plus, he should've been able to sense they were one. Like he could sense witches and other creatures out there. It was why she cloaked she was a witch, so other creatures would never find out her secret. As long as she wore her necklace, which had the spell woven in it, she was protected from revealing what she was.

"They're animals," he added when she didn't respond fast enough to his liking. "Sure, Mona and Mason can understand them, but they're animals."

They were. Which was unheard of. Guardians usually didn't take the form of animals. They were fierce humans with wings. Some creatures saw them as angels, though they had never admitted to being such things. Which was how they'd gotten the moniker of guardian—a guardian angel watching over you.

And to have two guardians. Unprecedented.

Mona raised her hand as if they were in a classroom and she needed permission to speak. "What's a guardian?"

"Protectors. Large, fierce warriors with wings," Joe answered in a much softer voice than he used with her. "Not animals. They chose who they wish to protect. They come from out of nowhere and they stay, making sure no harm comes upon the person, until they're not needed any longer."

"Oh." Mona's hand slid into her pocket, grabbing another piece of licorice as she looked at the animals.

"Ask them," Stella prompted. "Ask them if they are what I say they are. Just because you've never seen them in animal form, doesn't mean it's not possible."

"How would you know if they are? I've seen a guardian once," Joe spat. "I sensed it was one right away. I've never sensed it with these two. Yes, they can speak to Mona and Mason, so that makes them magical of some kind, but not a guardian."

Right about now would be a fabulous time for the obstinate animals to speak up and prove her right. She even glared at them to do so. She swore the cat glared right back with a defiant glitter in its gaze.

A short laugh burst free from Mason. "I knew it." He pointed at the cat. "I've had to lock the door one too many times, Scatter, when I want to be alone with Mona. Tell the truth right now. Because we all know Stella has powers that eclipse everyone in this room. I bet even you."

Scatter strolled with an easy gait toward Mason and Mona, brushing his body against their legs, purring loudly. Then a quiet meow escaped.

Mona jumped and anger flared to life on Mason.

"No, it can't be," Joe muttered.

"I don't understand," Mona said right before she ran out of the room. Mason followed after her. The cat and wolf right behind him.

"Happy now?" Joe crossed his arms.

No. Not by a long shot. She hadn't meant to cause such a ruckus. How was she suppose to know none of them were aware what the animals were?

"I be welcoming you even if me friend doesn't have the manners to do so." Peter walked around Joe with an amicable gesture on his face. "I be hearing quite a lot about you, Stella. It's nice to meet ya."

Stella knew she was going to love Peter without a doubt in her mind. "I heard a few things about you as well. Protecting your friend Mona from an evil aunt or something."

"Or something is right," Giselle said with a shiver.

"When you said they mentioned evil, I didn't think it would be this bad."

Giselle wasn't wrong. Evil spilled out of every nook and cranny in the house. It overwhelmed to the point of suffocation.

"I be telling ya," Peter yelled at Joe, pointing a long finger at him.

Joe sighed, loosening his stance for the first time that night. "Is that why you're here?"

Stella smiled. "I'm not your enemy. While I never thought I'd work with a vampire on anything, I'm always willing to try something new."

Hell, she kissed a vampire tonight. That was definitely something new. Which brought the burning question to the forefront of her mind.

Where was Donnie? Why wasn't he here amongst his friends?

Maybe it was better he wasn't here. Less distraction to the matter at hand.

"As much as I don't want to upset your friend Mona further, she needs to address the evil aunt situation."

Joe ran a hand down his face. George didn't say a word. And Peter grinned like he was the devil himself.

Max cleared his throat, prompting her to look his way. "As much as I don't want to side with Joe on this one, even though he didn't say it out loud, I don't think now is the best time to do that."

Max and Joe shared a long look, surprise filtering in both their eyes.

"Why not?"

Max gave a humorless laugh. "Stella, you threw a wrench in their world by outing their animal friends as guardians. Remember that fairy we met in France. She wanted to murder her guardian because of how overprotective he was of her. She couldn't breathe from his suffocating presence."

Stella cocked a brow. Did he not see any resemblance to how he treated her?

When it dawned on him, his cheeks turned red, but he didn't apologize. "What I'm getting at is, one huge wrench at a time. Let them come to terms with two guardians in their mix and then we tackle the aunt issue."

Peter groaned. "I hate to be admitting you have a point."

Another throat cleared, this time from George. "Why are they animals? If it's not normal. And Bozo was originally with Marcella. Why would he protect her, then switch to Mona?" He looked at the three of them. "Bozo is the wolf. Marcella is the evil aunt."

Good questions, and Stella had no answer for any of it. How would she? All she knew was they were guardians. She sensed it the moment they walked into the room. While she couldn't understand them speak like Mona and Mason could, she knew without a doubt she wasn't wrong in her assessment.

"Where's your friend? Donnie?" Max snapped. "Why isn't he here?"

Oh, Stella would love to know the answer to the question as well. Dying to know.

10

THE FIRST THOUGHT that hit Donnie was did Jock know the man was a lycan? It was hard to tell with Jock because he was such an easy-going guy, accepting everything thrown at him as if it were no big deal.

"What's up, man?" Jock said in his usual jovial voice, standing up to clasp hands and do the quick one-armed hugs men did.

"Not much. How have you been, my friend?" The quick glance his way indicated the lycan was issuing a subtle warning. Hurt my friend and I hurt you.

Ditto, asshole!

"Work, work, work. That's what it seems like lately. Oh, hey, my bad." Jock laughed, not appearing to notice the tension at all. "This is my friend, Donnie. Donnie, this is my friend, Benny."

Donnie nodded but didn't move an inch. One wrong move and all hell would break loose. He knew it by the dangerous glint in Benny's eyes. He might appear all serene, but there was a fire brewing in his veins.

There was no way Donnie could walk away from

Jock without warning him what kind of creature he was friends with. No doubt, the lycan wouldn't leave without doing the same. Might as well get it out in the open.

"Please, why don't you have a seat?" Donnie suggested. "Jock knows I'm a vampire. The question is does he know you're a lycan?"

Jock flinched, and even backed up a step. Donnie could've kissed the man on the lips. Yes. Trusting a lycan was never wise. At least, in his experience. And it answered his question. He had no idea.

Benny sighed and took a seat across from him. Jock slowly sat back down in his chair.

"Since when have you been a lycan?"

Laughter filled the air. "Since I was born. Holstrom, you kill me with the funny shit you say."

Donnie took it more as a rhetorical question, but he remained silent on the matter. And he wished the man would stop calling him Holstrom. His brother was Holstrom. He was Jock. That's how Donnie differentiated the two, and he wanted it to stay that way.

The lighting wasn't the best outside, but Donnie knew Jock's cheeks brightened.

"Why are you conversing with a vamp?" Benny's eyes leveled a hard stare at him.

"Didn't you hear him?" Donnie feigned a relaxed posture, though was ready to attack in an instant if need be. "We're friends."

Benny inhaled a deep breath and released it before turning his attention to Jock. "I hate to break it to you, but vampires are killers. He will not hesitate to drink every last ounce of your blood. You would be wise to cut ties with him and let me deal with him."

Jock straightened. "He is my friend and you will not touch him. He would never kill someone."

He appreciated the confidence, but he had in the past.

"He's already killed."

True, but not in many, many years.

"There's two recent dead bodies to prove it."

Donnie's entire body went taut and ready. He wasn't positive how many packs were in the area. Generally, it was one pack per town because they didn't share territory well with others. But he'd seen stranger things before. Perhaps Benny was from the same one he had been intending to meet with? The same one that attacked Kade?

It suddenly seemed odd how he'd come across a lycan when he usually didn't, despite knowing there was a pack in the area. They knew how to keep their distance from other creatures.

Jock scoffed. "Yeah, I know. My brother is working the case. Donnie's helping him. He didn't do it."

"Your brother and his partner, Detective Waters, are two humans who can't handle this. Leave this issue to me."

At least this lycan didn't know Stella was a witch. He sure in the hell hoped Jock didn't spill her secret.

"No, Benny. I will not leave this issue to you. It's my brother's case and *he'll* handle it."

"Look, Holstrom, you—"

"You attacked my friend Kade, didn't you?" Donnie was finished listening and ready to start doing.

Benny turned his gaze toward him in slow increments as if that was supposed to frighten him or something.

"Anyone deemed a threat will be dealt with."

Not a yes or no, but it sounded like a resounding yes. What the hell did that even mean? A threat will be dealt with? How had Kade threatened them?

"A bunch of humans working with vampires." Benny leaned closer, the rage plastered in every corner of his face. "What kind of spell do you have on them? You're controlling my friend, Holstrom, somehow."

It was Jock, damn it! Not Holstrom.

"I'm not a warlock, asshole." He couldn't be, not if he was a vampire.

"Oh, no. I've heard of vampires putting spells on people. To do your bidding. To kill them easier. It's easy enough to do when you have a witch in your midst." Benny laughed, a vicious one. "Don't worry, Holstrom, the spell you're under will soon be broken when they're gone."

As if this asshole would be able to kill him.

"I want to speak to the leader of your pack."

Another evil, boisterous laugh came out. "You're talking to him. There's nothing you can say that I will believe."

Well, that sucked. There would be no reasoning this guy.

"Benny, there is no spell on me. Donnie is a good guy. Mona would not put a spell on us."

"He's a monster and will be dealt with accordingly." Benny slammed his hand on the table. "Two humans already dead, Holstrom. What more proof do you need?"

Jock drew his mouth into a thin line. "He did not do anything."

The expression was so foreign on his face Donnie wanted to laugh. Though the emotion didn't escape his lips. Now was not the time to be laughing.

"Your brother is safe, as is his partner. They're just trying to do their jobs."

Jock moved closer. "What does that mean? Who are you insinuating isn't safe? Is Donnie right and you hurt Kade? He has a wife and kid! He didn't do anything wrong either."

"Enacting a recon mission for a bunch of vamps is most definitely doing something wrong."

Shit!

Bailey's mistake was coming back to bite them in the ass. One error and it was turning fatal.

Jock slumped back into his chair as he rolled that information around. The man might not be around all the time, but his brother kept him up-to-date on the kinds of things they did.

"So let me get this straight so I'm not missing anything. Since you're not spitting it out. You tried to kill Kade and used his ex-best friend as a lure, which is insane. Now you plan on killing Mason, Mona, Bailey, and the other vampires, including Donnie here. Do you plan on killing little Emerson too?"

Benny flinched as if Jock had slapped him after the last question.

"To keep you safe. To keep the people in this town safe. Yes. I would eliminate all of them. Minus the child. He's innocent."

Well, at least the asshole wasn't a baby killer.

"Assuming you managed to do all of that,"—and Donnie knew he'd never lose against this piece of shit—"you'll lose a lot of people in your pack trying to do so. We won't go easy. What are your plans when the actual vampire killer resurfaces? You'll be down men, weak, tired, and very easy to finish off for that vampire. And if they're with a coven and not a rogue, you'll be in a world of shit."

Benny hesitated, as if the doubt were starting to creep in.

"I don't want a war with you. Even though you did hurt my friend. He's alive. He'll heal. I might be feeling differently if there had been another outcome. I want peace between us. Did Mason and Kade step on your property?

Yes. An honest mistake on their part. The moment they realized it, they left. The enemy we should be discussing is the vampire out there killing innocent people."

"I don't believe you."

No, he wouldn't be easily swayed to the truth.

"So my brother and her partner are safe?"

Benny gestured with a firm nod, but he didn't take his eyes off him. Not that Donnie thought he'd attack in public. That would give humans who had no clue about the paranormal world a show they wouldn't be able to handle.

Jock pulled out his phone and put it on speaker.

"Hey, Jock," Holstrom answered on the second ring.

"Warn Kade and Mason right now there will be another attack from lycans. Apparently, Benny, from the firehouse a town over, is the leader of said pack. He's issued a kill order on the asinine thinking that they're working with our vampire friends to kill humans."

Donnie grinned at the way Benny's eyes enlarged as Jock kept going on in his quick speech.

"He thinks they're under a spell or something from Mona. You and Stella are safe as humans. Even though Mason, Kade, and Bailey are human too. So if they were under a spell, it's not their fault. But I guess that doesn't matter for some reason because they have to die. So if you could kindly let them know they're about to be attacked, that would be great. Oh, and—"

"Enough!"

Benny pushed hard on the end call button.

Jock leaned back, looking pretty damn smug.

It might not be enough warning, but it was a warning so that's all that mattered.

"You were always a blabbermouth, Holstrom. You never know when to shut up."

"Tell me I'm wrong. Tell me which part is not true, and I'll shut up."

Benny rose from his chair. "Fine. Your human friends are safe. The four vampires though, and the witch." Benny looked him dead in the eye. "Are dead by sunrise."

Then he walked away with large strides. The man was on a mission.

"I can check that off my list. Thanks, Jock."

The man laughed. "For what? He still plans to attack you."

Donnie rolled his eyes. "I can fight him with my eyes closed and still win. I don't want to, of course. But if it's him or me, it'll be him. I had intended to request a meeting with the leader to talk this through and I just did. He backed off hurting the others. There is that. Without you, I doubt he would've conceded that part. So, yes, thank you. Not good though that he wants to hurt Mona as well."

"You seem unfazed by imminent death."

"It's not imminent. It's life. I've been hunted my entire existence. Benny's another one in a long line of hunters." Donnie stood up. "Don't worry about me and my friends. We'll be fine. Call your brother back. Ease his mind."

Though the phone hadn't rung, he knew Holstrom was going out of his mind with worry. No doubt, he was on the phone with Mason or Kade right this moment issuing the warning. That had to be his next stop as well.

Mason's house.

His friends were there and they would need the backup. So would Mona. He wasn't that close to them. They lived between this town and the town where Kade resided. It would take him far longer than he liked to get there.

"Can I borrow your car?" He was fast, but not that fast. He needed wheels to help him along.

"Anything."

Jock tossed him the keys.

"I'll even help you fight Benny. Now I want to get a few good licks in."

Donnie chuckled. "As much as I appreciate the sentiment, I have to decline. He'd crush you, Jock. I do hate admitting that."

By Jock's infuriated face as he walked away, he hated hearing it too.

———

SHE WAITED with bated breath for one of them to answer Max's question. Where was Donnie?

"Helping Holstrom. There's a vampire out there that needs to be caught," Joe replied.

But it was a lie. Donnie had been with Holstrom, but he wasn't anymore. Which meant Joe didn't know where his friend was.

"Well, we won't take any more of your time. We do need to find the vampire." Giselle gestured toward the door, as if Stella would follow.

She wasn't ready to leave.

Of course they had decided they wouldn't be touching the aunt issue yet, and she wasn't going to step in the guardian mess.

She didn't want to leave because Donnie could show up. Bottom line.

Joe nodded. "What part of the city will you be searching? We can take the other side."

"I be staying here, but it be a good idea," Peter added.

So they were officially working with all three vampires

on the case. She would've never guessed in a million years she'd work with a vampire for any reason at all.

"We already covered—" Max stopped speaking when Mason rushed into the room.

"We have a problem." Mason rushed out everything Holstrom had relayed to him.

First a vampire killer, and now a lycan problem.

Sure, it didn't affect her in any way. She was safe because they thought she was a mere human. But she wouldn't stand by while these people were attacked for something they weren't responsible for. She believed in justice. In the truth. In right and wrong.

Joe walked to the living room window, pulling the curtain aside. "I don't hear or sense any lycans outside." The curtain fluttered close. "Of course that doesn't mean they aren't. They could be on the edge where we can't detect them."

"What do we do?" Mason ran a hand through his hair. "Mona is not in the right mind frame right now to fight. She's so upset with Scatter and Bozo. I can't say I blame her. I'm pissed too."

"I be protecting her with me life." Gone was the friendliness in Peter's eyes, replaced with fury. "You as well, Mason."

"George and I aren't leaving either. Though that leaves Kade and Bailey unprotected. So one of us has to go there."

Stella was about to offer her help when Joe pulled his phone out of his pocket. "Donnie, where the hell are you?"

Donnie could protect them, and she could as well. It would give her time and the opportunity to bring up the kiss.

They all waited and listened to the one side of the conversation.

"Okay, so Jock got Benny to not hurt Mason, Kade, or Bailey. But us vampires and Mona are still in danger."

"Why, Mona?" Mason asked in a pained breath. "She hasn't done anything."

Joe walked closer, putting a hand on his shoulder. "They think she's helping us put a spell on all of you. So you do what we say."

"She would never...if I talk to this Benny guy..." But Mason's words trailed off, knowing it would be useless.

Then Mason turned his attention to her. "Scatter and Bozo aren't giving us the full story right now, but you're right, they're guardians. They've been lying to us. I'm so damn pissed it happened right now."

Meaning, he was pissed at her.

"Will you please stay and help me protect my wife? I can't lose her."

Since it was her fault she put Mona in such a frenzied state, she should stay and help.

Before she could respond, Max stepped in front of her. Full protective mode activated. There would be no stopping him when he got this way.

"Stella doesn't use her powers unless necessary. Nothing good happens when she uses them. I'm glad your friend Kade is okay, but I don't agree with what she did. She exposed herself. She put herself in danger. Any one of you could hurt her now knowing what she is. I'm not about to let her expose herself to an entire lycan pack. It's not happening."

Giselle took a stance next to Max, letting everyone in the room know she agreed with him. This was what her friends did. Protected her from any possible threat.

She let them. Because they were right. She'd survived this long by rarely displaying her powers. And when she did, it was to a creature that was about to die. They couldn't share her secret.

Mason looked on the verge of tears. Joe clamped his hand on his shoulder. "We got this, Mason. It's okay she won't help. We will not let anything happen to Mona. I swear to you."

It wasn't that she didn't want to help...

None of them could understand what kind of burden she lived with.

Max shoved a hand behind his back, warning her off. How did he know she wanted to speak? To make them understand her position. He was telling her she didn't have to explain herself.

"We're leaving." Max turned, putting his arm around her waist.

She let him lead her out of the room, boxed in by him and Giselle. She felt like a coward retreating in such a manner. Not even speaking up for herself.

They were leaving these people to be butchered by wolves. Maybe three vampires and a witch would be enough to fend them off. But for how long? How big was the pack? Lives would be shed tonight. On both sides. She knew Mason wouldn't stand by while people attacked his wife. He'd be injured, or worse, killed.

"No, Stella," Max growled under his breath, opening the car door.

He knew her too well. Where her thoughts were taking her. What she wanted to do.

"Their deaths will be on our hands," she whispered, not getting into the car, despite the pressure he put on her back to do so.

"They can take care of themselves."

Giselle tensed on the other side of the car. "We might be too late."

Max's entire body froze as his eyes turned a bright, vibrant green. His wolf senses were on alert.

Stella saw them. Eight lycans crossed the street. The door shielded her, as did Max's body. Giselle was in more danger than she was by herself on the other side of the car.

"Benny said you weren't to be touched. A human doing her job. Yet, here you are at the traitor's house and surrounded by a lycan and a witch," the blonde man with a bushy mustache said, standing as the leader in the large group. "Care to explain?"

"I don't even know who you are or what you're talking about," Stella replied, her heart beating steady and clear. It would trip them up, wondering if she were telling the truth or not.

His gaze leveled at her. "Are you telling me you don't know you're standing next to a lycan and a witch? Or you don't know that we're about to kill the vampires you're looking for? The ones who murdered your two victims?"

"How do you know it's these vampires who did such a thing?"

His gaze turned even more murderous. "We know." Then he looked at Max. "Who are you?"

Max laughed. "I don't answer to you. Who I am is none of your business. My friends and I are leaving."

Oh, Max.

They couldn't leave these people to fend for themselves. What would Donnie think of her then? To leave his friends to die.

Max put pressure on her back to get into the car. She didn't budge.

Then everyone turned their attention to the front door. Joe, George, and Peter had emerged. No Mona, though.

Joe stepped off the porch first, George and Peter standing behind him. "We don't want to fight you. We are not the ones who killed those humans. If you look in the fridge inside this house, you'll see we drink blood from a bag, not a human."

The blonde man inhaled deeply, then released a heavy sigh, a chuckle floating out as well. "As if we'd believe the lies from a vampire."

"We will defend ourselves. But it's not what we want to do."

Stella gave Joe credit. He was trying his hardest to avoid a fight.

"Don't worry. It'll be over before you know it," the blonde man cackled.

Then they rushed forward.

Stella couldn't allow this to happen. A deep ache in her gut told her she'd regret it if she let this go forward.

"Stella, no," Max whispered in her ear.

He didn't understand.

Hell, she barely understood.

Before they could morph, they hit an invisible wall, making them stumble backward. They turned their attention toward them.

"Witch!"

DONNIE ARRIVED moments before the fight broke out. Or would've, anyway. He'd never seen such a large protective barrier erected in his life. It covered the entire house, including his friends, protecting them from anything outside of it.

"Get that black-haired bitch!"

Stella had protected his friends, so he would return the favor.

He zoomed toward Giselle, taking position in front of her. Though his entire body and mind screamed he should be standing in front of Stella.

Except these lycans thought Giselle was causing the protective barrier. That she was the only witch outside. He had no idea Stella could be so powerful. To enact a spell and keep her identity hidden at the same time. She looked deep in concentration, but her heartbeat was steady as a drum, not giving away her emotions.

Stella...

She twitched.

As if she had heard his plea.

But that couldn't be.

The blonde-haired guy in the lead laughed. "I bet you wish you were standing next to your friends right now. But it doesn't matter. As soon as we kill this witch, you're all dead."

"You can try, but none of you are getting past me to her."

"One vampire against eight of us."

"Make that nine." Benny stepped onto the sidewalk, taking a position next to his friends.

Donnie's lips formed into a cocky gesture. "Well, I beat you here. What makes you think you can beat me in a fight?"

"I ran into a few red lights." Benny shrugged. "But I will best you in a fight."

"The blonde bitch should die too. She's clearly working with the vampires," the man next to Benny said.

"Oh, but Benny already gave his word she wasn't to be touched." And Donnie swore he'd make their deaths that much more painful if they even looked at Stella in the wrong way.

Benny nodded. "I did. She can't help it if she's under a spell."

If they only knew the truth.

"But the witch and lycan she's with can die. They're working with these vamps," Benny added.

"Actually," Donnie started, "we just met them. We're not even friends. Your issue is with us. So they're leaving and then we can finish this fight you're dying to have."

Benny cackled. "You expect me to believe that?"

"You're a very obstinate man. I bet your pack hates having to come to you with issues. I bet you never listen to what they have to say. You make up your mind and never budge from it. How infuriating that must be for them."

A muscle ticked on Benny's cheek.

"I am friends with Mona and Mason. Mona is a good witch. A kind woman. She would never hurt anyone. I am not lying when I say I just met the witch behind me and the lycan over there. I can't say I like them. They don't like me and my friends either. Do you, Max?" Donnie looked at the man for him to verify.

A smirk punctured Max's lips. "I hate you."

Donnie swept a hand outward as if revealing the magic trick. "See. The man hates me. And come on, have you ever heard of a lycan and a vampire working together? Have you?"

Benny looked doubtful again. The same expression he had when he tried to reason with him at the cafe.

"Then why are you protecting them? If you all don't like each other."

Because he'd do anything for Stella. Anything.

"Because while you might think I'm a killer, it's not the truth. I protect people who need protecting. Why would I idly stand by so you can hurt innocent people? You claim to want to keep people safe? Yet, you're acting like a monster."

A car rumbling down the darkened street had them all freezing. The car stopped in the middle of the road. When Holstrom exited the car, he wanted to scream at the man for walking right into danger.

He'd be the hardest to protect. A mere human. The witch and lycan would be able to hold their own, but Holstrom didn't stand a chance. He couldn't trust Benny to keep his word not to hurt any of their human friends.

"This...looks intense," Holstrom said, shutting his door and stepping closer to the fray. "Benny."

Benny inclined his head toward Holstrom. "Detective. You shouldn't have come."

Holstrom cleared his throat. "Well, my partner is here."

He threw a hand toward Stella. "Considering I just received a phone call of another dead body, we need to get to work. To find the *real* vampire out there killing people."

Benny's stance loosened. "Excuse me? Another person has been murdered?"

Holstrom shook his head rapidly up and down. "I got the call not that long ago. Another woman. Two small puncture wounds in her neck. Her sister called it in. From the information I got from the responding officer, she got off of work two hours ago, and her sister arrived an hour later. That means she died within an hour of getting home. Her sister is lucky she didn't get there sooner. Donnie was with me this evening, and when he left, he was with my brother. Which you know because you saw him yourself. Since you've suspected all of these vampires to be the culprits, I imagine your men have been keeping an eye on them. So they can tell you what those three have been up to." Holstrom gestured toward Joe and the guys still standing by the porch.

Benny looked at his friends, then at him before turning to the blonde guy next to him. "Report."

The blonde guy huffed in disgust. "They've been at this house all night. None of them left. These three arrived a little bit ago." The guy motioned to Max, Stella, and Giselle.

"We want the same thing, Benny," Holstrom stated. "To get a killer off the streets. But these vampires are not the ones we're looking for."

"They're still killers."

"If you want to believe that, sure. But they're not." Holstrom put a hand on his hip, near the gun that rested there. Not that Donnie believed he'd pull it out and start shooting. "In any case, they're not the threat right now. This rogue vampire is. You want to be useful, you want to help the people in this area, then help find *that* vampire. And leave these ones alone."

Benny stared at Holstrom for the longest time before jerking his attention toward him. They maintained eye contact with each step he took toward him. "You and your friends are safe for now. But don't think we won't be back. One wrong step and you're dead."

Donnie didn't think the statement required a response, so he remained silent. The lycans left.

As soon as all of them were out of sight and hearing distance, Holstrom let out a huge breath.

"Holy shit. That was intense."

The man's heart rate was through the roof.

Donnie chuckled, walking toward the detective, clamping a hand on his shoulder. "You're much braver than I gave you credit for. Good job, detective."

"Umm...this barrier." Joe waved his hands at the shield still erected. Nothing could get in or out. They were trapped.

"Stella!" Max shouted, which jolted her out of her trance she must've put herself in.

The shield fell.

So did Stella.

Donnie was by her side in an instant, though Max caught her before she hit the ground. The man glared at him, but it didn't make him back up even an inch. He wanted her in *his* arms.

"I'm fine." But the way she whispered it, her eyes barely staying open, told a different story. She wasn't fine. She'd exerted way too much energy trying to protect his friends.

"Bring her inside."

Max was startled at Joe's quiet command, but listened without argument.

They all filed inside the house and into the living

room where Max laid Stella down on the couch. Donnie wanted to be by her side. But without causing another potential war, he couldn't do as he wished. Max stayed by her, and Giselle took up position behind the couch to protect her from behind. None of them had anything to fear though.

Joe, George, and Peter stood on the other side of the room, while he, Mason, and Holstrom stayed near the entrance.

"I'm fine. Holstrom and I should go. There's a crime scene that needs our attention." Stella tried to sit up but failed. The exhaustion was evident.

"I can handle this, Stella." Holstrom looked at Mason. "Want to tag alone?"

"Of course."

"I'm taking Stella home." Max looked around the room, keeping his gaze on him longer than anyone else. As if he'd be the one to argue. "Then I can meet you at the crime scene. Track the scent of the vampire."

"George and I will go as well," Joe offered.

"No," Mason cut in, "I need two of you here. To protect Mona. She's not in the right frame of mind, and if...if something happened with her aunt, I need two of you here."

"George, you stay with Peter." Donnie wanted to be with Stella, but it wouldn't be happening tonight. "I'll go with Joe. We'll track the scent with Max."

"Max," Giselle said with a firm tone, jolting his attention off him. "I'll take Stella home. They need you more here. I've got her."

Donnie could tell he wanted to argue. So did he. Because he wanted to be the one to take her home. To see to her needs.

Neither man argued.

They all left to find the vampire causing havoc in their lives.

The crime scene had been chaos. Police personnel combing the entire neighborhood. He, Joe, and Max had to wait quite a bit before they could get close enough to detect a scent.

Once they did, the hunt had been on.

They were quiet the entire time. Even on the ride to the scene, no one had spoken.

The vampire's scent took them through the entire city. Going down one street, just to take an abrupt turn down another. At times it felt like they were going around in circles. When the scent ended at another abandoned building, except this time on the other side of town from the other one, Donnie knew they'd been led on a merry chase.

"This vampire is smart. It knows how to dodge us." Donnie couldn't wait to get his hands on the bastard. For the mere aggravation he was putting him through.

"It won't work forever." Joe crossed his arms, sighing. "We'll get this vampire."

"I'll let Giselle know this location. She can do more digging." Max tossed one shoulder up in a careless gesture. "Probably won't mean anything though. The vamp most likely used these locations to drown out their scent. Too many smells here. But I'll let her know anyway."

Donnie wanted to add that he ask about Stella, but refrained. It wouldn't do well for this man to know his feelings toward her.

Max shot off a text.

Silence filled the alleyway where they stood between the two vacant buildings.

It stretched.

And stretched.

They were done here. They could part ways.

Donnie was about to suggest that when Max broke the silence.

"I want to say thank you for stepping in front of Giselle. For protecting her." The aggrieved expression on Max's face said it was a hard thing to admit. "You didn't have to, and yet you did."

Joe scoffed. "Yeah, when you would've left us high and dry."

Max threw him an angry glare. "I was protecting my friends."

"You're welcome."

His simple remark had the ire in Joe deflating.

"When Stella recovers, I want to wish her a great deal of thanks as well." Joe uncrossed his arms, letting them fall to his sides. "She didn't have to protect us, and yet she did."

Donnie nearly laughed at Joe's almost identical phrase Max had given him.

Max's own anger lessened. "She never thinks of herself, always putting others before her. It drives me up the wall. You're welcome. Accept it from me because I doubt she'll say it. She doesn't like the praise. She doesn't do it for the praise."

Joe swallowed hard, looking sheepish for the first time that Donnie could ever recall. "Her secret is safe with us. Donnie already told you he'd lay down his life for her. I'm telling you the same thing now. No one will touch her if I have anything to say about it. With this lycan pack on our tails, who knows what they're capable of."

"Yes, that is an additional worry I didn't want to have." Max blew out a breath, shuffling his feet. "Once we find this vamp, we'll be on our way. We never stay in one place for very long."

Donnie was not looking forward to that day. Would he be able to let her leave? Would he be able to not follow her?

"We would be much obliged if you helped with Mona's aunt before you leave." Joe shrugged. "Well, if Stella would help. She mentioned stripping her of her powers. I don't doubt anymore that she can do it. That woman is capable of anything."

"That's why we stopped by the house. Stella wanted to help. I know we won't be leaving until that happens."

"Now what?" Joe asked, looking at him as if he had all the answers.

Now he wanted to be by Stella's side until she regained her strength.

But he knew that wasn't what he could say out loud.

"Now we continue our search."

12

A POUNDING ECHOED LOUDLY. It took her a moment to realize it was coming from inside her head and not from anywhere else.

She didn't move, hoping it would go away.

Lying there, waiting for it to recede, was taking too long. Opening her eyes felt like trying to pry iron bars apart. But she managed to create tiny slits to see her room was shrouded in darkness. That didn't tell her much, whether it was night or day, because the curtains were closed. Though she was grateful for the low lighting as it didn't increase the massive headache beating her to a pulp.

Several more minutes went by before she could open her eyes all the way. That helped her to determine it was daytime. Small wisps of light poked through above the curtains.

It took another few minutes to sit up in bed. The movement caused the pain to ricochet from one part of her body to the next. From her head to her arms to her legs and back up again, repeating the pathway. Though it didn't stop her from scooting to the edge of the bed and standing up.

She wobbled on her feet, having to press her hand to the bed to keep herself upright. When she felt more stable, she put one foot forward. Then another. And another. Until she made it to the door.

The knob twisted with ease even as her body screamed with pain. The flight down the stairs wasn't any better. By the time she made it to the kitchen, she wanted to cry from the exertion it took to make it that far.

"Holy shit, you're awake." Giselle pulled out a stool, helping her to sit down. Then she made her way back to the coffee machine, pouring a cup, and grabbing two pain pills before setting all the items before her.

God bless her best friend for knowing what she needed. She downed the pills with a large gulp of coffee, drinking over half of it before setting it down. Giselle refilled it to the top.

"Where's Max?"

Giselle grabbed her own coffee mug, lifting it to her lips. Either because she wanted to take a sip or to hide the smile that burst across her face.

"A lot has happened while you've been resting."

Nothing bad if her devious smile was any indication.

"How long was I out?"

Some of the laughter disappeared from her eyes. "Stella, you need to promise me you'll never do something like that again. It was dangerous and reckless and you could've been killed."

That didn't answer her question.

She knew she'd do the same exact thing if the need arose. Giselle knew it too.

"Three days."

Her brows shot up in disbelief.

"Yes, Stella. The stunt you pulled took you out of

commission for three whole days. For a while there, I was worried you weren't going to wake up. Especially since you were conscious right after it happened. You fell asleep on the ride home and I couldn't wake you up. It scared the living hell out of me. That's why you can't ever do it again." Giselle leaned across the island counter, the fear ramping up in her eyes. "You put a protective spell over an entire house. A freaking huge-ass house! You're lucky your necklace kept your cloaking abilities working. You could've killed yourself from the immense use of power alone! You've never done something of that magnitude before. You had no idea how it would affect you."

Well, she knew now. It knocked her on her ass and then some. The headache still waging a war inside her head said she would contemplate it a little bit more next time. Her body felt like she'd hit a brick wall at high-speed impact.

"So where's Max?"

Giselle rolled her eyes that she dare ignore the plea to not act so recklessly again. She couldn't promise such a thing or lie to her friend.

"You'll never guess."

She didn't have the energy to play games. Her mind wasn't intact for it. "Okay." She stood up. The shower was calling her name. She didn't need Giselle ripping into her.

"Where are you going?"

Wasn't it obvious?

"I can't think right now. I can't do this with you."

Then she left the kitchen, walking to the bathroom without grabbing a change of clothes.

The hot water helped soothe her somewhat, but not as much as she hoped it would. She stood under the spray until the water turned lukewarm. Even then she didn't want to get out, but she did. Wrapped in a towel, she left the bathroom and headed for her room.

Instead of getting dressed right away, she sat on the bed. She didn't even care it would make a wet spot on her bed from the damp towel.

That's how Giselle found her. She sat next to her and grabbed her hand, squeezing hard. "I'm sorry. I know right now is not the best time to get in your face, but you scared me. You really, really scared me."

Her head fell to Giselle's shoulder. "I'm sorry too. I didn't mean to scare you. But I couldn't let them get hurt."

"Why do I sense it wasn't about them? That it was about Donnie."

Her instincts were spot on. She didn't need to voice her affirmation about it. Giselle didn't press the issue, for which she was grateful.

"That whole evening changed everything. I can't say we're best of friends, but we are on friendlier terms with that whole crew now. Max is with Donnie and the rest of them searching for this vamp killer."

That had her lifting her head. "It's daylight."

Giselle grinned. "And Donnie's house is vampire proofed since ours isn't. They have a map of the city. They've been searching it grid by grid each night. We will find this vampire and kill it. We will find where it's hiding."

Unexpected, but very welcome news. She didn't like being at odds with her friends. The more people helping on the case, the faster they could close it.

"Max left about an hour ago. They'll map out what area they'll search tonight and then head out afterwards. It's late afternoon. You were gearing up for day four of not waking up."

She clutched Giselle's hand. "I am sorry for scaring you. I will try not to let it happen again."

Giselle didn't look convinced, pursing her lips in a thin line. "I guess I'll have to accept that."

"I should get dressed. Join them in the search."

A slow, rising brow said she was being presumptuous in her abilities to return so fast. Yes, she had to agree she still felt weak as hell, but she was awake now. She couldn't sit idly by while everyone else did the work.

"What did you tell my boss?"

Because she knew Giselle handled her absence at work. She surprised her again.

"Holstrom took care of that. Not sure what he told your captain. But he said not to worry about it."

She was starting to like Holstrom. How could she not, especially how he'd driven right up to a battle about to begin between lycans and vampires with no thought to his own safety.

"He's been worried about you."

Holstrom? Sweet, but not necessary. She didn't need another overprotective macho male in her life. One was enough.

"I'll let Holstrom know his worries were appreciated, but not needed."

Giselle laughed, bumping her shoulder with hers. "Not who I was talking about. But, yeah, I'm sure he's worried about you too."

Max? Well, duh. Of course he worried about her. That was a never-ending, daily occurrence with him.

"I'm talking about Donnie."

Oh.

Well.

That one shouldn't surprise her either, but it did.

"He's been here every evening. Max and I have never extended an invitation inside." Giselle hesitated, as if embarrassed Donnie had welcomed them into his house but they couldn't offer the same courtesy. "But he's never asked for one either. He stares at the house, at the window where he knows you sleep, for the longest time. Then he leaves. He doesn't mention you often with Max. He comes by the house, does his intense staring, and that's it."

She didn't know what to think about that.

"But I can see the worry on his face. The pain, as if he can feel what you were suffering. I don't understand this pull you two have with each other."

"I don't either."

While she wanted to admit they kissed, she stopped herself. That was between her and Donnie.

"You know I hate it when I don't understand something. I research it. I dissect it. I obsess over it until it makes sense."

Yes, that's why Giselle was their technology gal. She was good at ferreting out the information.

"My search started with you, being a cosmic witch. I was worried why you weren't waking up. I had to dig in the old archives about cosmic witches. It wasn't easy. But I found a few things. Enough to make me lessen my worry that you would wake up. You needed to recharge. You exerted so much energy it wiped you out. I understand that now."

She waited for Giselle to continue, but she felt nervous energy erupt in her veins.

"Then I came across a section about cosmic witches and finding their soulmate. It says that when a cosmic witch meets their soulmate, their power is a hundred times greater. There was no mention of *actual* documentation of a cosmic witch ever meeting their soulmate, but I wonder what one would look like when they do. I wonder if that's something that frightened people even more about them. That they could be even more powerful than they realized. That they tried to prevent them from meeting the love of their life. That's why so many have died."

She wasn't sure she liked where Giselle was going with this.

"Of course, their power isn't magnified until they declare their love for each other."

What was she supposed to say to any of this?

Did Giselle honestly think Donnie was her soulmate? A vampire?

Giselle leaned in closer. "It doesn't specify that it's a warlock that is a cosmic witch's soulmate. It doesn't specify any kind of creature."

"He's a vampire."

Why pretend she didn't know what Giselle was alluding to?

Giselle nodded, rubbing her free hand over their clasped hands. "There's a powerful connection between you two that you can't deny. What else could it be?"

Her soulmate?

Donnie?

"Do we even believe in such things as soulmates? That would mean fate is involved. What is fate but a way to take the power away from you on how you live your life."

A grim expression emerged on Giselle. "If magic can exist, then so can fate and soulmates and destiny and all that stuff that sounds ridiculous." She gripped her hand. "You never date. Max and I are your only friends. You keep a hard shell around your heart. All for good reasons. I know this. I know why. But if there is a small chance that love is possible for you, that you could be happy, then why not jump right into fate?"

"I'm happy," Stella responded as she frowned.

"Yes, you're beaming with happiness." Giselle rolled her eyes. "Do you think I like the thought that your possible soulmate is a vampire? I'm not too fond of it." Her brows drew low, the worry creeping into her eyes. "It's something I would conjure in a nightmare." Then her tightened expression relaxed. "But for a vampire, he's not that bad. He's even had Max laughing a few times, and you know how difficult it is to get that man to loosen up for even a moment."

That was surprising to hear. Max ventured through life as if a stick lived up his ass. Always so rigid. Always surrounded by worry.

"What am I supposed to do with this information, Giselle?"

She shifted away, tossing a lazy shoulder up. "Whatever you want to do with it. It's your life. You can tell fate to go suck it if you want."

DONNIE STEPPED BACK from the map, content with the plan for the evening. Though neither Joe nor Max would express it out loud, they both knew his first stop would be to Stella's house. To check on her. From afar, of course.

To hear her heartbeat, steady and strong.

That's all he needed to know that she was all right. Actually laying eyes on her in such a sedate state might put him in a frenzied mode he'd never been in. Panic.

Giselle had told them she would wake up. Her body was recharging. Considering how much power she had wielded, he understood why it was taking so long.

It didn't mean he enjoyed the wait.

Max walked back into the study, the room they'd turned into their command center after leaving to take a call.

"Stella's awake."

Donnie's eyes flashed red, making Max flinch. In one split second, he'd wanted to dash out the door and to her side. Then he realized the sun was out and couldn't without burning alive.

"She's sore and moving slowly, but she's awake, ready to get to work."

"She should rest." Then Donnie turned his attention back to the map as if he needed to remind himself of his route tonight.

"Yeah, well, what Stella should do and actually does usually doesn't match."

Joe chuckled. "Women. Gotta love 'em. Glad to hear she's awake and on the mend."

"I'm going to head out. We can meet up later to chat about our findings. Or hopefully one of us finds this bastard and we can take care of the problem."

And Stella would vanish from his life.

He would never wish a vicious vampire on any town, but he wasn't ready to find the culprit. Not if it meant Stella would depart.

Donnie turned around, hoping he'd removed all traces of his turmoil going on his mind. "Sounds good. Tell Stella we're glad to hear she's better."

A sly grin morphed on Max's face as he walked backward toward the exit. "Yeah, I'll do that. See ya."

Then he was gone.

"I thought you'd be a lot happier to hear she's awake. You haven't been yourself since she..."

Got hurt? Put herself in a coma? How did one describe

what happened to her? None of them even knew how to help her. Not even her friends, who had never seen her exhaust herself so much before.

"I am happy. It's wonderful news."

"Then why don't you look or sound happy."

Donnie threw an agitated hand toward the heavy curtain covering the window. "Because I nearly rushed out of the house to her side. That's how elated I was to hear she awoke. While I'm rejoicing deep inside, I'm angry I can't leave the house. Something's wrong with me, Joe." With unsteady feet, Donnie shuffled until he found a chair to sit down on, shoving his face into his hands. "I don't think I can bear to see her leave. I'm afraid of how I'll react when she does. She has this power over me I've never experienced before."

He didn't hear Joe move, but suddenly he was by his side. A cold hand touched his shoulder. Yet he didn't look up from the floor. He couldn't see the disgust in his eyes. That he could...love?...a witch. He didn't know what these feelings were, but they were intense and they were not going to go away. He feared nothing would make them disappear.

Only death would rip him apart from her.

Joe said nothing. But his hand on his shoulder was solid and strong. A comfort he didn't know would work to soothe the turmoil going on inside him.

"I kissed her."

Joe's hand went rigid.

"I turned while doing so." Donnie looked up at him. "Has that ever happened to you before?"

"Never. But I've also never had such a connection as you do with her." Joe moved closer. "You would never hurt her, Donnie. You know this, even if you're thinking you could.

Stop thinking about why you feel a pull toward her and let it be."

He could not walk away from her. Joe didn't understand.

Joe's hand on his shoulder went from light to heavy, as if a rock had descended on him. "I didn't mean let it be as in let her go. I meant, go with the damn flow. See where the shit takes you. Get your head out of your ass, stopping over-analyzing it, and let it be."

"You hate her."

A heavy sigh echoed between them. "I can't hate someone who risked their life like she did for me. She nearly exposed her true self to a pack of lycans. For me. For George and Peter. And I think she did it because of you. So the connection is on both sides. When the sun goes down, go to her. See for yourself she's okay, and then get your head back in the game. As she said a few nights ago: one thing at a time. We can only tackle one thing at a time. So take this thing—whatever the hell it is between you two—one day at a time. One moment at a time."

Sound advice. And from his friend, who warned him off her days ago, was mind-boggling.

But it scared the shit out of him.

What happened if he turned again while kissing her? Because he knew he wouldn't be able to keep his hands to himself once he saw her. He needed to touch her. To assure himself with the touch of his hands she was okay. From top to bottom.

One moment at a time.

He needed to repeat that to himself.

Then he stood up and flew across the room, stopping at the doorway. "We should order more blood. Because I'm about to drink way too much before I leave."

Joe grinned like the devil. "Way ahead of you. Already

did two days ago. Drink away, my friend. But fear not, you won't hurt her. I know you won't."

Donnie wished he held the same belief. Because he might hurt her. Take a bite that he shouldn't. If it happened, if he lost control...he'd kill himself. He'd step into the sun and let it fry him to dust.

13

A DOOR CLOSING echoed through the room. It took longer than she figured it would've for Max to appear in her doorway. She thought he would've rushed to see her, except he'd taken his merry time.

"You look exhausted. Still."

She continued brushing her hair as she rolled her eyes. "Thank you for the wonderful compliment."

Max chuckled, stepping inside the bedroom. "I thought after three days of sleep, you wouldn't have dark circles under your eyes." Then he turned grim. "You can't ever do that again, Stella. Promise me you won't."

She looked away. It didn't work because she saw him in the mirror, the same foreboding, determined expression on his face. So she turned her gaze down at the contents on her vanity table. Lotion, hair accessories, makeup. None of it would make the exhaustion he still saw disappear. Because she felt it deep down in her bones.

He was right.

Giselle was right.

She couldn't do such a spell of such magnitude ever again.

But she couldn't promise such a thing. If they were in a dire situation like that again, there was no way she could stand there and do nothing. He had to know that.

Soft steps padded her way.

"Stella, you have to promise me. I won't accept anything else."

She stood up and twisted around, boxed in by his large body and her vanity. "Don't demand that of me. You know I can't."

"You could've..." He sighed. "Died. Never woken up. I don't know. But something bad could've happened, and I can't handle that kind of worry. It was hard to leave this house knowing you were unconscious and unsure when you'd wake up. If you even would."

"Giselle said it was normal. That I needed a recharge. I'm sorry I worried you." She reached up and brushed his cheek. "You know I'd never intentionally worry you. Please forgive me, but don't make me promise something I can't keep."

Max backed up a step, letting her hand fall away. "It was worth a try. You should take the night easy. Stay here."

"I should be helping. I'm fine."

Max looked her up and down, no doubt noticing the way her legs trembled. Not from fear. From standing too long. Her legs wanted to cave in on her. He was right. Again. She wasn't up to full power yet.

She plopped her butt back down on the seat.

"We have it covered. Holstrom and Mason have been working hard during the day, while me and the vamps are doing the night work."

Her eyes narrowed. "Don't call them that."

A low chuckle rented the air. "They are vampires."

"Yeah, but..." Well, she didn't like it. It sounded like a derogatory term. One they'd use on a vampire they were about to kill. These ones were different. They were...friends.

"I'm sorry. You're right. I won't say it again. They're not that bad. I'm getting used to them."

She smiled. "I heard Donnie has even made you laugh a few times. What a rarity, and I'm sad I missed it."

Max scoffed. "He's also a dumbass at times, so don't get too excited."

An awkward silence settled in the air.

She shouldn't have bought up Donnie. She wasn't ready to talk about him. Not again. Though he just got home, knowing Giselle, she had shared her findings with Max about a cosmic witch and finding her soulmate.

"He says he's glad to hear you're better."

Her brows pleated into a frown. That's it? Glad to hear she was better. Nothing else? Of course, why would Donnie share his feelings with Max? That was a ludicrous thought to begin with.

"I doubt he'll admit it, but he was worried too."

"You all worried for no reason. I'm fine." She stood back up to prove her point, wobbling on her feet.

"Yes, you appear so fine." Max crossed his arms, shaking his head. "Please stay home tonight. One more night. That's all I ask."

Her rebuttal was on the tip of her tongue. She didn't want to stay home.

But the overwhelming concern in his eyes had her conceding. One more night wasn't going to kill her.

"Okay. You win."

"Thank you." Then he moved toward her, kissing her forehead. "Now rest. Nothing else."

He left the room.

Yeah, well, giving in to staying home and not doing anything in general were two different things. She agreed to one, but not the other.

She needed food, stat!

Giselle must've read her mind or knew she'd need sustenance once she finished getting ready because she smelled the makings of spaghetti the closer she got to the kitchen.

Comfort food.

Her friends were too good to her.

She dug in, consuming seconds before taking a seat on the couch. Max fussed over her some more, even grabbing her a blanket and tucking her in. Then he was out the door to start his grid search. Giselle made sure she didn't need anything before hiding herself in her room where all her computers were set up. She didn't ask what she planned to work on. Because if it was more information on cosmic witches, she didn't want to know.

She called Holstrom for an update. Not much to report that she didn't already know. With Holstrom on the case, she had nothing to worry about. Hell, with all her friends— new and old—doing their part, it was as if they didn't even need her help. For the first time in her life, she felt utterly useless. Inessential.

Before she knew it, her eyes got heavy, and she fell asleep.

She jolted up on the couch, blinking. How much time had passed? What did she miss? How could she have fallen asleep so effortlessly? That's all she'd been doing the past three days. Enough was enough.

Her hand patted around the floor before she felt her phone, picking it up. The time on the screen said it was two thirty in the morning. Was Giselle still awake? Had Max returned home?

No missed calls or texts. So no one had reached out to her.

And what for? She was useless. How could she forget that?

A shiver rushed down her spine.

Why had she woken up in such a panic? That never happened to her.

Stella!

She looked around the room. The sound of Donnie's voice was clear and distinct, yet he wasn't in the area.

Or maybe she was creating things in her mind. He still hadn't reached out to her, and it hurt. It hurt more than she cared to admit.

To hell with fate!

That man wasn't her soulmate. Because if he was, he would've been at her door the moment after the sun set.

He stood in the shadows, staring as usual upon Stella's house. It was already the fourth time he'd been by her place and still he couldn't find the courage to walk up to the door.

For someone who never shied away from anything, this was unusual behavior.

But if he hurt her...

If he bit into her delicate skin...

He'd hate himself.

The moment he laid eyes on her, he knew what he'd do. He'd go to her. He'd touch her. And he could very well lose control.

So he remained outside, across the street, and in the

shadows where no one would know he was even there. Giselle didn't have acute hearing, so it wasn't because of her he maintained such a long distance away. But Max was another story. If the man came home, he didn't want him to know he was in the area. He could very well invite him in. Then he'd be screwed.

He'd searched his grid already. They'd all check in soon to report their findings. Since no one had called, that meant there wouldn't be much to report. Nothing had been found.

But he couldn't stand outside her house the rest of the night. Talk about pathetic.

He could hear her steady heartbeat. She was safe. Resting, as she should.

There was nothing else for him to do but return home.

He turned to leave when he went still as a statue.

Her heartbeat that had been a steady rhythm went into a chaotic mess. Like her adrenaline had shot through the roof. *Stella!*

His feet flew across the ground before his mind had given the order. He was at her door in under two seconds. Then he was pounding on it with a desperation he'd never felt.

"Stella! Let me in. Let me in right now."

Her heart rate was still erratic and out of sync. She was in trouble and he was helpless to do anything. Until she let him in, he couldn't enter the house.

A vampire had to be invited into a person's home. He'd never been bothered by such a rule before until now.

He pounded again, the fear suffocating him.

All she had to do was whisper the words. As long as he heard it, the invisible barrier keeping him out would evaporate.

"Let me in, Stella." He leaned against the door, his hands seized in their torment. "Say the words, my love. Let me in."

He'd never felt so powerless before. How could he protect her if he couldn't reach her?

The door swung open, and if there hadn't been an invisible wall, he would've toppled into her arms. Her hair was mussed, her eyes filled with tiredness. The dark circles coating them added to the exhaustion he saw imprinted everywhere.

If his heart could pump blood and beat as if he were alive, he knew it would be thumping double-time. In tune to hers that still battered out of control.

"What's wrong? What happened? Please let me in." He couldn't hide the desperation in his tone. He didn't even try.

"Nothing's wrong. I was sleeping."

"No, not possible. You went from a steady heartbeat to what I hear now."

Her hand touched her chest, over her heart. "Hmm. Yes, it is beating pretty out of control. I don't know. Maybe I was having a nightmare. I was jolted out of sleep. Then I heard pounding on the door." A wry grin framed her lips. "You startled me, Donnie. I didn't expect you to be standing on my doorstep."

Yes, well, he never intended to knock on the door either.

"So you're okay?"

"Yes."

Then that's all he needed to know.

"Good."

He turned to leave.

"Wait."

He froze.

"That's it? You pound on my door like a maniac and now you're leaving?"

Hell, yes. And it was a damn good thing she didn't let him in. He couldn't get to her now. Couldn't touch her. Couldn't test his resistance.

"I didn't mean to bother you. You need your rest."

His foot hit the pathway, but before he could take another step away toward freedom, a warm hand grabbed his arm. Damn it. She left the safety of her house.

"Look at me, Donnie. Don't you dare ever walk away from me like that."

He turned around gradually, gritted his teeth, forcing himself to not flip into vampire-mode.

"Stella, for your own safety, I need you to go back inside the house."

Confusion lit her eyes. "What are you talking about?"

He could feel the ache pulsing in his bones. His gaze flashed to the vein pumping a cool, steady rhythm in her neck. It didn't matter she'd calmed down. His senses zeroed in on it, watching the regular beat, mesmerized by it. One taste. One bite was all he needed.

Two warm hands grasped his cheeks. "It's okay, Donnie. You're okay."

"I'm two seconds away from hurting you. Back away from me slowly and go inside the house," he growled in a low voice, feeling his fangs slide into place. He knew his eyes glowed a bright red as well.

Too late.

He couldn't control the vampire side of himself.

"You won't hurt me."

"I would like to think the same thing, but I don't trust myself. Why do you think I've stayed away from you as long as I have? I want to kiss you. I want to touch you. Everywhere. Leave no spot untouched. I want to claim you. Brand you as mine. I want to sink my teeth in that vein singing a tune just for me and see how you taste. I'm barely holding on to my control. So for the love of God, Stella, get back inside your house."

She removed her hands and took a step back, finally understanding the danger she was in. Then she stopped, crossing her arms with a defiant look on her face.

"Good. It's about time we talk about that kiss we shared."

This woman...

...was going to be death of him.

"You walked away from me then too. I will not stand for it. You don't ever walk away from me."

"I would've bitten you then. My fangs came out. You felt them."

"I did. And it didn't frighten me. Not nearly as much as it did for you." A tender smile appeared. "I can't explain it, but I know you won't hurt me. Because more than two seconds has gone by and yet you still haven't moved."

"Because I'm exerting all my strength not to do so." He swallowed hard. "There isn't anything to talk about. That kiss was a mistake. It can't happen again."

Pain morphed into her features, and he felt like a bastard for hurting her this way. But could she not see how impossible anything between them could be?

"A mistake?"

He never lied. Being honest had always been important to him. A moral code he lived by. Lying never got a person anywhere but closer to hell.

But he couldn't tell the truth. Not about this.

"Yes, it was a mistake. One I won't repeat."

To save her from herself, he fled. Walked away from her like the asshole he'd been since she opened the door.

14

SHE SHUT the door with a quiet click, but it didn't matter. Giselle was standing there when she turned around.

"I won't pretend I wasn't listening to all of that. You should've listened to him."

Not her too.

Stella walked around her toward the kitchen.

"If he says he's losing control, listen to the man. At least he had the decency to warn you."

She pulled a glass from the cupboard, slamming it to the counter. Luckily, it didn't break.

"Though, I also agree with you. If he wanted to hurt you, he would've. Which means he doesn't want to. The pull between you is way stronger than we realized. He's misunderstanding what he's feeling."

Stella paused with the water pitcher suspended in the air, though not tipped enough to let the water out. "Excuse me?"

Giselle grinned as she sat down on a stool. "He's thinking he's going into blood lust, when really, he's flipping horny. And you, missy, did not mention you kissed the man. These are things your best girl friend needs to know."

The pitcher plopped down onto the counter with a loud thud. "He called the kiss a mistake."

"He lied. I could see it in his red, beady eyes. He was lying through his teeth. To protect you. To protect himself."

"Protect himself from what?"

"From..." Giselle shrugged. "Falling in love? I don't know. I don't know what he's thinking or feeling, but what I saw out there wasn't a vampire about to feast on a human for the mere sake of drinking blood. He wanted to devour you from head to toe with his lips. With his delicious cock."

Stella spewed out the water she'd taken a sip of. "Please do not talk about his cock."

"Possessive, are we?"

She tried to maintain a stern expression, her lips in a thin line, but the comical look on Giselle's face was too much. She burst out laughing. Giselle joined her.

"Maybe I am." Stella grabbed a paper towel to wipe up the water mess. "Possessive. So don't say the word cock in association with Donnie again."

An evil smirk answered her.

Then Giselle bobbed her eyebrows up and down. "I bet it's impressive. Like, super impressive. He has that look about him."

"How did we go from he's a vampire, keep your distance, to he's got an impressive cock and one he knows how to use well?"

More boisterous laughter filled the air.

After they both got ahold of themselves, the teasing laughter died in Giselle's eyes. "He's afraid. Just like you were expressing your concerns earlier. He's feeling the same thing. Whatever is going on between you two is new. For both of you. He doesn't understand what's going on. You, at least, have a little clearer idea about it." Giselle stood up. "I know I said to do what you think is best. If that was to tell fate to suck it, then so be it. But I'm changing my mind. You should go suck it, and I'm not talking about fate anymore."

Stella would not laugh again. She pressed her lips together so hard, they hurt. A smile did break free but that was it.

"Have you talked about this stuff with Max?"

Giselle's eyes enlarged. "Are you nuts? That man would have a coronary. It's one thing to be amicable and friendly with vampires, but he'd never agree with a relationship. Even if it's destined."

Stella shook her hand, waving that ridiculous notion away again. "I don't want my life to have a specific ending. I don't want to have a destiny. Or fate to be steering the way. Stop it."

"I don't think you have a say in the matter. Or maybe you do." Her wicked grin made Stella's skin crawl. "Ignore the man. Believe his lies. See that fate doesn't get its way."

Then Giselle left the kitchen with her ominous statement hanging in the air.

Was that what she should do? Tell fate it couldn't win.

That meant Donnie was her soulmate. The love of her life. The one she was meant to be with. Forever.

What would happen if she denied herself happiness she was meant to have? How would her life turn out then?

More miserable than it already was.

Had he been lying? Truly? That he didn't believe the kiss had been a mistake? Because it didn't feel like a mistake.

She took another shower to clear her mind. The water did nothing to help soothe her troubled thoughts, though her muscles felt more relaxed than before. The weariness she'd been feeling all evening was starting to ebb away. By the time she'd dried her hair, re-dressed in a new outfit, and donned a small amount of makeup—enough to cover the damn dark circles—she was ready.

Ready to confront a vampire on the verge of losing its control.

She knew he wouldn't hurt her. But on the off-chance she was wrong, she could hold her own. She'd protect herself if the need arose.

She didn't bother telling Giselle she was leaving. The moment she heard the door close, she'd know where she was going. There was no other reason for her to leave the house. Not at four o'clock in the morning.

When she got to his house, she didn't even need to press the button to the gate before it swung open. For a man who wanted her to keep her distance, he was making it very easy to disregard that request.

Before she could knock on the door, it opened. To her surprise, Joe stood there. Donnie was nowhere in sight.

"I'm glad to see you're doing better." Joe swept a hand for her to enter, then shut the door after she stepped inside. "I also want to thank you for...protecting me and my friends. You didn't have to, but I appreciate it."

She nodded, not needing his thanks. They hadn't done anything wrong, therefore, they should've never been threatened by the lycans in the first place.

Joe crossed his arms in a nonchalant way, a wry grin puncturing his lips. "I imagine you're not here to see me. Donnie got home a little bit ago and in a very strange mood. Didn't say a word to me. I know he saw you because I could smell your scent on him. Care to explain what happened since he won't tell me?"

No. It wasn't any of Joe's business. Where was Donnie?

Why hadn't he appeared yet? He had to have heard someone entered the house. The voices in the foyer. Her heartbeat that he loved to listen to. That sang a tune just for him.

"Maybe it's because of what you did. I don't know. I don't want to examine why I've change my mind about you. But I'm not opposed...to you entering his life as more than a friend. Everyone can see there's something brewing between you two. But I ask you not to hurt him."

"I would only defend myself if he attacked, which I don't believe he'd ever do."

He didn't trust her if he had to ask such a thing of her.

Joe shook his head. "You misunderstood me. I meant, don't break his heart. He's more fragile than he appears. And I agree, he would never hurt you either, despite his fears. Hell, he threatened me if I ever hurt you that I would pay."

Interesting.

She thought it was the case, but to hear it confirmed surprised her.

"I'll sleep the day at Mona's. Give you two some space." Joe headed for the door.

"Wait. Where is he? If he knew I was here, why hasn't he appeared?"

Joe grinned. "Oh, he knows you're here. He was probably hoping I'd get you to leave, and I'm not doing that. I'm not getting in the middle of whatever is going on with you two. You can find him in his room. With the door locked. Up the stairs, down the hallway, last door on the left. Good luck."

Joe was gone before she could ask any more questions.

Then she turned toward the stairs, wondering if she'd lost her damn mind.

Walking straight into a vampire's lair.

JOE WAS RIGHT. He'd lock his bedroom door the moment he shut himself inside it. He hadn't wanted Joe to bother him. Inquire why he came home in such a foul mood, downed two more bags of blood—on top of the three he consumed before he left.

He never expected the lock would keep him away from Stella too.

Waiting by the bed, he listened to her footsteps as they made their way up the stairs. He'd give her credit. Her heartbeat was steady and serene, as it usually was. Why wasn't she afraid of him? His behavior at her house should've scared her enough to stay away.

A soft knock echoed in the room.

"Donnie? Can I come in?"

No!

She needed to stay far away from him. His fists clenched as her scent—despite a door standing between them—drifted his way. It filled his senses, making his fangs emerge. He wanted her blood. To sink his teeth deep inside her skin and drink until he was sated. He didn't think he'd ever be sated with enough. He'd drain her dry and kill her.

The knob wiggled.

Brazen of her. To attempt to enter when he didn't answer her question.

"Let me in, Donnie."

Words he'd hollered a few hours ago. Thank goodness she hadn't listened to him then. And he wasn't going to listen to her now.

"This is ridiculous. You're acting like a child. Let's talk about this like rational adults. Unlock the door and let me in."

And hurt her? Rip her apart with his teeth? No.

He tilted his head to home in on the new sound permeating the air. The click of the lock registered a second too late. His feet flew across the carpet and he stopped a breath away from her before he would've collided into her warm, soft body.

A twisted smile pierced her lips as she lifted a set of bobby pins in the air. "I have many talents. A lock isn't going to keep me out."

"Leave. For your own good."

He zoomed back to the bed, leaning stiffly against it. As long as he maintained a standoffish, aloof, I-don't-care-about-you attitude, she'd leave.

She ignored his request, tossing the pins into her purse, then set her purse on the small table near the door. Then she kicked the door closed with her shoe. Her gaze darted around the room.

"Dark tones. Black curtains. Black comforter on the bed. No knickknacks anywhere. You can only see darkness, why in the world would you live in it too?"

That's what he was cursed with. Darkness. For eternity. Why pretend he could have anything else?

Plus, he liked the color black. It looked well on him. Most of his suits he wore were black. He owned a few blue suits. But black was his go-to for most days.

"I don't want you here."

He didn't even bother to control his emotions. His fangs remained out, even visible for her to see, his eyes a deep red, like the color of blood that he feasted on every single day. If she feared him, she'd leave faster. He would only be able to control himself for so long before the urge took over.

And he consumed her.

"You're lying. Like you lied about that kiss. It wasn't a mistake."

Hell, yes it was. Because the kiss had caused this intense ache inside his gut. He wanted more from her. That one taste had not been enough. Did he have to spell it out for her?

Of course, that would be admitting it wasn't a mistake to kiss her. He had enjoyed the kiss. It was the way it made him feel that had been his downfall.

She walked toward him.

"Don't come any closer, Stella."

Her feet kept moving.

"Please," he pleaded. "For your own safety."

Her stride didn't lessen or falter.

What had Max said to him earlier this evening? *Yeah, well, what Stella should do and actually does usually doesn't match.* No words had ever been truer than those.

She stopped in front of him. Close enough he could feel her breath on his lips.

"Giselle heard our conversation outside."

And if she told Max what happened, he was a dead man. He wouldn't like to know he'd nearly attacked Stella. Lost control.

"We had an enlightening chat about it all." A devious grin spilled across her lips. "Do you want to know what she thinks?"

He did not.

And he didn't respond because he didn't trust himself.

Stella reached up and cupped his cheeks. He closed his eyes, hoping that would drown out the desire he saw reflected in her eyes. That it would make the scent of her swirling around him disappear. That he wouldn't be able to hear her heart thumping a steady tune.

It did nothing but make him ache for more.

"I think she's right."

His eyes snapped open. It sat on the tip of his tongue to ask right about what. He refrained—barely.

Her hands slid from his face to his chest. He'd taken his jacket off, but the black velvet vest he still wore. Her fingers fiddled with the buttons before unsnapping the first one.

"Stop, Stella. You need to leave."

That same devious smirk brightened even more. "If you truly believed that, you'd stop me yourself. Yet, you're standing there not moving a muscle."

"Because one wrong move and I'll lose it."

She'd gotten four of the five buttons undone. "Good. I want you to lose it."

A heavy sigh escaped. This woman drove him insane.

The last button came undone. Her hands slid underneath the vest and circled around his waist. "Kiss me, Donnie."

"I can't. Don't you see I have my fangs out? Do you want me to bite you? Is that what you want?"

Her hands drove a sensuous path from his back to his front, settling her fingers on his belt buckle. "See, Giselle and I talked about this very thing. It's not bloodlust you're feeling, it's desire."

No.

He knew the difference. He'd never gotten this way with a woman before. Bedding someone was about sex. Finding pleasure and moving on. Not this intense need to consume, to ravish, to lose complete control of himself.

He'd been waging such a war with himself, he didn't realize she'd undone his buckle, the button to his pants, and pulled the zipper down until her hand snaked inside and grabbed him.

His eyes closed again as she stroked him.

Or maybe he wanted to pretend he didn't notice what she was doing because he wanted what she was offering.

"Kiss me, Donnie. Don't make me beg."

Never. He would never make her beg.

He moved so fast, a startled squeak fell from her lips. He had her in the middle of the bed, trapped with his body above hers before she finished the sound. Then his mouth was on hers, drowning out any other sound.

He did what he feared he'd do. Consumed her.

His lips plundered deep inside. She met him every step of the way. Her tongue even grazed his fang, inciting the desire to dangerous levels.

The sound of fabric tearing filled the room. He gave no care to her shirt. Her bra didn't survive his hands either. Then his lips went from her mouth to her breast, sucking hard, biting her nipple. But not enough to draw blood.

She arched her back, lifting high off the bed at the touch. While his powerful hands divested every article of clothing off her, she was doing the same to him. They were both naked before he knew it.

His mouth touched every spot he could see. Her mouth, her cheeks, her arms, her shoulders. He even eyed her neck, but refrained from that spot. The temptation would be too great, and he didn't trust himself as much as she seemed to be trusting him.

Then he retraced his path, peppering gentle, soothing kisses until he reached her mouth. They were once again fused together as if they were one and the same.

Her hand snaked between their bodies, grabbing ahold of his cock. Hard and ready for her. She must've been ready too because she guided it to where it needed to be. He plunged inside her with one strong thrust.

She cried out, and he silenced her scream with another twist of his lips.

Then the duel between them really started. He pumped furiously while she dug her nails into his ass, holding on and meeting each powerful thrust with vigor.

"Harder," she mumbled between the meshing of their lips, urging him to lose himself even more.

He was barely holding on. Why was she tempting fate? He could hurt her with his power and speed. Why didn't she understand that?

But he listened, thrusting deeper, more ferociously.

He was swallowed up in lust, working his hips so fast, he had to stop kissing her. The wicked smile on her face urged him on. Maybe kissing her would be better than to see that look of triumph.

"So close, Donnie. Keep going. Harder."

God. This woman. Did she know what she was doing to him? Driving him wild with an even deeper need than he knew he possessed.

Then she cried out his name, tensing, the bliss spreading across her face. It was the most damn gorgeous sight he'd ever seen in his life. He swore he'd repeat this over and over just to witness it again and again.

Staring into her eyes, seeing the same wild desire, hit him square in the chest. Then the pinnacle struck him as well. He let the orgasm sweep him away to a place he'd never been before.

After the pleasure receded, he lost his strength, cocooning her into his body. The damn temptation still beckoned him. Her neck in his view. Her vein pumping with that sweet tune that put him in a trance.

She caressed his cheek. "See. Not blood lust. Desire. And I asked for a kiss. You gave me so much more."

He was still buried deep inside her, his cock stirring to life once again. "You stroked me. What did you think was going to happen?"

"I didn't say it as a complaint."

What was he going to do with her? She stirred his blood, his emotions into a frenzy that he didn't understand.

"Did I hurt you?" He'd run away and never let her find him if he had. "I wasn't gentle. I should've been more gentle."

"It was absolute perfection." She lifted her hips, moaning in delight. "You can't hurt me. It's not in you to do something like that."

"Stella..." His gaze trailed to the vein throbbing in her neck. "The need to bite you right now is strong. I could hurt you."

"I think you think I should be worried. But I'm not. I refuse to be." Then she pushed on him until she was on top.

He was stronger than her. No doubt about that. The only reason she changed the position was because he allowed it.

He felt bereft the moment she disengaged from him. But the cunning smirk on her lips as she moved lower had his skin prickling with ecstasy. The moment her lips clamped onto his cock, all coherent thought fled his mind.

15

IT WAS strange to wake and see no sun filtering through the windows. She loved feeling the sun on her skin. What must it feel like for Donnie to never know that feeling ever again? To live in darkness for the rest of his life?

She didn't want to know the answer enough to ask.

Who knew? Maybe the sun hadn't even come up yet. She hadn't bothered to check the time.

Her hand wove a tender stroke up and down his chest, knowing he wasn't asleep despite his eyes being closed.

She shivered.

His eyes snapped open.

"You're cold."

"I'm fine."

His lips were in a tight line. Not the first look she had wanted to see waking up with him.

"You're shivering."

He propped up on an elbow as if to shift away from her, but she rolled on top of him to stop the movement.

They were both naked. They'd come together too many times to count, exploring every nook and cranny on each other's bodies before exhaustion hit her. He, no doubt, could've kept going. So there was no barrier between them. And she didn't want one between them.

And yes, the cold from his body seeped into her bones. Not an ounce of warmth emanated from him.

Another tremble hit her skin.

It was like sitting on a block of ice.

His frown intensified.

She reached down, smoothing the fierce expression from his face. It worked somewhat. He wouldn't be swayed from his sudden dark mood.

"We've been in this bed for hours. It's fine. I can handle a bit of coldness."

"Perhaps I will chalk it up to a lapse in naivety. But I thought when you trembled in my arms earlier, it was from bliss, not because I made you cold."

She leaned down, brushing her lips with his. Despite the turmoil he was navigating within himself, he responded. Giving as much of himself in the kiss as she did.

"The hazards of being dead."

He flinched at her words.

Yes, they were abrupt and to the point. But no less the truth.

"Do you want me to leave?"

Donnie stared at her, the severe frown still there.

"Because I can. I can leave and we can pretend this never happened."

She was flipped onto her back and him on top in a split second. It wasn't the first time he'd moved so swiftly, adjusting their positions. It startled her every time. A tiny squeak escaped before she could stop herself.

"I will never forget a moment of this. I could never." He held her trapped between his body and the bed, but he wasn't holding her down with force. Nor touching her as closely as she wished. "You're not leaving. I fear you're going to have a hard time getting rid of me from your life."

Not something she wanted. Ever. But they weren't diving down that path. Not yet, anyway.

"But I don't like knowing I..." A muscle ticked in his cheek. "That I make you feel that way."

Since he wouldn't close the distance between them, she solved the problem herself by reaching up and wrapping her arms around his body and hooking her legs behind his. He was forced to get closer. The coldness wrapped around her, swallowing her whole. She couldn't stop the shiver from escaping. He tensed while she strengthened her hold on him.

"You can't change who you are, Donnie. If I had a problem with that, I wouldn't be here right now."

Part of her might not even have a choice. If fate had a hand in what was going on.

His answer was a kiss. A long, deep kiss that had her insides melting and her body singing with joy. They went from drowning themselves in the erotic kiss to connecting as one as he slid inside.

All the other times before were hard and fast, full of frenzied need. This joining was slow and sensual, as if they were focusing on each tiny movement they made together.

He zapped her skin with coldness at every corner. She, in return, warmed him in the exact same spots.

A negative counteracting a positive.

There was no escaping it.

The pleasure that always erupted between them was close to the pinnacle once again. Her moans got louder. His breaths a bit heavier. They would soon come together in glorious bliss.

He pumped leisurely, but with purpose. She met each thrust, dying and wishing for the next one.

Then it hit her.

The powerful feeling tore through her body, making her cry out his name and shuddering from the aftereffects.

Her trembles were not always a bad thing.

He followed her, shortly after.

She sensed he wanted to move away, but she refused to move her arms and legs, keeping him trapped in place. Well, he gave the illusion she trapped him. He'd proven time and again that he dominated what took place in the bed. If he wanted to be free from her, he could do so at any moment without much fight from her.

Unless she used her powers, and she wouldn't in a situation like this.

He kissed her temple. "I don't think I could ever tire of this. It's something beautiful and new every time with you."

She would never tire of the sweet words he bestowed upon her.

They twisted until they were lying on their sides, though still wrapped in each other's arms.

"I hate to ask, but what time is it?"

Donnie looked over her shoulder, giving her the impression there was a clock on the wall somewhere.

"Eight o'clock. Not time to get up. You need more rest."

She cupped his cheeks, pressing a hard kiss to his lips. "We both know I will get no rest in this bed. I need to get back to work. I should already be at the precinct by now."

The hard expression on his face said he wanted to argue. Instead, he jerked his head in a tight nod, rolled away, and got out of bed. She hadn't expected him to capitulate so easily.

She should follow his lead, except the view was too good

to look away from. A sculpted back, rigid in all the right places. An ass made for grabbing, and fit perfectly in her hands. When he turned around, she continued her perusal. Abs that were rock solid. A sprinkle of hair, leading a trail down to his cock that had already sprung back to life, ready for the fifth or so round they were on. She had lost count hours ago.

A brow cocked as a silky smile appeared on his lips. "Are you going to stop staring and get out of bed?" A predator look snapped into place. "Or am I going to prevent you from leaving?"

She scrambled out of bed because she knew that hadn't been an innocent question. He'd keep her here if he got back in the bed.

They both dressed in silence. Though she had to borrow some of his clothes since he'd ripped hers apart in a frenzied need. He walked her to the door, also without speaking. It was the first weird awkwardness they experienced since they shared intimacies.

"I wish you'd stay."

She also wished she could.

"I can come back later."

He pulled her roughly into his arms, his expression telling her he would come to her if not. "I've never hated the daylight as much as I hate it right now."

She translated that into he would miss her.

They shared a kiss that curled her toes and turned her insides to goo. Before she caved and stayed, she left.

Max was waiting in the foyer when she opened the front door. He winced, groaning. "I can't believe you. You reek of him."

She would not apologize for putting herself first for once. Not to him. Not to anyone.

"And should I even ask why you're wearing his clothes?"

"Are we going to have a problem here, Max?"

Because Giselle's absence spoke volumes. She had no issue. Hell, she'd told Stella to go jump Donnie's bones. If she were worried about what happened and that she hadn't returned home for the night, she'd be standing next to Max.

"I hope you know what you're doing, Stella. He's a vampire. You're not."

She knew the specifics of the relationship. He didn't need to remind her.

"He'll live forever." Max sighed. "You'll grow old."

"But in the meantime, the sex is phenomenal."

She walked around Max's stunned expression that she'd say such a thing. She laughed on her way up the stairs at the way Max feigned gagging.

Was there a future with Donnie? Even if he was her supposed soulmate? She had no idea. But she sure in hell would enjoy the ride for as long as she could. It was a new experience for her. Putting her needs first before anything else.

"SO, WE NEED TO TALK."

Donnie stood staring at the map of the city, deciding that was a better view than whatever expression Joe had on his face. Never a good sign when the conversation started that way.

But he never shied away from anything.

He turned around to witness a goofy-ass grin on Joe.

"The walls are sort of thin around here." Joe chuckled. "I'm getting sick of listening to you two get it on every night. Perhaps we should invest in soundproof walls."

Not the chat he expected to have, but it was a good one.

In the last two weeks, he and Stella had been inseparable. At least after they hunted for the vampire killer. Once he returned home, she came over and they shared a lovemaking he'd never had before. He felt things he'd never felt before. Even with his wife, and at times, that made him feel guilty as hell.

"I won't be kicked out of my own home because you want to have sex." Joe crossed his arms, but the stupid grin said he wasn't angry at him for the changes that had taken place.

Donnie wanted to maintain the happiness displayed on his face as well, but it was difficult.

Joe sensed his unease right away. "What? I don't mean to be an ass about it. I'm glad you two are connecting. That you found someone who...makes you happy. It's been a long time since I've seen you this happy. No nightmares either since you started seeing her."

"You're not being an ass. It's a solid idea. Truly, Joe." Donnie glanced away, training his eyes on the map. "But once we find this vampire, she'll leave. That's a lot of work to do for someone who has no intention of sticking around."

He understood her need to move from place to place. It was safer. He knew that feeling well. He, Joe, George, and Peter had done the same for many, many years. Always hiding. Always running. Always vigilant for hunters in the area. This was the first time in a long time they had felt safe. Mona helped in that sense. Putting protection spells on the house. The security system was top notch. They still hid in the shadows, keeping a low profile, but he felt more secure than he had in ages.

"So how long do you think I have to endure listening to you go at it like animals?"

Joe had lost his smile just to reignite it with a cocky-ass grin. He was trying to make light of a serious situation.

Donnie would let him because thinking about Stella leaving never put him in a good place. He knew he wouldn't handle her departure well.

"Perhaps you need to get laid as well. Fair is fair in the listening game."

Thundering laughter filled the room.

"Time to cease whatever you two are talking about now." Max walked into the living room with his fingers plugging his ears.

That garnered more laughter around the room.

While Max seemed to be joking, Donnie knew the man wasn't too keen on the idea of him and Stella together. But he wasn't getting in the middle of it. Surprisingly.

What was also surprising was how fast they'd all become friends. How the trust had come so quickly. They'd given Max and Giselle the gate code, giving them free range to step onto their property whenever they wanted. They didn't give that to just anyone.

But when Donnie gave it to Stella, he knew he was also handing it over to her friends as well. He trusted her, so he was also putting his trust into them.

Joe stood near the bookshelf, arms still crossed and the same annoying grin. He stood across the room. Max took a spot between them, looking at the map.

"We've covered the entire city. The question now is where do we go from here? The vampire is not hiding out in the city. It also hasn't killed anyone else." Max looked at him. "Maybe it left the area, which is why we've been out of luck the last two weeks."

Donnie doubted that. It didn't feel right. He couldn't

explain why he felt that way, but his gut said this vampire would reappear.

"We expand our search. The vampire is in the area. Now we start in the surrounding towns."

Joe moved away from the bookshelves, closer to them. "Can we not start with the town where the lycans reside? We've had such peace with them. I'd hate to start it back up. Plus, I imagine they've done their own searching in their town."

Yes, they hadn't heard from that pack since the showdown at Mona and Mason's house, but it didn't mean the fight between them was over.

"I tend to agree." Donnie glanced at Max. "Your thoughts?"

They were a team now. He wouldn't discredit anything Max had to say.

"Not a bad idea. I'd like to avoid a fight with them as well."

Joe perked up, his smile growing even more. "My favorite person has arrived."

Thirty seconds later, the front door opened and closed. Another thirty seconds passed before Bailey and Kade walked into the room. Bailey had Emerson in her arms.

"How's my favorite nephew?" Joe held out his arms.

Bailey giggled. "On the move." Then she set him on the ground and they all watched in fascination as Emerson zoomed, somewhat awkwardly, on his hands and knees toward Joe.

Joe swooped him up as soon as he got near, laughing and whooping with joy. "I'm so proud of you, Emerson! You're crawling like a big boy. Uncle Joe-Joe is so, so proud."

Emerson started babbling and giggling, then grabbed

Joe's finger and sucked on it like he loved to do every time Joe picked him up.

Donnie greeted Bailey with a hug and clapped Kade on the back. "You look well. How are you feeling?"

Kade let out a long breath. "Like I was torn apart by a lycan." Bailey circled his waist and he leaned into it. "I'm feeling much better. I'm healing well. I'm ready to get back in the game."

"We're happy to have you back."

Bailey held out her hand, as if to hold him back from Kade. "He means during the day and non-dangerous stuff. Not out there searching for this vampire."

"Bailey..." Kade started.

"I think Emerson is due for a bottle. Joe, help me in the kitchen." Then Bailey kissed Kade on the cheek and walked out of the room with the diaper bag slung across her shoulder as if the conversation was settled and over. Joe followed, giving all of them a mischievous grin.

Kade let out another tired breath. "If it were up to her, I wouldn't even have left the house yet."

"You almost died, Kade." Donnie waited for Kade to meet his eyes. "She was alone a very long time. Then she finds you. She falls in love. You're everything to her. If she lost you, I know she'd be lost too. Let her worry about you. It'll help her." Then Donnie winced. "She also feels guilty. Even though it's not her fault."

"Yeah." Kade cleared his throat as if that would help the sudden tears that were building in his eyes to disappear. "We've had that conversation too many times. No matter what I say, she feels guilty. I hope both of us getting out of the house will help lessen her worries and guilt."

Kade tossed a lazy hand at the map behind Donnie. "I

know I'm useless in this search. But I want to help in any other way I can."

This time Max cleared his throat, garnering Kade's attention. "We haven't met yet. I'm Max." He held out his hand. Despite the small moment of panic Donnie saw in Kade's eyes, he shook his hand. "You know I'm a lycan."

Kade nodded.

"Then I'm the perfect one to teach you how to defend yourself against one." The shock hit not only Kade, but Donnie as well. "I'm not saying you could win a fight against a lycan, but knowing the weak spots can help. You should know how to defend yourself against any creature." Max jabbed a thumb at Donnie. "Even vampires."

"He has a point. We've never done any training with you. We should."

Kade laughed. "When can we start?"

Donnie loved his eagerness. It would help Bailey's nerves with Kade getting hurt again, and give Kade a confidence boost in not feeling as helpless as he felt when he got attacked.

"Tomorrow morning." Max looked at Donnie. "You got a gym in this huge-ass house?"

"Fully stocked with whatever you might need."

Max clapped his hands. "Let's start putting up a new map of the next town we're searching. We have a lot of work to do. I say we start where Mona and Mason live. It's the next closest town."

"I can help with that," Kade said as he rolled up his sleeves.

Donnie glanced at the time while Kade and Max tackled removing the old map. Too soon for Stella to arrive. She'd be busy working with Holstrom.

Time couldn't move fast enough.

With the sun still out, he couldn't even venture outside and watch her from a distance. He hated the moments she was out of his reach. Without his protection.

He had no idea how it'd happened so fast, but he'd fallen in love. And he never thought he'd ever experience that emotion again. Not after the tragic way he'd lost his wife.

Of course, what he felt for Stella was different than he had for his wife. It was more...consuming. Overwhelming. Suffocating in a way. But in a good way.

She was his everything, and the day she left, he knew he wouldn't be able to let her walk away. Not without him by her side.

16

STELLA PRESSED HER LIPS TOGETHER, trying to hide her smile. It didn't work. Laughter spilled out. Giselle stuck her tongue out and went right back to her computer while simultaneously munching on cheese puffs.

"How are you not getting orange sticky stuff everywhere?"

Giselle cocked a brow. "It's an art that can't be taught." She eyed her up and down. "You look different tonight."

Stella joined Giselle in perusing her person. Tennis shoes—boring, but comfortable. Jeans—not too tight, but made her ass look great. Pink T-shirt—loose but the V-neck showcased her breasts in the right way. Her hair was out of its ponytail. That's the sole thing different than how she normally left for the evening.

Donnie liked her hair down. Removing her ponytail had been one of the first things he did when he saw her. Running his hands through her locks with a delicacy that sent a weird joy through her system.

Then she saw it.

"Ketchup stain. I had a hot dog." Stella rubbed at the small mark on her T-shirt.

Giselle laughed. "Nope. It's not that." She set her computer to the side and stood up, her hands on her hips with her head tilted as she stared. "I know what it is."

Her lipstick was off. Her makeup too heavy. Maybe the dash of perfume she sprayed on her wrists was too strong of a smell.

"You look happy and free of worry. I can't remember the last time you looked like that."

The sudden nerves that had attacked her fell away.

She *was* happy. Life didn't seem so bad when she had something wonderful to look forward to. Focusing on crime and who she could save wore on a person. Looking over her shoulder. Constantly watching what she said or did. It battered her nerves until they were so taut and strung, she felt helpless.

Giselle walked around the coffee table, hugging her. "Seeing you happy, makes me happy."

Yet, she didn't look happy as she headed for the kitchen.

"He's an idiot, you know. That he can't see what's right in front of him." Stella followed her, knowing she shouldn't bring it up.

They'd had this conversation too many times to count. Every time, Giselle told her to forget it, leave it alone. She didn't want to mess with the easygoing flow they had. But every time, she couldn't help herself.

Giselle grabbed a glass from the cupboard, offering a light smile. "Some people aren't meant to be. Not like you and Donnie."

Stella still wasn't sure he was her soulmate. That meant giving fate control of her life and she didn't like the idea of doing that.

But when she thought of losing him, in any sort of way, her heart shattered in a million pieces. She couldn't envision any other way of life but with him in it.

Not wanting to focus on that train of thought, she brought it back to Giselle.

"Max will eventually come to his senses."

Giselle slammed the glass down. "I don't want to be a last resort for him. If he's never had feelings by now, it's never going to happen. He doesn't see me as anything more than a sister. Like you." She shook her head, grabbing the pitcher of lemonade from the fridge. "I don't want to talk about this. I wanted you to know I like the happiness on your face. Keep it there."

Stella rounded the island counter, wrapping Giselle in a warm hug. "I'm sorry. I didn't mean to bring it up. I know how it makes you feel. We'll keep ignoring the elephant in the room. But, Giselle, how long are you going to live with a man and hide your feelings from him? You like seeing me happy. I'd love to see the same expression on you."

Giselle kept her eyes trained to the floor when Stella let go. She remained silent as well. Stella's cue that Giselle was not going to give in and respond.

With that, she left the house.

Donnie opened the door before she could do it herself. She was in his arms, and for the smallest of moments she forgot what happened before she left.

Then he released her and cupped her cheeks, his stare intense and unyielding. Before he could ask what was wrong, she put a finger to his lips, shaking her head. Not with Max in the house. Since his car was outside, she knew he was somewhere.

Donnie conceded, though she knew he'd bring up his questions later.

Max and Joe were in the study. The three of them showed her the new map they were searching. Part of her was ready to get this over with and part of her never wanted it to be solved.

For the first time, leaving didn't sound so great. Because, for once, they were putting down roots. Making friends. Being accepted. Having a life that didn't involve just work.

Last week, Holstrom had her, Max, and Giselle over for supper. Met his wife and enjoyed the evening with nothing but laughter and light conversation. It'd been a nice change of pace.

It was going on two o'clock in the morning. She'd taken a nap before coming. She always needed it before she came because they never went to sleep right away. By the time they did, she got an hour or two before she had to get up and go to work.

"Well, I should get going. Another busy day tomorrow." Max finished the drink he'd been sipping on and set it back down on the table.

"Take Giselle out for breakfast tomorrow."

Max's brow rose with confusion. "Why?"

This man was as dumb as a box of rocks. The only why he should be asking is why he couldn't see how special Giselle was?

"Because I think she's getting burnt out. A break from everything is needed once in a while. Holstrom and I are interviewing a witness in one of our cases that I can't get out of, otherwise I'd do it myself." And she would. If nothing other than an apology for bringing up Max and her feelings she had for the idiot.

Max shrugged as if that made sense. "Yeah, okay. I can do that. I've been wanting to try out the diner near our place. Looks like a neat place from the outside."

Such indifference. She wanted to punch him in the face to knock some sense into him.

Max left and she wanted to follow to do that. Beat the sense into him.

Joe excused himself, surprising her by saying he was spending the night at Mason and Mona's. She had gotten over the embarrassment of him hearing the things her and Donnie did together. What else could she do but that? She wasn't going to deny herself or Donnie the pleasure because Joe could hear every single sound. She could make a protective bubble, but that would also drain her and exert energy that would be better used for other things. Like pleasure.

Suddenly, she was trapped between the desk and Donnie. The house was empty besides them.

"Now tell me what's wrong? We have no audience. What happened?"

"Nothing happened."

His hands tightened their grip on her hips. "Your heartbeat was steady as normal. Your smile as beautiful as always. But the way you trembled in my arms, it was different. Not from the way I make you cold. Not from anything I've felt from you before. I know something is wrong. Please don't lie to me."

He knew her so well. Down to the slightest movement she made.

"I brought up an old argument with Giselle and she didn't appreciate it."

His gaze remained intense and unyielding. He expected more of an explanation. She brought up her hands, smoothing them through his hair. "It stays between us."

He gave a sharp nod. "Always."

"Giselle has feelings for Max, and he's a damn idiot for

not seeing how amazing she is. How amazing they could be together."

A perplexed expression spread across his face until his lips widened into a devious grin. "I'm not so sure about that. I've spent quite a bit of time with him. Do you know who he mentions more than anyone else?"

"Me? Because he's a damn worrywart."

Donnie chuckled. "No, he never mentions you. That appears to be an off-limits topic between us." His hands wove around to her back. "Giselle this, and Giselle that. It's all I hear. Sure, it is related to the business at hand, but there's something in his voice when he says her name." He lowered his head. "I only know this because I can hear it in my own voice when I say your name."

Then his soft lips were covering hers and the conversation ended.

She didn't want to talk about those two anyhow. Not when she had this sexy man all to herself. The entire house empty and theirs to do as they will.

Donnie made quick work of removing her clothes. She did the same. Thankfully, he did so without ruining anything. She'd already lost a few shirts and bras from his frantic need to get her naked. Not that she ever complained about it. Sometimes, he forgot about his strength, his desire for her so overwhelming.

He lifted her to the desk, sliding into her with one strong thrust. For a moment they stared, frozen, holding each other in a death grip.

"Stella..." he whispered in her ear. Then his teeth grazed her neck.

She swallowed hard, wondering if this would be the moment he lost his control. And what her reaction would be.

Instead of two long fangs digging into her skin, his hips moved, thrusting quick and deep. She held on for the ride as he pounded in and out of her.

He was always careful to avoid her neck with his lips. She knew he worried he'd fall over the edge and do what he feared the most. Bite her.

There were times when his eyes trained on her neck where she wanted to lean her head to the side, give him full access. Let him bite her. Let him release some of the agony she knew he lived with.

But she never did.

Because a part of her also feared what would happen. Would he be able to control himself? Would he be able to stop in time?

Their heavy breathing filled the room along with the slap of skin against skin. She closed her eyes, enjoying the beautiful sensations ricocheting throughout her body.

Stella...

"Yes, Donnie. Harder, faster."

He tensed, stopping for a moment. Her eyes popped open and they shared a look before he was pumping his hips once again. What was that about?

Then it didn't even matter because she could feel the pleasure rising. Then it exploded. She screamed his name, holding on for dear life as the orgasm tore through her.

He grinded several more times before joining her. She sensed he wanted to kiss her neck. He settled for her forehead instead.

"Hang on tight."

Then he was zooming out of the room. She felt like she was flying, rushing through the air as if on a roller coaster that twisted and turned. Yet she didn't get that same feeling in her stomach when she rode the intense ride. She never felt off-kilter or like her stomach had dropped and she would get sick. She felt safe and secure and like nothing could touch her.

One second she was sitting on a desk in the study. Another second later she was laid out in the middle of Donnie's bed.

"Do you do that to impress me?"

A silky smile appeared before he kissed her, thrusting, starting round two. "Not at all. I was eager for more of this, but in a soft bed."

17

THEY WERE RUNNING out of time.

Donnie hated thinking in that sense, but he knew it was dwindling.

Everyone was in the study. Joe was on the couch, holding Emerson, with Bailey and Kade next to him. George and Peter were on the far side, next to the bookshelf. Mona and Mason close-by. Max stood by the newest map on the wall. Giselle had taken a spot in the soft leather chair close to Max with her computer open on her lap. The woman never went anywhere without her laptop. Holstrom and Charly stood behind the couch. Even Jock was in attendance, standing on the other side of his brother. He leaned against the desk with Stella wrapped in his arms. Her back to his chest, cocooned in his embrace.

She shivered every once and awhile, and while he hating feeling her react in such a way to him, he also couldn't seem to let go. He liked her in his arms. Way too much.

"Okay, welcome, everyone," Max started, as if he were the ringmaster to this unusual circus. They sure made up a crazy group of people. Vampires, witches, former ghosts.

Regular humans, a psychic, and a lycan. A very eclectic group of creatures. One he never envisioned himself being a part of. Now he wouldn't trade it for the world.

"We thought"—Max gestured toward him, then Joe, since they'd been the main ones out there searching for the vampire—"that a group meeting was necessary. To get everyone's input." He waited as if giving someone time to object, even though he hadn't gotten that far in his speech. "We need to make a big decision, and we can't make it lightly. So everyone needs to speak up."

It had taken them over two weeks to search their city for the killer. From top to bottom. Every nook, every cranny, every possible place a creature could hide. Nothing.

Then they moved on to the next town over to the north, where Mona and Mason resided, another two weeks to do so. Same results. Nothing.

Then the town to the south. Two more weeks of nothing to show for it.

On to the town to the west. Of course, two more weeks of no progress.

It had been two months since the first murder occurred. Two months of searching the city, the surrounding towns, coming up empty. The only positive thing was no other murders had occurred. Three victims. No other incidents had popped up.

"The last surrounding town we haven't searched is to the east. It's the same town occupied by the lycans that attacked Kade." Max paused, as if again, waiting for someone to speak up. "They did step into our town, stepping on our toes when these murders didn't even happen in their town. They stepped into our space again when they tried to attack at Mason's house."

Donnie hid his grin behind Stella's shoulder at the

choice of words Max used. Our town. As if those three had decided to make this their home. To stay in a place for once.

He could only hope.

"While they don't own it, we would be stepping into their territory if we conduct a search there. I don't know if they are going to care what the reason is." Max clapped his hands. "So, do we risk it? Or do we throw in the towel and assume this vamp has moved on?"

Jock's hand went up. Holstrom knocked it down, rolling his eyes. "This isn't a classroom. You got something to say, say it."

"Okay, bro, I will. I would like to think it's safe to say the vampire has moved on. Two months is a long time to go without another killing. Unless I'm wrong in my assessment and you guys can live off that for that long."

Hell, no.

Donnie had been drinking more blood than he ever had since Stella walked into his life. It kept the urge, the craving attacking his system to a level he could control. Every day. Every second he was with her, he wanted to bite her. Suck her sweet blood and know how she tasted.

"No, Jock," Joe jumped in, "we need more than that to survive. If that vampire stopped drinking blood, he'd go into a state that would be dangerous. For everyone around him. Bloodlust. A severe case of it."

Jock waved a hand in the air. "Then it moved on."

"It's possible," Joe agreed.

Kade raised his hand in the air, twisting his head to smirk at Holstrom, who rolled his eyes again. Though he didn't knock Kade's hand down. "I'm leaning toward it moved on. I personally don't want to risk stepping on the lycans toes again. Once was enough."

Bailey nodded, agreeing with her husband. Donnie wasn't surprised.

"We could at least warn them," Mona said, "or ask them if it's okay we search the area, to be on the safe side."

When no one spoke up, as in, who would be the person to do that, the idea fizzled before it could get bigger. Mona looked crushed that no one jumped on her suggestion. It didn't help her in the slightest, especially when in the last two months she'd gone back into her shell, shutting all of them out.

Scatter and Bozo weren't even here tonight. They wouldn't tell Mona more about themselves. They admitted to being guardians, but that was it. No other details. Since the day Stella ripped a wide gap between them—unintentionally, of course—Scatter and Bozo had even distanced themselves from everyone else.

They still hadn't tackled the issue concerning her aunt either. But soon. They would soon.

Stella straightened in his arms, but he didn't lessen his grip on her. She didn't fight him.

"Holstrom, Mason, and I have kept our eyes and ears out around the surrounding areas for cases similar to ours. There are no open murder cases suggesting the vampire has killed somewhere else. At least not in a fifty-mile radius from here. We can expand our search. If it left the area, which it's pointing to that, then..." Her hands gripped his that were holding her in place. "Then it might mean we need to follow."

Giselle didn't look up from her computer. "I've been keeping an eye on cases beyond the fifty-mile radius. There are two possible towns we could venture to. Both murders seem to meet the criteria, based on the evidence I see. One is a hundred miles west. The other is one hundred fifty miles or so to the south. No known covens in either area."

Not that creatures broadcasted their existence in an area, but most of the time other creatures knew when it was occupied by another. To not step into the zone unless invited in.

Charly's face lit up with a gentle smile before speaking. "Seeing as you three have been doing the majority of the work, what do you three think?"

He, Max, and Joe shared a look.

They couldn't agree on the matter, which was why this meeting had been called.

"I," Max said, pointing to himself, "think we should check out the two unsolved murders farther away. Giselle mentioned her findings to us yesterday."

Joe bounced Emerson on his knee. "I think it wouldn't hurt to check those two cases out, I don't think it's our guy. It's only two cases and they happened in the past week. I think this vampire is way out of range. Somewhere far away. Maybe I'd think differently if those two cases happened shortly after ours. As if he was finding a meal as he traveled toward another destination."

Donnie tended to agree with all of that. At least the part where it couldn't hurt to check the cases out.

But he didn't think this vampire had left. Not yet.

Charly met his gaze. "Donnie? Your thoughts?"

His decision had nothing to do with Stella. Not with the thought of her leaving him altogether. It was all gut instinct.

"This vampire is hiding somewhere. In town. Or maybe in the town we haven't checked out, but I doubt it because the lycans would've sniffed him out by now. No other dead bodies have popped up because he got smarter. He knew drawing attention to himself wasn't wise. So he's still feeding on people out there, he's just not killing them."

Bailey was tapping her leg incessantly, staring at him with wild, scared eyes. "Max and Joe aren't agreeing with you. Is that it?"

Donnie offered a tender grin. "A difference of opinion. I have no facts to back up my theory. Only a gut feeling." Then Donnie's gaze darted to Charly.

So did Joe, George, Peter, and Max. They all zeroed in on her.

Nervous laughter escaped as she curled into Holstrom's arms when he threw them around her. "You all need to tone down your hearing."

Impossible.

It was a part of who they were.

When one's heartbeat skyrocketed without warning, it meant something happened. Trouble was on the horizon.

"Did you have a vision, Charly?" Donnie asked.

Not a vision at the moment because they all would've witnessed her experiencing it. She lost consciousness for a while as it played out in her mind. Since that didn't happen, it meant she had it before she came and was now finding the courage to tell them about it.

Which suggested it hadn't been a vision she wanted to share. She saw something bad happen.

She forced out a smile. "Donnie's right. He's here, hiding somewhere. He's feeding off people, not killing them anymore." Then she looked at Mona. "But Mona also is right. We need to speak to the lycans. We'll need their help."

Kade twisted his head at her. "Please expand on that."

Yes, Kade would be the last person who would want to come face-to-face again with them.

"All I know is in my vision, Donnie's in the woods, I

don't know which ones. Maybe the land where the lycans reside. He's with Benny, the leader of the pack. They aren't fighting. They're searching together. It's evening." Charly sighed, closing her eyes as if she couldn't believe she even said that last part out loud. Of course it would be evening. Donnie wouldn't be able to be outside otherwise. "The short snippet of conversation I got was they were tracking a vampire."

Max crossed his arms, scowling. "You saw Donnie and that jackass working together?"

Donnie knew the only reason Max gave a fellow lycan such a moniker was because the man would've killed him and Giselle. Max was firmly on their side, which Donnie would never doubt. Not after getting to know him so well.

"Yes. It was the weirdest thing that's happened to me." Charly gripped Holstrom's arm. "Breck told me this meeting was scheduled, and then the next thing I knew, a vision hit me. I've never had a vision hit me when I needed it to happen. So my vote is to talk to the lycans. The vampire is still around. In order to find it, we need to work with them."

"It's one vampire." Giselle shut her laptop with a hard slap. "I think this entire group can handle one vampire together. I think at this point, we know it's not a coven because our extensive search would've found one. Kade, Mason, and Holstrom having been training hard. Even those three could hold their own against the vamp."

Donnie wasn't ready to agree with that statement, but since the three had started training with him, Joe, and Max, they were much better prepared to defend themselves than they were two months ago. It was something they should've started learning long before now. Even Bailey and Mona joined them on occasion. Charly didn't touch other people, so she remained away.

Charly shrugged. "I'm relaying what I saw. Do with it what you will."

Joe handed Emerson to Bailey and stood up, taking a spot by Max. "It could be a very powerful vampire." He shared a look with Donnie. "A very old vampire. They are the hardest to kill, if not damn near impossible."

For the first time that evening, he wanted to let go of Stella. She gripped his forearms holding herself in place as if she sensed his need. As if to say she wouldn't let him escape. To run away from whatever hit him.

Except he was stronger than her and he needed to do something. He moved away from her, ignoring the disapproval in her groan. Or was that more like pain that slipped from her lips? Well, whatever it was, he couldn't focus on it. He'd apologize later.

He stopped in front of Charly and held out his hands.

Holstrom stepped in front of Charly. "What the hell are you doing?"

"I was in her vision. Not Joe or George or Peter. Not Max or Giselle. Nor Mona or Mason. Me. Out of everyone here." He could forcibly remove Holstrom out of the way. "Do you know why my friends and I have moved so often? Have you ever wondered about that?"

Holstrom squinted his eyes as if pondering the question. "Hunters or whatever you call the people who want to kill you."

"And my master. The one who turned me. The one who didn't give me a choice when he turned me. If it's him who's doing this, then I need to know. I've been running from him for a very long time. I will not get stuck in his clutches again."

Charly peeked around Holstrom. "I don't know how to

show you that, Donnie. I didn't see the vampire in my vision. Only you and Benny."

"Try. For me. I need to know."

"What for? So you can run?" Stella asked with a bite to her tone.

Maybe. But he didn't voice it. He'd never put her in harm's way. If it was his sire in the area, that meant he had already put Stella in the crosshairs. He'd never forgive himself if something happened to her.

"I could see more than you wish for me to see."

Donnie smiled. "I'm not proud of some of the stuff you might see. But I can't fear what you might think of me because of it. It happened. It is what it is. This is more than that."

Charly nodded and grabbed his hands.

18

STELLA WATCHED in horror as they stood there holding hands. Charly wincing, as if in pain, and Donnie watching her as if in a trance. No expression marred his features. She couldn't tell what he was feeling or thinking.

Stop it, Donnie! What are you doing?

He flinched, glancing at her.

Odd.

It's as if he heard her thoughts. Her desperate plea.

What was even odder, it wasn't the first time she sensed he might've heard her thoughts. Or that she had sworn she'd listened in on his thoughts as well.

But it wasn't possible.

It couldn't be possible for them to read each other's thoughts. She was powerful, but not that powerful. Nor had she done anything to make it happen.

Then Charly was letting go, stumbling into Holstrom's arms.

"Oh my...Donnie." Charly looked on the verge of tears.

He closed his eyes, pain filtering everywhere. "I'm not that person anymore, Charly."

She straightened her stance, reaching out, then stopping herself from laying a hand on his shoulder. "It's not that. I didn't see any of that."

He blinked, as if confused.

"I tried to focus on your master. On what you wanted me to focus on." A bubbly laughter escaped. "It worked. It's so amazing. I'm getting so much better at it." Her laughter died. "The way he treated you... I'm in awe of the person you are. That you managed to get away from him."

Donnie looked away and Stella wanted to move closer. Remove the ache she saw trying to swallow him whole. What had he been through? Their past was not something they talked about. They didn't even graze the surface on it. On either side.

"I saw all of that, but I still can't say whether it's the same vampire we're looking for. I don't know."

His attention drew back to Charly, a grimace on his face. "I'm about to suggest something that will make Holstrom upset. Very, very upset. And something you won't want to do either."

"Then don't say it," Holstrom said through clenched teeth.

Charly laid a hand on Holstrom's chest. "Go on. Say it."

"If you touched something that this vampire had, maybe you could get a sense if it's the same one from my past."

Charly frowned. "I might. I can't be sure until I try. Is there something in evidence that I can try?" Charly tilted her head up at Holstrom.

"There's nothing. They didn't leave a trace behind."

"It left one thing behind," Donnie counteracted to Holstrom's terse words.

"Like what?"

"The body."

"Hell, no!" Holstrom roared, shoving Charly behind him. "You are not digging up a dead body so Charly can touch it. Have you lost your damn mind?"

"I am so proud of how steady your heartbeat is right now." Donnie grinned. "You've come a long way, detective."

Stella could see the fury rising up in Holstrom's chest. The man was going to explode sooner or later. "Enough. We're tabling this conversation for now. I think we all have what we need to muse on this situation. We can come back for a vote later on what we plan to do."

Everyone must've agreed because the room dispersed. Stella didn't care where anyone ventured off to but Donnie. She followed him. The audacity of him to think he could walk away from her—again. Though she couldn't see him since he'd used his vampire speed to get away, she focused her senses. It led her to his room.

She closed and locked the door behind her. He stood by his oblong dresser, a large mirror behind it. They stared at each other through the mirror. She held his gaze as she walked closer. He didn't avert his eyes until she was upon him.

He refused to turn around, and he stood too close to the dresser for her to get in front of him. She could fight him to make him shift his stance, but she knew that would be the wrong move.

"Talk to me."

Anything. She didn't care what he said as long as he spoke. This silence. The tension in the air needed to evaporate. She didn't like it.

Sometimes, moments like these called for magic. She waved her hand in the air.

"I've created a bubble. This is a safe space. No one can

hear us. Giselle and I do this all the time when we don't want Max to hear something."

His eyes met hers through the mirror.

"You hate the idea too. Don't you?"

To dig up a dead body so Charly could touch it and sense something he wanted way too much? Yeah, she didn't relish the idea one bit.

But it wasn't something she'd get in the way of. At least he was speaking to her now. She wouldn't risk anything, otherwise the conversation would cease.

"I will stand behind you on it."

On everything. Why couldn't he see that?

She placed a hand on his back, needing to feel some sort of contact. "We never talk about our past."

His entire body tensed.

"Maybe we should."

"You want to hear about the people I've killed. The need for blood, no matter how I had to get it."

They all made mistakes in life. She couldn't hold his against him. He'd found a better way to live. She was proud of him for that. Sure, there were times she forgot he was a vampire. That he could kill without breaking a sweat. When reality slammed back into her, it still didn't make her fearful of him. Why was he trying to push her away like this?

"Donnie, don't do this. Don't turn away from me. Don't try to scare me as if that will work."

He swiveled around so fast, she stumbled backward. Of course, he caught her, pulling her savagely into his arms.

"You want to hear then how one man controlled me like I was a puppet on a string. Is that what you want?"

She brushed her hand across his cheek, trying to soothe the agony she heard in his voice. "Only if you wish to share it with me."

"I lived a simple life. I worked for a merchant. Got paid very little, but it was a job. I cared for my...my wife as best as I could." He closed his eyes.

She hated that he shied away from her like this. Did she want to hear about the woman he must've loved with his entire heart before her? If the pain that crested his features was any indication, he loved her dearly. No, she had no desire to hear a word about her. But it was a part of his past and she couldn't change it any more than he could.

She swiped her hand across his cheek again, the only way she knew how to ask him to continue.

His eyes remained closed for the longest time, before he opened them again and forged on. "I closed the shop down one evening. Left out the alleyway as I normally did. I was accosted by two men. They brandished a knife and took the few coins I had, leaving me with a wound deep enough to do damage that could not be repaired in that time period.

"In those last moments, I felt a sort of peace I hadn't in a very long time. Life was much harder than I would've wished for anyone. I felt remorse leaving my wife alone, but I wasn't going to fight death. Then he appeared out of the shadows. He didn't say a word, nor even make a sound as he approached. One second he was standing, and the next he was feasting on my neck. As much as I hate to admit it, there was peace in that too. He was making my death faster. I welcomed it, even as I regretted that feeling. God, I hated leaving my wife all alone in a cruel world."

He stopped speaking and she figured she knew why. This was where, at the last minute, he begged the vampire not to kill him. To save him. She'd heard several different versions of this kind of story from others right before she killed them. Right before they then begged her not to kill them. As if she'd grant mercy after the carnage they left behind.

She didn't know how to feel about what he was about to confess. If he hadn't done so, he wouldn't be standing before her. So how could she regret that?

"He stopped before I lost consciousness. He stared at me for the longest before asking why I wasn't fighting him. Then that's when the most wicked smile I've ever seen appeared. That was the moment he turned me. If I would've fought death, he would've given me it. But because I didn't, he decided I should live in hell. I started fighting once he started the process and all he did was laugh. He loved a challenge, and I was nothing but a challenge. From that point on, he made decisions for me as if I couldn't be trusted to make them myself."

She sucked in a sharp breath as the truth hit her. "He didn't give you a choice?"

"I wish he had. I would not have taken this life. I would not have said yes to this existence."

Knowing that about him made her love him even more.

Because while she resisted the notion for the first month. This second month with him she'd embraced that turbulent feeling swirling in her veins.

She loved this vampire with her entire body and soul. She ached for the man who wasn't given what he wanted. Death.

"It took me years, more than I want to admit, to break free from him. But I did. For a while he left me alone. But he always reappears, tries to sway me back in his clutches. I've tried to kill him. I'm not strong enough. I don't know how old he is, but if I had to guess, I'd say more than a millennium."

That would suggest more than a thousand years old. A vampire that old would be damn near impossible to kill. The older they got, the stronger they became.

"He'll never stop trying to control me. Never."

She cupped his cheeks, bringing his face closer. "It's a good thing you happen to know a cosmic witch."

His grip on her hips tightened, his fingers digging into her skin so hard it hurt. "I would never let you take him on. If he hurt you... No, Stella, promise me you'll keep your distance."

"I can't promise you that, Donnie."

He picked her up and flew to the bed, trapping her between the edge of it and his rigid body. Summer had arrived and she wore more dresses because of it. And it made it easier for Donnie to gain access.

Her panties tore as he ripped them from her body. His pants tore as well as he whipped them away. Then he thrusted hard and deep inside her. Pounding into her several times before stopping, holding so still she was worried he'd gone into a far place where no one would be able to reach him. Not even her.

She clutched his forearms, digging her nails into his cold skin. "Donnie?"

He blinked several times, before his eyes came back into focus. "I would never risk your life for anything."

"I know this."

"You're mine." He pumped ferociously into her. "Only mine." Another hard thrust. "I've never felt this possessive of something or someone before." More deep, thorough thrusts. "When you leave this earth, then so shall I."

She knew without hearing the words themselves, that was his way of telling her he loved her.

"I will do anything to stop you from putting yourself in

harm's way." He thrusted so hard, it was as if he needed to ram the truth into her. "Anything."

A sliver of fear hit her body for the first time in his presence. What could he do?

One thing entered her thoughts. He'd leave her. Run away from her.

She clung to him, afraid this would be the last time they ever enjoyed themselves in this way again.

"What are you doing?"

Donnie didn't look at Joe, who stood in the threshold of his room. He hadn't been as quiet as he thought he'd been. Where was a magic bubble to hide the sounds when he needed it?

Another shirt hit the suitcase. He grabbed one more from the closet, folding it with careful precision, but before that one could join the others, it was snatched out of his hands.

The shirt was clutched in Joe's fist, creating wrinkles that annoyed him. He liked his outfits nice and pristine.

"Why are you packing?"

A rhetorical question. Because the answer had to be obvious. He and the guys had done this many times over. Fled when their position had become known. They were lucky. Their masters either were dead or didn't care what the hell they did with their vampire lives. Joe hadn't seen his since the day he was turned. He'd struggled as a newbie vampire because he had no one to lead him. George and Peter shared the same master. The man was dead from crossing the wrong witch.

"Does Stella know? Because the way she left this

morning suggests she doesn't. I haven't gotten any phone calls all day from Max or anyone else suggesting you told her during the day either."

Leaving without saying goodbye was the best option. The safest one. She'd fight him tooth and nail at this decision, and he wouldn't be swayed.

He had to keep her safe.

"Damn it, Donnie!" The loud sound of the shirt ripping in two filled the room.

No, damn it, Joe! That was one of his favorite black shirts.

"You can't leave like this. You can't leave Stella without telling her." Joe whipped the mangled shirt to the floor. "Were you even going to tell me? George or Peter?"

He had no idea. When the sun started setting, he knew it was time to get his things in order and be out the door the moment it disappeared under the horizon.

As soon as darkness set, he would be gone.

Joe grabbed him by the front of his shirt, picked him up as if he were as light as a feather and threw him clear across the room. Of course, he did all that in a split second, Donnie had no time to counter the attack.

"You want to ignore me? Fine. Let's talk a different way."

Joe zoomed his way and Donnie met him halfway there. They threw punches and jabs, kicks to the stomach that felt like a tiny slap to the face. Joe managed to get a good grip a few times, throwing him in one direction or another. Donnie returned the same move in kind.

Furniture splintered in two. Pictures fell to the ground. His dresser mirror shattered into a million pieces. A shard of glass even cut him on the forearm. A slice from wrist to elbow. Blood dripped on the floor and smeared on Joe as they continued to fight.

One moment they were fighting, the next they were leaning against the bed, then sliding to the floor with clothes scattered around them.

Donnie stared at his arm as the cut healed in real time. Only remnants of blood remained. No more wound. No scar. Nothing to remind him he'd fought his best friend. And for what reason?

"She would fight him. For me. I could never allow that."

Joe sighed, resting his head against the mattress. "She's very strong-willed. I get it. But she would do it because she cares."

"I will not allow it."

What part weren't they understanding?

"So that's why you're leaving? To stop her from taking on that asshole? What if he doesn't follow you? We don't even know if he's the vampire out there. You could be running for no reason."

Donnie had pondered that very question all afternoon. One answer came to him. He had to forget about his friends and Stella and leave. Because deep down in the pit of his stomach he knew it was his master playing games with him. As soon as Joe put the idea in his head, he knew. His master loved to toy with him. Make sure Donnie knew who was in charge. He had to leave, and his master had to follow him. Do what he always did to Donnie. Make him see reason.

Of course, Donnie would fight him as he always did. As long as Stella was safe. If her life was threatened? Well, if he had to go back to being a puppet, he would. For her.

As he told her last night, he'd do anything for her.

"Oh, no, Donnie. No, you can't." Joe gripped his shoulder, forcing him to look at him. "You can't bend to him. Don't do this."

"I will leave. He will follow. You will all be safe. All of

you. If he doesn't follow, I will do what I have to to keep you all safe. I should've seen this from the beginning. He's been toying with us this whole time. That's why we haven't found him. He didn't want to be found."

Joe's fingers dug into his shoulder. If he wasn't a vampire that didn't feel pain like a normal human, he would've winced. Except he felt nothing. "You've never walked away like this. You've never let him win like this."

"It's for the best, Joe." He placed his hand over Joe's and stared straight ahead, eyeing the destruction they caused. "If I don't leave now, I'll break apart. I won't survive her leaving me."

"Like you wouldn't go with her."

"But where could this relationship go? How long could it last?" He patted Joe's hand. "She'll grow old and I won't. There's no future. I will watch her become a frail old lady with gray hair, and then when she takes her last breath, I will wish to do the same. I can't watch her grow old. I can't do it." He dropped his hand to his lap, losing the rest of the fight himself. "I'm afraid even walking away, I will know when she's gone from this earth, and I will walk into the sun. It won't even matter I've walked away."

"So you lov—"

"I don't wish to speak of such things. Don't say it out loud. Please. Let me finish packing and let me go."

"I don't agree with this decision. And when Stella hears you left, what do you think she's going to do? Do you think she'll let you disappear? You're an idiot if you believe that."

"You and I both know I can vanish without a trace and be found when I want to be found."

Joe gave a merciful laugh. "Except you're wrong. You can't do that. Because if you could, he wouldn't have found you again. Assuming this vampire is him."

Well, Joe wasn't wrong there. He hated to admit that.

"She'll find you too. We both know she will. You'll have hell to pay when she does. You're better off telling her before you go. For your own safety."

Donnie couldn't help but chuckle. "There's nothing she could do that would hurt me. I wouldn't fight her if she found me. But I would disappear again. You know it's for the best."

Joe stood, flexing his arms as if gearing up for round two. "No, Donnie. On this, we disagree. It's the worst possible decision you've ever made. You'll regret it. In more ways than one. This is a mistake."

No, this wouldn't be a mistake. His mistake was losing control. At that very first kiss they shared. If he had maintained his distance, he wouldn't be in this spot now.

One mistake too late.

"You're not going to see reason." Joe shook his head, frowning in disgust. Then a hundred different flashes and blurs filled the room as Joe ran at top speed. He didn't know what he had done until the carnage was over.

Every piece of clothing he owned—but the ones he wore —were torn to shreds. Shirts, pants, vests, and every coat were in shambles, spread across the room in disarray.

"Go ahead and pack now. Have fun."

Then Joe was gone, leaving him alone in his turmoil.

He stood up, eyeing the mess.

Damn him!

Donnie looked behind him to the clock on the wall, except it wasn't there. It had fallen in the argument. He couldn't locate his phone either in the mess. So he walked over to the clock on the floor.

Another thirty minutes until the sun would set. All he had to do was wait.

He'd be leaving with nothing in his possession. Ruining his clothes would not deter his original goal.

Get as far away from here to keep Stella safe.

KNOCK, knock.

"Come on, Giselle. Open the door, please."

Stella swiveled around, deciding not to leave her room yet, and placed her back against the wall. She didn't want to walk out into the hallway and disrupt Max from having a conversation with Giselle. But she also didn't want to eavesdrop from her room.

Eavesdropping won, of course.

"Please. Open up."

The hinges creaked with a short huff following. Giselle had done as he wished.

"How can I help you?"

Stella imagined Max crossing his arms in annoyance at such a ridiculous question. Especially with how Giselle said it so sweetly as if she wasn't pissed at him.

Since the day, nearly two months ago, when she told Max to take Giselle to breakfast, things had been stilted between them. He'd taken her to breakfast. That much she knew. What happened after that day, she wasn't sure. Not even Giselle would tell her anything. Giselle had even been a bit annoyed with her too.

"How much longer are we going to do this?"

"Do what?"

Stella had to put a hand over her mouth to stop the snort that wanted to escape at Giselle feigning confusion.

"I hate this tension between us. I'm sorry if I upset you somehow. Tell me what I did and I'll fix it."

"Nothing's wrong. I'm not upset."

This would be where he'd frown, his brows drawing low and his hands fisting while his arms were still crossed.

"I know your moods. I know you. Something has been bugging you, and I think it's time we talk about whatever it is. We can't go into a fight with shit between us. We all need to be at top form."

"Who says we'll be fighting anyone? I thought it was a group decision."

"Yeah, well, I think it's leaning towards a fight. We both know that. We need to do one more search where the lycans reside, and we know it won't go over well with them."

"I don't know that."

Stella wanted to chuckle again, clamping her hand even tighter over her mouth. It was nearly impossible to argue with Giselle. She never gave an inch, and she was so damn good at pretending not to be affected by anything.

"So you're telling me I've done nothing wrong?"

"Yes."

Liar! Stella heard the falsehood of that from the tone of her voice.

"Then what's been bothering you?"

"Max, I am fine. Nothing has been bothering me. I would like to keep researching before we leave for Donnie's.

For the record, I will be voting that we do not search the last area because I believe the vampire has left the area."

"What about the things Donnie thinks? That it's his master doing all this shit? I don't think he left the area."

"If that's the case, he's not hiding in lycan territory. So contacting them is a moot point."

"I want to make sure you're okay. I don't like seeing you like this."

"Now you're upsetting me. If I told you I'm fine, then you should believe me."

Stella flinched when a door slammed. She waited for a good minute, wanting Max to depart, before pushing away from the wall and turning toward the doorway.

Max stood with his arms crossed and his lips in a stern line. She wondered if he had even unwound his arms walking toward her room or kept them in that position the entire time.

"You're not as quiet as you thought you were. Did our conversation amuse you?"

"Some parts, yes." Why lie? He heard her struggling to hold her laughter in.

"Something is up with her. I don't know what."

Could be anything. But since it started around the time she told him to take her to breakfast, she assumed it was Giselle's feelings about Max that were putting her in such a state. Not that she would share that with him. If Giselle wanted him to know how she felt about him, then she would've told him.

"It's been a stressful time around here. We've all been working hard. I'm sure it's nothing more than that."

At least, Stella hoped so.

Max relaxed his stance, glancing at the watch on his

wrist. "I doubt she wants to ride with me right now. Can she catch a ride with you over there? I'm going to head out now."

"Sure."

Max headed down the hallway.

"Max."

He stopped, twisting to see her.

"Men can be such idiots. Maybe you should stop being one. Open your damn eyes." Then Stella stepped back into her room, wanting to avoid adding anything else.

She'd already said too much, hinting at Giselle's feelings. But enough was enough. Max was right about one thing. They couldn't go into any kind of fight with this sort of tension between the three of them. They worked better as a team when they were in top form.

When they got to Donnie's, she hoped Donnie was more receptive to talking than Giselle was. Because she needed to fix the tension between them as well. Sure, they had come together in fabulous lovemaking like they always did. But that was sex. That was never an issue between them. It was explosive and all-consuming and never filled with awkwardness. It was when they broke apart that it filtered between them.

She hadn't spoken to him all day either. Not even little texts here and there, and that was something they'd gotten in the habit of doing—maintaining contact as much as they could.

Like Max, she was ready to leave. But she needed to give Giselle time to get her bearings back. She knew interactions like the one she had with Max never put her in a good headspace.

Stella heard the front door close. Max had left. Okay. She'd give Giselle five minutes and then they'd leave too.

Setting a timer even crossed her mind, but she refrained.

Barely. It didn't mean she didn't watch as the numbers rolled past one by one on her phone until five minutes had gone by.

She banged on Giselle's door. "Let's go. I'm ready to leave."

"Coming!"

Good. At least she didn't have to argue about that.

"I'll meet you in the car."

Stella grabbed her purse from the living room, tossing it over her shoulder, and opened the door.

The sight before her had her heart thumping to a dangerous beat and her eyes blurring from the sudden onset of tears.

"Giselle! Get down here now!"

Stella raced down the porch and to Max's side, throwing the strap of her purse over her head and tossing it away. Then she tore her T-shirt off as well, shoving it hard at the large wound at his neck. As if an animal had taken a large bite.

He opened his mouth to speak, but nothing came out but tiny croaks. The wound at his neck was one of the most vicious she'd ever seen, but she knew right away a vampire had caused it. The large gashes across his chest were uncommon but were the markings of a vampire as well. Whoever this vampire was, it had wanted to cause the most damage it could. It hadn't been about feeding off the blood. It had been about the pain it could inflict.

"Oh my God, Max!" Giselle screeched, rushing to his side.

"Help me get him inside."

Stella was forced to stop putting pressure on his throat as she grabbed under his armpits to lift him up while Giselle took his feet. They had him in the house in under a minute. Of course, if the vampire was still in the area, it had time to attack them. They'd been alone long enough to do so. So why hadn't it? The only reasoning could be was it left. Not that they were going to take that chance. They were safe in the house.

As soon as they had him on the living room floor, she resumed pressure on his neck. He groaned at the contact but still didn't speak. Giselle, instead of removing her shirt, grabbed a blanket from the couch, pressing on the wounds on his chest.

"What the hell happened?"

Stella shook her head. How could she know the answer to that? He'd obviously walked outside and was attacked. Laying there bleeding to death until she walked outside. If she hadn't wanted to leave so soon after him, he'd be dead.

He could still die.

A hospital was too far away and would never be able to save him.

His neck was so torn to shreds, she wasn't sure what could save him.

"Stella..."

She didn't know if Giselle's plea was to save him or to let him die. Because this would not be easy healing his wounds. The gashes on his chest were much deeper than even Kade's had been, and that had taken a toll on her. She even bore the scars to prove it. Then in addition to the neck wound...

But she had to try.

Oh, Donnie. I need you. I wish you were here. I love you.

"I CAN'T BELIEVE you're leaving."

Donnie descended the staircase, empty-handed, since

Joe had ruined all his clothes. Did he think that would stop him? Joe didn't know him as well as he thought he had then.

Joe stood in front of the door, arms crossed, as if that would also stop him.

"You have about ten minutes before the sun is gone to keep me here. Are we going to do this again? I don't want to fight you, Joe."

"Then don't leave like this."

He had to. It was the only way to keep Stella safe. It was for her own good. She would never back down from a fight, and he couldn't allow her to take on his master. If that man found out what she was, she would die. He would make sure of it.

Oh, Donnie. I need you...

He looked around the foyer as the voice echoed around him.

His feet flew toward the door, stopping inches from Joe. "Move. I need to get to Stella. Something's wrong."

Joe's brows drew inward. "What the hell are you talking about?"

"I can't explain it. I know something's wrong."

"In case you forgot, the sun hasn't set. Ten more minutes. You said so yourself."

Donnie grabbed him by the shirt and tossed him behind him. Joe crashed into the wall. "It's a chance I'm willing to take."

He was already so far away from her. By car would be much faster if he knew he wouldn't run into traffic. But he would, especially near the bridge close to her house.

Dusk was nearly gone, replaced by the night. He could avoid the patches of sun where it landed in certain spots. He had no choice if he were to reach her as soon as possible.

He raced like he'd never had before. His shoes barely

touched the ground. It was as if he were flying. Stella needed him. He swore he heard her plea. Despite still wanting to leave, he couldn't do so when she was in trouble. He'd leave after.

He had one goal in mind: get to her house. Though, he didn't actually know where she was, his instincts told him she'd be at home. He was focused, but he still sensed Joe right behind him.

Thank goodness for friends. It didn't matter what happened between them, they always stepped up to the plate.

Too much time had gone by since he heard her cry for help. But he made it to her house, smelling the scent of blood before he even hit her yard. The door was wide open, a trail of blood leading from the yard, across the porch, and through the foyer where it disappeared into the living room, which he couldn't see.

He didn't stop his pace until he was forced to, hitting the invisible force field like it was a brick wall. He was propelled backward and landed on his ass in the yard.

How could he have forgotten? Despite being together for the past two months, Stella always came to his house. He never ventured to hers. He had never wanted to. Stella having one safe spot from him in case he lost control had always been a good idea.

Until now.

He went back to the door, Joe right by his side.

"Stella! Let me in! Let me in right now!"

Silence greeted them. Not a peep. Not one tiny sound.

Where was Max and Giselle? Whose blood were they smelling? Donnie inhaled again.

"It's either Max or Giselle. It's not Stella's blood."

"I believe you." Joe nodded as if he knew that without a

doubt. Donnie would know Stella's scent from anywhere. He was confident in his assessment.

"Stella! Let me in!"

So if she wasn't hurt, why wasn't she letting him in?

"Come in, Donnie and Joe."

At the sound of Giselle's voice from somewhere in the house, the shield dropped. He raced inside and found them in the living room.

"No!" Donnie dropped to his knees by Stella's side. He had to push Max out of the way to be closer to her. There was a large nasty wound on her neck and several deep slashes across her chest.

It couldn't be.

It wasn't her blood he smelled outside or in the house. He knew her scent. It enticed him every single day to take a bite. He would've known it was her.

Donnie cradled her in his arms. "Stay with me, Stella. I'm here. I came as soon I heard you. I'm here. You can't leave me like this."

Not like he was going to do to her. That would've been different.

"Donnie..."

"Yes, my love, I'm here." He kissed her forehead, hugging her tighter. "I came. Stay with me."

"What happened?" Joe asked.

Giselle shrugged, shaking her head. Max crawled to her side, pulling her into his arms. His shirt was torn to shreds with blood covering his body everywhere, yet no wounds.

"Something attacked me the moment I walked outside. I didn't even hear them coming. I was on the ground before I could even make a sound, bleeding. I couldn't even call out for help. Thank God Stella came outside a few minutes later and they dragged me back inside. Stella...she...healed my wounds."

Donnie looked him over. "You have no scars. You don't look like anything happened to you!"

Max's head dipped once, wincing, as the tears welled in the corner of his eyes. "She absorbed it all. Giselle tried to stop her, but she wouldn't listen."

Stella moaned in his arms.

She was still alive. There was still time to save her.

He made a slit in his wrist and put it to her mouth. "Drink, my love."

Max shoved his hand away. "What the hell are you doing? You are not turning her!"

Donnie would fight him if he had to, but it would waste time. "I would never turn her. Tell him, Joe."

Joe looked ready for battle, his body taut and rigid, his expression that of a warrior. "Never. He had that choice taken away, so he'd never do the same to someone else."

"Then what the hell is he doing?" Max shouted, throwing a hard gesture at his wrist that bled.

"She's losing too much blood. I'll give her enough to help sustain her, not turn her." Donnie put his wrist back to her mouth. Max must've believed him because he didn't protest again.

"More, Stella. You need to drink more. Please."

She was losing consciousness. And way too much blood. The amount he could give her would not be enough to save her. While his blood could heal his injuries, he doubted it would help her do the same thing.

"Donnie, I—" Joe stopped speaking, and Donnie didn't care what he was going to say. There was nothing he could say that would change what happened. What would happen if she died.

Her lips stopped moving, taking in the small amount of blood he'd offered. He was losing her.

"Don't die on me, Stella. You can't die on me now. It's too soon. You're supposed to grow old with beautiful white hair. I've already seen that imagine of you in my mind. It's the most gorgeous thing I've ever seen. That's your destiny. Not this. I love you. I love you so much. So I beg you not to do this to me." He pushed his wrist against her mouth, urging her to drink.

A low moan escaped. Her eyes even fluttered for one tiny second. She resumed sucking on his wrist before stopping again.

No more sounds from her. No movements of any kind.

He'd lost the woman he loved. The woman he had planned to walk away from. He now understood how foolish that would've been. How devastating to realize too late.

Giselle's heavy sobs filled the room. Max's own quiet tears merged with hers. Joe dropped to the floor, putting a hand on his shoulder.

"I can smell him," Donnie said with no inflection in his voice. He'd lost all the will to live. But he'd do one thing before he died. "I will kill the man who sired me for this. And then I will step into the sun."

Joe squeezed his shoulder. "I will help you kill him. And I won't stop you from seeing the sun one last time."

Because his friend knew that was how strong his love was for her.

"Are you sure it was him?" Max asked.

Donnie nodded, on the verge of tears himself.

"It happened so fast. I can't believe I didn't sense him or hear a sound."

"It's not your fault, Max." Donnie would never hold what Stella did against him. She had made the choice to save her friend. "He's very powerful. I've never succeeded in killing him, but I will not lose this time."

"I won't let you lose because I'll be right by your side." The fierceness in Max's expression said there was no use arguing. Why would he? The more people, the better chance they had at beating him.

"Umm...guys." Giselle sniffed, pointing at Stella. "What's happening?"

Donnie looked down at Stella to see the wounds on her neck and chest, closing. In the exact same way his injuries healed themselves. Even his wrist had stopped bleeding and the wound gone as if it never had appeared.

He watched in awe as they closed up and vanished. Not even one scar remained.

20

STELLA GROANED at the ache in her back. There was something jammed there...a knee? Her eyes fluttered opened to see Donnie staring at her as if he'd seen a ghost.

"Stella, my love." He pulled her up and into his embrace, squeezing her hard.

And she didn't care because it felt good to have his arms around her, even if they did chill her to the bone. Of course, she shivered, which caused him to loosen his grip, but he didn't release her.

"What happened?" she asked as she positioned herself better in his lap. She looked at her friends who had tearstains on their cheeks and at Joe who looked like he'd seen a ghost as well. "What's wrong?"

"Stella!" Giselle leaned forward. "You healed yourself."

She looked down at her chest. No gashes. Then she smoothed her hand across her neck. No injury, as if someone had taken a large bite out of her.

No, she couldn't have healed herself. She had healed Max like she had the one time with Kade and absorbed his wounds. All of them. She left nothing behind, and not because she didn't want her friend to have any scars, but because she hadn't been able to stop herself. She'd been consumed with the power, and it had been impossible to stop until she'd collapsed to the ground.

She had felt the pain. The blood running down her neck. The life draining from her body. She had even noticed the moment Donnie arrived and pulled her into his arms. The coldness that wrapped around her hadn't frightened her. Oddly enough, it had warmed her. Filled her with a sense of peace she hadn't ever felt. She knew she was where she belonged.

She even remembered the taste of his blood. Not bitter and metallic like her own blood tasted when she had pricked her finger or cut herself a time or two and shoved it in her mouth. No, it had tasted strong and bold, like a classic red wine that aged well. The urge to have another taste hit her.

But at no point in time did she heal herself. It wasn't possible.

"I didn't do anything, Giselle."

"Maybe it was Donnie's blood," Max said with a genuine smile before frowning and grabbing her arm. "Just making sure you feel warm still. He promised not to turn you."

"I would never," Donnie growled low under his breath.

No. No, he hadn't turned her. She was still herself. Alive and breathing. Her heart pumping—a bit faster than normal, but working like it should.

"Oh, he..." Giselle stopped speaking, and they made eye contact.

He what?

Stella felt like she should know what Giselle meant to say. She tried to rewind everything that happened and froze when it hit her.

Had Donnie spoken his true feelings? Told her he loved her? While she didn't say it out loud, she had thought the words for the first time in her head right before she healed Max.

Could it be possible?

That I hear you in my head. I'm afraid it must be possible because I can hear you again.

Stella looked at him, grasping his cheek.

Again?

You called my name. You said you needed me.

She had said more than that, but he'd heard the beginning part. In. His. Head. And he had come running to her side.

"Okay, you two are staring at each other weird, and like you're having a conversation without us," Max commented.

Because they were.

I also told you I love you. You didn't hear that part.

I did not. Donnie slid his hand behind her head, his fingers sliding into her hair. *But I love you too. Perhaps you didn't hear me say it either.*

No, she hadn't.

When?

When you were dying in my arms.

"Okay, you both are freaking me out. Stop it," Max demanded. Giselle giggled.

"I have to kind of agree with Max here. What is going on?" Joe asked, moving away to give them space.

"Fate."

And boy, she hated admitting that.

Donnie chuckled. "I doubt that."

She needed to be away from him when they had this conversation. Because in his arms, she felt comfortable. Safe. And when he heard what she was about to say, he might not feel the same way. When she moved to want to get up, he helped her. When she took a few steps toward her friends, he didn't stop her. But she could see it in his eyes he wanted to. That he was confused she wanted space.

She got a hug from Max and Giselle, needing it with a desperation that clawed at her soul. If she had lost either one of her friends, it wouldn't have been pretty how she would've responded.

Then she looked at Donnie who stood with an unreadable expression. It's as if he sensed she was about to say something he wouldn't like, but he wasn't positive. Hence the neutral expression.

"Giselle did some research a while back about cosmic witches. When I did the protective spell. She was worried how long I'd been out."

"Yeah, well, she needs to do more after what happened here," Max said with a relieved sigh.

"She found that when a cosmic witch finds their soulmate their power is hundred times greater."

Joe chuckled. "So you're saying Donnie is your soulmate and you did heal yourself?"

She shook her head. "I couldn't have healed myself. I absorb wounds from the other person, not heal them without consequences. I've never healed myself before. And the extent of my injuries—impossible."

"But you're saying Donnie is your soulmate?" Joe looked skeptical, if the arched brow and wide eyes were saying anything.

"I don't know if I believe in soulmates. That means fate is involved, and I don't like to think fate controls my life. But I love him." She turned her gaze to Donnie. "I love you. You said it in return. The moment you did, I was healed. And it says that when their love is declared, the power is magnified. So maybe I did heal myself without realizing it."

Donnie moved with caution, and the movement looked odd on him when she was so used to him flying in a blur. He took ahold of her hands. "I don't care what you want to call it. If fate had a hand in it. If my words of love saved you, I'll take it. Because I will not live in a world without you."

I won't leave either until I kill that bastard.

I'm sorry, what? You were planning on leaving?

A look of terror entered his eyes.

Yes, Donnie, my dearest. I can hear your thoughts more clearly now, remember? What more do you need to tell me?

He chuckled, pulling her into his embrace, and kissing her. *I will not forget again. And as for leaving, I told you I'd do anything to keep you safe. At the time, that was the best way to keep you safe. He changed all my plans. Because I will hunt him down for what he did.*

You and I will talk more about this later. I told you once before never to walk away from me. How dare you think you could do it again?

He placed another gentle kiss to her lips. *Forgive me, my love. Never again.*

"Okay," Max clapped his hands. "Enough talking in your heads. It's freaking me out and it's annoying as hell."

You're forgiven. I kind of like being able to have a conversation no else can hear. She felt his cock harden, pressing against her with eagerness.

I like that you can create magic bubbles where no one can hear what's going on inside of it. We should venture to your room and you make a bubble.

She slapped his chest, laughing. *Not right now.*

"Yep," Joe said, emphasizing the 'p' with a pop. "I'm agreeing with Max on this one. Stop it right now, you two."

They answered with laughter.

"SORRY, WE'RE LATE," Max started off. "As you all know, we had an incident tonight."

Donnie's arms wrapped around Stella in an even more fierce grip. Incident didn't begin to describe it. He'd almost lost her, and he still couldn't wrap his mind around everything that had happened.

"It's been confirmed." Max grinned at Holstrom. "No need to dig up any dead bodies. It's Donnie's master. He attacked us tonight. He's the one we've been looking for."

Jock's hand went slowly up in the air.

Donnie grinned at the sight, especially when Holstrom looked like he wanted to whack his brother in the back of his head again.

"I'm new to all this and all the things you all are capable of. But how do we know this? You mentioned you didn't see him."

"I smelled his scent," Donnie replied.

"Right, of course." Jock smiled as if that made sense. "But you tracked the vampire scent from both crime scenes. I would think you would've noticed his scent then."

Jock made a good point.

"It wasn't his scent at the crime scenes."

Holstrom groaned. "You have got to be kidding me."

"Look," Joe jumped in. "We've dealt with this asshole before. This is what he does. He plays games. Just because he wasn't the one who killed those humans, doesn't mean he wasn't involved. He had one of his minions do it. They may or may not still be in the area. They do not matter. We can take them without blinking. But this guy." Joe shook his head. "He's going to take a lot of power to defeat. Max didn't even hear him coming." Joe shared a look with Max. "And I know it's not easy to sneak up on you. Don't blame yourself for anything. This guy is old. The older the vampire, the harder they are to kill."

Donnie wasn't even positive he got his age right. He could be off by a few hundred years. He could be way older than he thought.

But it was time.

Time to confront his past and be free of him once and for all.

They would never be safe—him and Stella—if he didn't.

Jock's hand went up in the air again.

This time Donnie chuckled out loud.

Jock grinned. "So, with all that information, I think we ask the lycans for help."

Silence descended as if they did not agree with that suggestion.

Jock forged on. "I spoke with Benny today." He waved his hands down as if people started berating him for such a stupid move, yet no one had moved or said a word. "He approached me, not the other way around. To be clear. They were on a job, helping a farmer out with some issue. He didn't see anyone, but he smelled the scent of a vampire near the property. That property isn't too far from his. I told him point blank none of us have stepped into their territory. I even told him I haven't traveled through his town."

Donnie's gaze traveled to Charly. She met it, offering a small smile. "Charly saw the future. She told us yesterday what happens. We're working in tandem with the lycans. Maybe that was Benny offering an olive branch. He knows all of our scents. He would've known it wasn't us near that farm."

"Okay," Max said with a jerk of his head. "So we're going to combine forces with the lycans? Is everyone in agreement?"

The low murmurs in the room said yes.

Max crossed his arms. "Who's going to reach out to them?"

"I will." Donnie assumed that would be obvious. Charly saw him with Benny in her vision.

"Me too."

His embrace strengthened around Stella, kissing the side of her head near her temple. "Not a chance."

Yes, and we will not argue about it.

Not happening.

I'm going with you and you can't stop me.

If they find out what you are, we're going to have more than just my sire on our hands.

You're not going alone.

"Wow, you guys weren't kidding about how they can talk to each other in their thoughts," Kade mused with fascination. "It's freaky."

Donnie cleared his throat. "Sorry, Kade. Minor side conversation. Max and I will talk to them."

Stella shoved out of his arms, and he was surprised by how strong the push felt. It had never felt like that before. She'd gotten much, much stronger.

"I can do this out loud too. I'm going, not Max."

Patience. He needed an abundance of patience right now.

"Should I remind you that I witnessed you die in my arms tonight? Because I can't see that again."

The ire in her evaporated. "If I died I wouldn't be here. My heart was still beating. Barely."

"Are you arguing semantics with me right now?"

"It's important to distinguish the differences, so yes."

Max moved closer, throwing an arm around him, then one around Stella. "Huddle time. I can see we are not going to come to an agreement on the matter. So how about we compromise."

"The only compromise will be Stella stays and I go." He would beat that answer into Max if necessary.

"Yes, and her compromise will be she goes and won't stay back. Stalemate on both sides. So my compromise is to invite Benny here."

Donnie thought it over for a second.

"Then she leaves the house."

Stella threw Max's arm off, making him wince. "You are being ridiculous. That was a very nice compromise suggested by Max." Then she shoved him in the chest, making him stumble backwards. "We compromise or I'll do it myself."

She pushed him away. He felt the force of her hand shove against his chest, and he had been powerless to stop it.

"Shit, Stella. When did you get so strong?" Max rubbed his arm, staring at Donnie as if he couldn't believe he'd been pushed by her as well.

Stella shrugged. "The whole, 'she's more powerful once love is declared thing,' I guess. I'm a bit stronger. So what?"

"So it's kind of a big deal," Max said, cocking a brow.

"Only if you want me to kick your ass. Otherwise, it's not."

Joe stepped into the fray. "I'm going to try to be the voice of reason here. But keep in mind, the obstinate man wasn't listening to me earlier, so..." Joe looked at Donnie. "Sometimes, keeping people close to you is safer than having them as far away as possible."

Tell that to his wife. She hadn't been safe being close to him. Only distance from him had kept her alive.

His gaze glided to Stella.

She wasn't his wife. The two women were nothing alike. They were more different than two women could be.

Stella could hold her own. And then some.

If her newfound strength was any indication, she was going to be a force to be reckoned with.

"Fine," Donnie conceded. "Me, Stella, and Max will meet with Benny." Donnie caught Jock's eyes. "And Jock. Benny approached Jock today, so I think it's a safe bet he should come too. I think it's better we go to them. Make them feel better. Show them they have nothing to fear, because I don't think they would feel comfortable coming to us."

"I am fine with that decision," Stella confirmed.

So was everyone else.

They were about to walk into the wolves' den.

21

"Do you think it was his blood that did it?"

Stella tossed a glance at Jock where they sat in the back seat together. Donnie drove with Max in the front passenger seat. They hadn't delayed with their plans. They couldn't afford to. Jock called Benny right away and he agreed to a meeting with the four of them. They were off in the car no more than fifteen minutes later.

"What are you talking about?"

"Your new strength they mentioned. And the whole healing yourself." Jock rubbed his hands on his thighs as his brows pursed in concentration. "I want to understand more about...everything. This whole new world is so fascinating."

"I would love to understand it more too." Stella shrugged. "I don't remember drinking any blood."

Such a lie.

She remembered. Every tasty drop she had. The flavor still lingered on her tongue. Or at least, she salivated thinking about it, envisioning it there.

"It could be a possibility," Max said, jumping into the conversation. "When Donnie gets injured, the wound heals itself. It's why vampires are so damn hard to kill unless you chop off their head or stake 'em in the heart. And you were pretty damn strong at the house. A lot stronger than I've ever felt."

"I didn't give her that much. She lost too much strength to take a whole lot. She could've endured even more before even being threatened with turning."

Max shuddered. "Imagine if she got even more. How much stronger that shove would've felt."

She punched Max in the shoulder, causing him to groan and rub the spot. "Damn! See, that hurt. I'm going to have a massive bruise there now. What was that for?"

"Because I could. You irritate me sometimes."

"So you told me. I'm an idiot," Max mumbled under his breath, then turned to stare out the window.

And had he understood what she meant by that? So much had happened in the last few hours it was hard to tell. The tension the three of them had was gone. Nearly dying would do that. Changed one's perspective.

"We're coming up to the property. Stella, do not reveal yourself." Donnie looked at her through the rearview mirror. "Promise me. Giselle's not here this time for them to think it's her."

"As long as there is no cause for me to do so, I won't. That's the most I can promise. I won't stand by while my friends, while *you*, are being threatened."

He should know that's the most she could commit to. When he didn't respond, she figured he had agreed with her.

Donnie parked in front of a large, white two-story house. Four men stood on the porch with two standing at the bottom of the stairs. One of them was Benny. She recognized the other one as the main guy at Mason's who wanted to kill her friends.

They all got out of the vehicle. Donnie stood on her left side while Max took position on her right. She knew that was to form a barrier around her to keep her safe. They couldn't help themselves. Jock either didn't notice the tension filling the air or didn't care. He walked right up to Benny with a jovial expression on his face.

"Nice place, Benny. I bet it looks gorgeous in the daylight. All this land and space."

Benny returned a smile while shaking Jock's hand. "It's nice and quiet. Peaceful. The way I like it."

Jock stepped back and gestured at them. "Let me introduce my friends. That's Donnie, Stella, and Max. They are the good guys you want on your side. Not the enemy."

Benny didn't look like he believed that quite yet. Then he pointed at the man by him. "This is Kurt. My right-hand man and best friend. He's also not an enemy you want to have."

Jock tossed his head back and forth. "Not quite how I said it. But we'll move on to another topic—the reason I asked if we could all meet. So we have two vampire issues at hand. One is the vampire who killed three citizens in *my* town."

Stella found it comical how Jock had to point that out. He was right, of course. The murders happened in the town where Jock lived. As did her and her friends. Even Donnie on the outskirts of town. While Benny lived in the next town over. He and his friends had taken it upon themselves to cross over into another territory, messing in a case that wasn't their problem.

"The second vampire issue is Donnie's master." Jock waved two fingers with his thumbs up in the air toward

Donnie in a teasing manner. "Not his master anymore. But the dude who, you know, turned him. Not by choice, I will add. That's important to note."

Stella didn't think these lycans cared one bit about any of that information. But she was fine letting Jock handle this. He was doing great so far, in her opinion. There wasn't bloodshed going on.

"So what we're figuring is—" Jock waved his hands in a frenzied manner. "I got ahead of myself. Let me rewind. Donnie doesn't like this dude. Who would when you have no say in what you can and cannot do. No, thank you. So he left. And this guy follows. Imagine your worst nightmare of a stalker, and like, multiply it by a thousand. That's this guy. Okay. You following me? So wherever Donnie goes, this guy eventually shows up. Talk about having to live with one eye over your shoulder. No one wants to live like that. Not even a vampire. Or a lycan. Nobody. Donnie wants to live in peace, be left alone. This guy isn't having it.

"So what we're figuring...back to what I originally wanted to say...is he finds Donnie again. Because that's what psycho stalkers do. Instead of..." Jock gestured at Donnie. "He didn't go into specifics of what his master normally does, but we'll say it's not pretty. So instead of doing what he normally does, he has another vampire kill a few humans. Toy with Donnie a bit. I don't know. Who knows what's going on in this dude's head. Okay. Still with me?" Jock met each lycan's eyes before continuing. "So, while this low-level vamp is killing people, the crazy dude is watching Donnie. He's seeing how much Donnie hates some humans got killed. He's seeing that he's made friends. That he's established himself in a town. Making a new home. Living his best life. That pisses him off. As it would any psycho stalker. That shit drives them insane. What does any crazy stalker do when they see something they don't like? They do something even more terrible. He attacked my friend Max here."

Jock moved closer to Max and clamped a hand on his shoulder, then pulled him in a hug. It took all of Stella's strength not to laugh. Jock was a hoot. He had such a masterful way of telling a story. She couldn't wait to see how it ended.

Jock let go of Max, blew out a breath, then went back to his spot. "Thank goodness for friends and a smart witch. Because she saved his life. As you can clearly see." Jock wove a hand up and down Max's frame to show he was uninjured.

Jock had the good sense not to share it was her who saved him. They would've been in a world of shit then. She would've had to reveal herself, and that would not make Donnie happy.

"But the gauntlet was thrown. War was initiated because Donnie recognized his scent. Then I got talking about how you dropped by the station telling me about the vampire in your territory, and well, here we are. Because why did a vampire stroll near your property? Don't you want to know that? Donnie can take a quick sniff and tell you which vampire it was. Human killer or psycho stalker. But the bottom line is, this crazy dude has roped you all into this nightmare. And nobody wants a crazy psycho stalker pulling them into anything. I hear he's pretty damn old, which makes him harder to kill, and that means all hands on deck to take the asshole down."

Jock clapped his hands merrily. "So what do you say?"

DONNIE REALIZED as Jock took control of the situation that he didn't even need to be here. Jock was handling it all and with a finesse he'd never seen before. He had everyone's attention. All eyes on him, listening intently to everything he said, even as he made half of it sound ridiculous. But no less the truth.

"Has anyone ever told you that you talk too much?" Benny replied.

Jock's lips turned up into a cocky grin. "All the time, man. It's my best trait I possess. What part didn't you understand?"

Benny chuckled. "Oh, I didn't misunderstand any of it. It's too fanatical to be a lie. You always tell a story with a flare, but you're never wrong in how you tell it."

"Good. So we'll work together to take this asshole down?"

Benny glanced at the three of them, staring at Stella a bit longer than he liked. "Why didn't the witch come with?"

Jock shrugged. "Her best friends almost died. She's still reeling from it all."

"Best friends?" Bennie zoned in on the mistake right away.

Damn it, Jock.

Cool it. He doesn't know anything yet.

Don't reveal yourself no matter what, Stella. Because I swear...

Your threats don't scare me. So stop worrying. It'll be fine.

Jock stole a glance at Max, then moved closer to Benny. "His hearing is impeccable, like yours, so it's like impossible to tell you this without him hearing. But...you know. She..." Jock raised his brows as he mouthed 'likes him.'

Benny burst out laughing. "Oh, your secret—her secret —is safe with me. I get it. She's distraught and all that."

Donnie was damn glad he didn't possess a beating heart because he knew it would've been running like a hamster on a wheel. Damn it, Stella was cool as cucumber. Not one change in her beat. How had Jock managed to distract Benny so easily? He had charm that was impressive. And did he know Giselle liked Max, or had that been something he made up on a whim?

I'm amazed with your strength to remain calm.

Many years of practice. Watching Jock navigate this is a true masterpiece.

Agreed.

Jock turned back toward them with his eyes wide, flashing an apology. Max looked confused by everything.

Benny shifted his attention to him. "Didn't have a choice, uh?"

"Have you ever stopped to ask a vampire before you kill them if they had a choice? Or do you assume we all want this life?"

Benny's eyes squinted as if pondering the questions. "Well, whether we like it or not, this crazy, psycho stalker"— Benny smiled goofily at Jock—"has brought us into the fight. How dangerous is he?" Benny gestured at Max. "He couldn't have been too badly injured if your witch friend healed him."

Oh, he had no idea how bad it had been. Or how truly powerful his *witch friend* was.

"She got lucky healing him. It was pretty bad. Have you ever come across a vampire over a thousand years old?"

Benny staggered back and shared a look with Kurt. "You've tried to kill him before, haven't you?"

"Tried and failed. Why do you think I keeping running from him? I like living, even if it is in the darkness."

His friend, Kurt, decided to speak. Surprising he'd been so quiet this whole time, since he had much to say last time they saw him. "We came across the low-level vamp Jock mentioned two days ago. Took care of him already. No need to sniff anything out to confirm it's your master. I imagine it is. If you go behind the house, you'll smell him there though. We detected the scent today. That's how close he got to us. We pissed him off, hurting one of his minions."

Donnie nodded. "Yeah, you sure did. And I'm sorry we didn't find the low-level vampire first. I wouldn't wish my master on anyone."

"You would've." Benny crossed his arms as a wily smirk emerged. "If you would've had the balls to step in our town, you would've found him. You had an excellent routine searching each town. But you looked in the wrong one. He hid well, I'll give the vamp that. It took us far longer than I liked to get him." He laughed. "We kept an eye on you. I was surprised when you didn't venture into our territory."

"And cause you to have another tantrum? No, thanks."

Donnie grabbed Stella's hand, squeezing hard. *Are you trying to piss them off?*

He's an asshole and you know it.

Benny's eyes zoomed in on them holding hands, though didn't comment on it. "Touche. Now what do we do? If you've tried to kill him before and it's never worked, how is it going to work this time?"

He wouldn't let it fail this time.

"I was on my own a few times I tried. Or with my other three vampire friends. But now I have a lycan pack, a few witches, *and* my vampire friends. He's not impossible to kill, but he will be a challenge."

"How did he attack you?" Benny asked, tossing his head toward Max.

"Out of nowhere. I didn't hear or see him coming. I was down on the ground, bleeding before I even knew what hit me."

"Surprise attack," Kurt commented. "Which means he wanted to send a message, not get into a full-on fight. Because if the witch had heard, she would've jumped in."

Benny gazed at Kurt. "We have to treat this like a hunt." Then he looked at the four of them. "We get aggressive elk sometimes on our land. Thinks it's their territory instead of ours. Even a few wolves who think they're alpha here. Coyotes too. When they get to be too much of a nuisance, we get rid of them. We don't kill them, but we wrangle them up and move them elsewhere."

"Okay." Donnie wanted to hear more. "What's your suggestion?"

"We corner these animals. We surround them, so they have nowhere to go but where we want them to, which is a cage. My pack can help corner him, surround him. We'll set the trap. Your people can lure him here." Benny jerked his head at Jock. "You need to stay as far away as possible. I appreciate you being the middleman here, but this is way over your head."

Jock held up his hands in surrender. "Wasn't planning on being here when it all goes down."

"I can work with this plan," Donnie agreed. "Send me the exact location you want, and I'll make it happen."

Benny eyed their linked hands again. Damn it. Donnie hadn't meant to keep ahold of her hand, but he was used to touching her in any small way when he was near her.

"Your lady friend, Stella, was it?" Benny said with a mischievous grin. "Should also stay away with Jock. Humans will be of no help in this fight."

For once, I agree with him on something.

I will be here.

And you'll reveal yourself to a pack of lycans.

I can't stay away while you do all the fighting. Not happening.

Max cleared his throat. "Right. That is a good point. Yeah, Stella should stay away too. So we'll be in touch. Thanks for meeting with us."

They bid their goodbyes and got back in the car. Nobody said a word until they knew they were out of hearing distance.

Max glared at him and Stella, darting his gaze at one then the other, back and forth. "You two cannot get into your own conversation in your heads when we're in such a serious meeting."

"Sorry."

Donnie snorted. She did *not* sound sorry.

"I know what Donnie told you. He doesn't want you there. And it's not a good idea. Those lycans think you're human. It needs to stay that way."

Stella leaned forward, inches from Max's face. "My strength has increased. I can heal myself. Imagine how powerful my magic is now. I could probably take this asshole down on my own."

"Absolutely not!" Donnie gripped the steering wheel, damn near driving off the road.

"But I won't," Stella continued in a strained breath. "But you would be foolish to hold me back from this fight. I could be what makes or breaks it. I can't be afraid anymore, Max. I hate looking with one eye over my shoulder as Jock described it. I shouldn't have to live like that."

"Charly saw me and Benny in the vision," Donnie voiced in a quiet tone. Any louder and he'd be screaming at her that she'd lost her damn mind.

"Yet, the entire pack will be in the woods. Our friends will be there. It doesn't mean it's just you two."

Don't fight me on this, Donnie. We'll be stronger together. You know it.

It might be true, but it doesn't mean I like it.

I love you. Let me stand by your side. Let's show the world how powerful a force you and I can be together.

Donnie looked at her through the rearview mirror. His guarded expression was the only thing he could answer with. Because he didn't want her to see that he might agree with her on the last point. They would be stronger together.

Unstoppable.

22

EVERYONE WAS IN ATTENDANCE. Even Scatter and Bozo. After they left the lycan residence last night, they all went home. To rest. To revive their energy. Once morning hit, they reconvened at Donnie's, going over the plan. The sun had set thirty minutes ago, and they were doing one more run-through to make sure everyone understood their role in it.

Stella blew out a breath, trying to display the most encouraging smile she could. But she knew it fell flat. Everyone was worried about the plan. About what could happen.

"It's going to be fine."

"I got faith in ya," Jock said, matching her smile.

At least she had one person who believed in her.

Not that she thought the others didn't trust her to get it done. They simply didn't want her going out there to begin with. No doubt her abilities would be revealed to the lycans and then they'd have another shitstorm to deal with. But she was done running. No more. She would live her life the way she wanted from now on. Someone wanted to pick a fight? Let them.

Max cleared his throat. "Okay, so Mason, Kade, Bailey, Holstrom, Charly, and Jock are staying here. None of you leave this house until you get a phone call from one of us. You're in as much danger as anyone in this room. If the plan fails and he doubles back here, you can't be in the crosshairs."

He waited for them all to agree that they understood. Because Donnie's master wouldn't be able to get to them inside this house without an invitation. Then he sighed, pointing at Mason. "What? I can see your irritation at the plan."

Mason crossed his arms. "I know I'm a human and have no abilities, but I'm always by Mona's side when something like this is going on. I don't like *not* being by her side."

Mona slid her hand into his. "He's right. I'm not feeling comfortable with it either."

"You're not strong enough for this," Max said. He wasn't mincing his words, and Stella didn't fault him for it, but she could tell Mason didn't appreciate it. "You could distract us."

"Let him go with," Donnie chimed in.

Max threw his hands up in the air, rolling his eyes.

"I agree with Donnie," Bailey said in a soft tone.

All eyes turned to her.

"When I...was on my way to heaven—I don't know what to call it." Bailey giggled, though the nerves could be heard. "Mona's mom saved me. She turned me back into a human. Gave me a second chance. She also told me to tell Mona that her and Mason are stronger together. They are meant to be fighting together, not apart. So I think Mason should be there too."

Donnie had his arms around Stella, her back to his chest, like they always stood together when they had meetings. His embrace tightened around her, his lips hitting her temple before he continued. "Bailey makes a great point. I hate our current plan. Stella out in those woods by herself. Acting like a defensive human to lure him to the spot. I more than hate it. I despise it. I don't care if she can defend herself."

She squeezed his forearms, trying to offer comfort.

"Mason and Mona are much stronger together. They never part in a fight. Mason might not be strong enough against my sire, but he has been working on defending himself. He can hold his own. What I'm suggesting is he and Mona join Stella."

"But that's a witch in the mix and he might not fall for it," Max said with the irritation laced in his tone that the plan was changing.

"Mason also isn't without powers," Donnie forged on as if Max never spoke. "His eyes glow a bright blue when danger is near. Hell, they glowed the first time he met Stella, and she was cloaking her abilities. But not even that power of hers could hide from Mason. He still knew there was a creature near him that he'd never met. They will have warning before he attacks. Because make no mistake, he will attack. I hate saying I don't have faith in this plan no matter how we form it, but I don't have the faith."

"And let me guess, Scatter and Bozo will tag along as well. One big happy group," Max chided.

Meow.

Max glared at the cat. Then waved his hand for Mona or Mason to translate.

"Where Mona goes, they go," Mason said. "I don't mind this new plan. It makes more sense for someone to be with Stella. On her own makes it obvious we're trying to set a trap. But if she's with a witch, it means we're trying to protect her—and me—while we search in the woods for him. Because that's what the goal is. We want him to think we're searching for him. That's why we're in the woods in the first place. Stella alone isn't the right move. Even the lycans would think it odd, I bet."

Giselle closed her laptop and stood up, brushing her hand down Max's arm as if to get his attention. "Mason's right. Those three should be together. Donnie's master doesn't know how powerful of a witch she is. It will look way more normal than Stella alone. You, me, and Joe will form another group. George and Peter will be together, and that leaves Donnie with Benny."

"Just like my vision," Charly added.

"Then it's settled," Stella said, ready to get this show on the road. "Jock, text Benny we're on our way. To set it all up. Let's do this."

Everyone dispersed, yet Donnie held her back before she could get into the car with Mona and Mason.

"Hold back using your powers as long as you can."

She brushed his cheek, kissing him. "We'll be apart, but it doesn't mean we won't be together." She tapped the side of his head. "I'll be right here with you at all times. If I need you, I'll say it."

He closed his eyes. "I love you. I'm not ready to lose you."

She wasn't either. But that did pose a problem with their relationship. She was mortal, while he wasn't.

"I love you too."

She had to pry his hands away, and he chuckled. "I still can't believe how much stronger you are."

He reluctantly let go, getting into his own vehicle so he could meet Benny at the designated spot. They would all enter the forest from different points.

Stella got into the back seat, scooting next to Bozo and

Scatter. "Gentlemen." A soft meow and low bark filled the small space. She didn't need anyone to interpret they had returned a greeting.

Mason followed the cars out of the driveway.

The battle was about to start.

Stella leaned forward, touching Mona's shoulder. "You up for this? Do you have the potions I told you to make?"

Mona twisted a piece of licorice in between her teeth as she munched on it like a rabbit chewing on a carrot. "I do. I memorized all the spells. I wish I could just do something without all that like you can. That protective spell was amazing. You didn't make a sound or flick your wrists. The shield just appeared."

The wonders of being a cosmic witch. It had its perks. But it also had its downfalls. Not that she'd go into all the pits of it right now.

"You got this. I hear you can make fireballs." Stella turned her hand in a circle, creating a tiny one.

Mona giggled, twisting her hand as well, making her own. "It is pretty neat. I've been practicing a lot with it."

Stella made hers disappear, then moved her other hand with a bit of flare. A tiny blue blame appeared.

Mona's eyes widened in surprise and a bit of awe. "What's that?"

"I guess you could call it ice." Stella made the fireball reappear in her opposite hand. "Fire and ice. When combined, it makes for a wonderful spectacle. Keep practicing." She flicked her wrists down to make them vanish, then touched Mona's shoulder. "Because if you can create a fireball, which shows such great power, you can make ice. Trust me on this."

Meow.

Mona jerked a tight nod at Scatter that she heard him.

But Stella could tell she still hadn't forgiven the animals for lying to her about who they really were.

"Scatter said my mom could make both. First time he's ever mentioned that."

"Hey, when this is all over, ask Giselle to do some research. She's amazing at finding out information. I know your mom didn't tell you much."

"She told me nothing."

Donnie had mentioned a few things about Mona, so Stella knew that, but she had been trying to be kind. Obviously, she had failed.

"Giselle could help you fill in the missing pieces. I'm sure of it."

"I'd like that." Mona inhaled and let out the breath with a huge blow. "And maybe some help with my aunt. I can't ignore her anymore."

"You got it."

From there, silence filled the car. They all focused on getting themselves into fight mode.

Mason parked the car and they all filed out.

"Okay, let's start searching and find this asshole. Take him down," Mason said, waving a hand for them to follow. Scatter and Bozo took the lead.

They talked as they walked, saying things they normally wouldn't say. But they wanted the vampire to hear. They wanted him to follow. Not attack, but follow.

But if he did, she'd be ready.

"My scouts tell me that your human friend came with." Benny shook his head in clear disgust. "Two human friends."

Donnie wasn't surprised by the fact Benny had eyes and ears everywhere. It was prudent of him to do so with so many unknown creatures in his territory.

"If Mason's wife—a witch—goes somewhere, he goes too. They do not part, especially in a fight. And trying to tell Stella what to do is impossible."

Benny laughed. "A stubborn one, uh?"

Donnie didn't think that required a response.

That didn't seem to deter Benny. "It amazes me that humans sleep with vampires."

Donnie had Benny by the top of his shirt, pressed against a tree without missing a beat. The lycan grinned like the devil.

"So she does mean a lot to you? I thought so. What boggles my mind is why you let her go alone without you by her side."

He let go of him, backing away. "Mona knows what she's doing."

Sort of.

Even if she didn't, Stella could hold her own.

They continued on. In silence this time.

For a while, at least.

"I know I haven't apologized, but I will now. I'm sorry for attacking your friend Kade. I'm glad he survived."

Without Stella, he wouldn't have.

But the lycan was offering him an olive branch. He'd be dumb not to accept it.

"Thank you. We're all glad he's okay as well. What Mason and them do is important in this world. They're helping creatures that can't help themselves."

"It's admirable. I'm happy to see it. I didn't believe it at first, but after digging more into them, I agree. It's a good thing."

Mason's eyes are glowing. He's near.

Donnie stopped walking. *Where are you? How far have you gotten into the forest?*

Halfway in our section. His eyes are getting brighter and brighter as the seconds go by.

"What's wrong?" Benny looked alert and ready to shift into wolf-form.

"He's close by Stella, Mona, and Mason."

Benny frowned. "How the hell do you know that?"

Donnie didn't have time to explain the love he and Stella had with one another. "Trust me on this. Alert your pack. It's time to coral this animal."

I'm coming, my love.

Hurry, Donnie!

He didn't need any more confirmation than that. He left Benny's side in a blur. The man could choose to follow or not. He'd decided to follow. In wolf form.

A large black wolf kept pace with the speed he traveled at. He knew lycans could communicate with their minds like he could with Stella. But only in wolf form. They had to be able to because Benny had followed without delay. He had no time to make a phone call. Yet he knew he had told his pack to do their role in the matter.

He knew he was getting closer to Stella's location when her scent drifted to his nose. So did his master's.

He abruptly stopped when he found his friends. Benny stopped right next to him, his mouth in a snarl, revealing his large teeth.

Stella leaned against a tree, holding her hand to her side. Blood seeped through her fingers. The scent of her blood ignited his senses. He wanted to lap it up until it stopped bleeding and his thirst was sated. Mason was on the opposite side, also leaning against a tree, but holding a hand to a wound on his shoulder. Mona stood in the middle, chanting, her hands ablaze with fire. Scatter and Bozo stood right in front of her feet as if they could deter an attack on her.

And his master, the man he would kill before the night ended, was right in front of Mona. His eyes a bright red. His fangs bared for all to see. No part of his impeccable outfit—from the long black trench coat to the black shirt and black pants—looked mussed up. His black hair was smoothed back in the way he always wore it, not a strand out of place. His skin flawless. He looked as Donnie remembered him. A man to be reckoned with. A man who always got his way.

Odd. He'd never noticed he wore black like his master. Good thing he had to replenish his wardrobe. He'd buy more color from now on.

"You've come. What took you so long? I am getting bored of listening to this witch." He lifted his hand, playing with the long nails that graced his fingers. His claws that grew when he went into vampire mode. His master loved slicing up a person before taking a long, powerful bite from their neck. Max was proof of that.

"I don't think she knows what she's doing." He paused in fiddling with his nails to look at him. "She keeps chanting and nothing's happening." He cackled. "What are you doing with these idiots, Donnie? Come back to me. Where you belong. You will always belong with me. Nobody else."

Donnie saw eyes appear from behind his master. Then another. And another.

The lycans had arrived, forming a circle around him.

His master delivered another evil cackle. "Oh, you think these beasts will best me? Have you learned nothing, Donnie? I will kill all your little friends, and you'll be left with no one but me."

"You're wrong. This time I will do what I haven't managed to do yet. Kill you." Donnie's own nails grew a little, something he rarely forced out. "You should've never attacked my friends."

"You needed to learn a lesson. You failed the first one. So I shall do it again."

His master moved in a blur, knocking Mona down before she could even throw one flame. She cried out, clutching her stomach where he'd slashed her.

Benny jumped in, as did him and the rest of the wolves. He didn't see Giselle, Joe, or Max, but George and Peter were also in the mix.

His master was strong. Way too powerful.

One by one, the wolves were knocked back, cuts marring their bodies. He even took a few marks himself. One on his cheek, another on his chest. Though he felt the wounds closing up as soon as they appeared. The wolves weren't as lucky. Blood filled the air. From everywhere. All around him. The different scents of blood were overwhelming.

As quickly as the melee started, it stopped. His master was near the outskirts of the circle with everyone else scattered around, but still within the bounds of the circle. Barely.

"This is sad none of you can even make one little mark on me." He looked up and down his body, then froze, fingering a tiny tear on the sleeve of his coat. He lifted it up and sniffed. "The wolf who made this mark will die first. The only woman I sense in the pack."

Benny growled next to him, his paws digging into the ground, his haunches arched and ready to propel him into action.

"You're surrounded. You can't escape. You can keep

making nicks here and there, but we will get you." Donnie threw his arms wide. "You can't win against all of us."

"I can turn around and walk away and we can pick this up another day." His master did turn and got no more than two feet before stumbling backward as he hit a forcefield.

"That stupid chanting that annoyed you? She was making a barrier, a cage, so you couldn't escape. There is nowhere for you to go. You'll be dead soon, and I never have to see your face again."

Not even in his nightmares.

His master twirled around with flare, his trench coat swinging with the motion. Then his eyes zeroed in on Stella.

"Perhaps I won't kill the lone woman wolf first. I'll take what you covet most." Then he was gone from his spot.

23

Stella wasn't afraid. Of anything going on in this circle.

She'd stayed back while everyone jumped into the fight. For Donnie. He'd asked her not to reveal her powers for as long as she could, and she wanted to try for him. Why jump in when they were making contact with him. Or at least she thought so. When the fighting paused, she'd been shocked to see him untouched, except for that one little tear in his coat.

He'd come out of nowhere, despite Mason's eyes warning them on his approach. She'd been shocked when his nails tore through her skin, stunned so much by the attack she hadn't returned the favor. He'd hit Mason in quick unison, and Mona started chanting. Then Donnie and Benny had appeared, and Stella didn't get a chance to retaliate.

But now he was gunning for her.

She braced herself to use her powers when Donnie moved like lightening, shielding her. They fought in a brutal battle. Fists flying through the air, though in blur as they moved so fast. Nails clawing each other.

It's as if the first battle with everyone had been on the lowest level, and now it'd been knocked up to the highest level it could go.

No one else ventured into the fray, letting Donnie have a go at it. She watched in fascination as they both held their own.

How could Donnie have lost in a fight with him before? It didn't seem possible with the way he was fighting now.

Then it happened. So swiftly, it stunned her. The tides turned without notice. His master threw Donnie clear through the air, pouncing on him, slicing him up and down his body, his nails going for his throat. They were long and sharp. So very long and sharp she knew one slice could take his head off. That's how powerful she sensed he was. That he'd done that very thing before to another unsuspecting vampire.

In that split second, one question popped in her head. Why kill Donnie now?

Perhaps he was done fighting him. A lost cause he got sick of dealing with.

One second for her to process all of that.

One second for her to jump into action herself.

Before his nails could even graze his throat, he was flung backward and suspended in the air.

His eyes rounded in fear, his body attempting to move but unable to do so.

She walked forward with slow steps, her hands raised, her heartbeat steady. She knew everyone's focus was on her. In fear? In awe? She had no clue, but she knew she was the center of attention.

"No," the doomed vampire whispered. "It can't be."

"Oh, but it is." She kept moving forward, holding him in

place. "Have you come across a cosmic witch in your lifetime?"

"Never," he hissed. "But I heard of you."

"I bet you're wishing you never did now. I bet you're wishing you would've walked away. That you would've left Donnie alone."

"It's not possible."

She cackled, imitating his vicious laughter. "And yet, you're at my mercy. I can do anything to you right now and there's nothing you can do to stop me."

Fear, for the first time—probably in his life—entered his eyes.

"I was going to let Donnie handle this without stepping in. But I would never stand back and let you kill him. He's mine. I'm his. And together we're—"

"Unstoppable," Donnie whispered as he drew near her. The wounds were healing, but not as fast as before because there were so many.

She lowered her hands a fraction, which made his master draw closer to the ground, yet still locked in her trap. "The honor is yours to be rid of him once and for all."

Donnie cupped her cheek, bringing her mouth closer, and kissing her. "Thank you, my love."

Then he grabbed a large stick from the ground and zoomed forward, piercing his master through the heart. He shattered into dust. Nothing but ash in the air.

Donnie glanced around the circle, eyeing each wolf. Mona stood with Mason on the sidelines, quiet, yet ready for more action. George and Peter were ready for anything. Even Max, Giselle, and Joe had arrived, though Stella wasn't sure when. They had been the last to the event. Everyone, all of her friends—new and old—were prepared to protect her.

"I'm sure you have all heard of cosmic witches," Donnie stated, his voice getting stronger as his body healed even more. "Stella is not a threat. She is a good witch. She may be more powerful than anyone can imagine, but she does not wield it unless necessary."

Benny transformed from wolf to human and didn't seem fazed one bit he was butt-ass naked. "She can shield she's a witch." He crossed his arms. "Though I sensed something was off about her. You grabbing her hand told me something was off. Her even joining our meeting was strange."

Donnie's eyes still glowed red, his fangs at the ready. "Are we going to have a problem, Benny? Because I had enjoyed our truce. The friendly conversation we had in the woods. The feeling we could be friends."

Benny eyed her, his gaze traveling up and down her body. "She was injured when we first got here and now that injury is gone."

Donnie waved his hands up and down his body. "So are mine. Does that make me a sudden threat as well?"

Then Benny's gaze looked around the circle, landing on each of the members of his pack, staring longer than any other on the female wolf. They were all still in wolf form, no doubt ready to defend their leader. "I suspect there would have been many deaths today in trying to defeat him. Yours would've been the first, Donnie." His attention shifted to Stella. "If not for you. Jock told me you all are not the enemy. Out of everyone in your group, I trust him the most. The man doesn't have a dishonest bone in his body. We're not your enemy either. As for friends? Don't push it."

Then Benny jerked his head away, directing his pack to vacate the area. The wolves were gone in a matter of seconds, albeit some of them slower than normal.

Donnie crushed her in his arms.

You scared me to death.

How? You were the one on the verge of death.

Exposing yourself. It will always scare me.

A throat cleared. She and Donnie turned toward the sound to see Max with his arms crossed, shaking his head. He was still dressed, which meant he hadn't transformed into wolf form. "Share with the group, would ya?"

Stella chuckled. "Nothing for the group's ears. Good job, everyone." Then she left Donnie's embrace to look at Mona and Mason's injuries. "Let me help with that."

She sensed Donnie's disapproval behind her, but she healed them anyway. Absorbing the injuries wasn't a risk anymore. Because as soon as they hit her skin, it healed. No scar left behind. She hadn't known if that would happen, but now knowing that, she went to Max and Giselle, checking out their injuries. They were untouched.

"Yeah, don't ask," Max groaned. "I blame it on Joe."

"Me? You were the one with the map for our area. You're the one who got us lost."

"I did not."

"I am so not taking the blame."

Giselle looped her arm through hers, taking them away from the men squabbling over the mishap. "Men. One wanted to go this way. The other that way. How they managed to search the towns on their own, I will never understand. They never asked for help. I could've looked at the map and saw we were going the wrong way. But you know how they are."

Stella laughed, squeezing her arm. "I'm glad you're okay."

"Same, girl. It's over now. We closed our case."

They did.

Which meant they'd move on.

For the first time, she wasn't sure she wanted to.

———

THINGS WENT BACK to normal as soon as they left the forest. George went with Peter to Mona and Mason's house. Giselle and Max went home without her, knowing she'd stay with Donnie. Last night she had gone home with them, but only because she knew if she had stayed they wouldn't have gotten any sleep. The time apart had been brutal on both of them, but necessary. They had won. So no more nights apart.

Joe also went home with them. Of course, both him and Donnie drank some blood first. She had never watched them do so, but she needed a drink of her own. She was shocked when she entered the kitchen to see them drinking from a glass.

"It's more refined." Joe lifted his glass in salute. "Don't you think?"

"It's the strangest thing I've ever seen." She retrieved her own glass. "But I like it."

Donnie pulled out a bottle of wine for her, uncorking it and pouring her a glass. They all enjoyed their drinks in silence. He'd given her a bottle of white wine. Her body was craving red.

And not from a bottle.

"I'm off to bed. Don't be too loud, kids." Then Joe was gone from the kitchen.

Donnie grinned from behind his glass. "We will need a magic bubble tonight."

Oh, definitely. The things she wanted to do to this man. She needed him more than she could express. To know he was alive—or at least, still with her, since technically he was dead.

When she polished off her glass, and he had three of his own, he whisked her into his arms and up to his bedroom. She created a bubble, cocooning them in their own space.

As soon as lights lit up the room, she laughed, scanning the disaster. "What is all this?"

Donnie winced. "Joe's way of convincing me not to leave."

"About that? Maybe it's time we talk about what you tried to do."

"It will never happen again."

Oh, no. He wasn't getting off that easy. "Because your master is dead and I'm in no danger? What makes you think another situation like that won't appear? Are you going to run every single time for my own good?"

I will always be with you no matter how far you try to run.

He stared at her intently, letting her words sink in. *I wouldn't have it any other way, my love. Forgive me for my faults. It will never happen again.*

"Make sure it doesn't."

Then their dirty clothes from the fight joined the rest scattered around the room. They should take a shower, but Donnie had her in his arms and in the middle of the bed before she could blink.

"I sort of love it when you do that."

"Move you at will. Make you do what I want."

"You're going a bit far at making me do something I don't want to do." She pushed against his chest, forcing him to move. "I am stronger now."

"Yes, you are." His intense stare strengthened. "I love you."

"I love you too. Now show me that love."

He needed no further demands. He guided his cock to where it fit perfectly and thrust inside. Closing his eyes, he moved leisurely. It gave her time to peruse him without him noticing. Her eyes trained on the vein in his neck, watching as it pumped in tune with his slow thrusts. Odd how his vein moved, displaying that blood pumped through his veins, yet his heart didn't beat.

Her fingers brushed against the spot.

His eyes darted open, dilating in pleasure.

"I have this ache inside me."

He paused his movements.

"My lips are dying for another taste. I don't understand why I feel this way. But ever since that first taste of your blood, I want more." She gripped his forearms, her nails digging in. It had never hurt him before. But the wince on his face said it hurt this time. "I need it again."

"That is the pain I live with daily. Every hour. Every minute. Every second. I've always lusted for blood. But never as much as I've ached for yours." He opened his neck for her to touch. One nail grew long before he cut himself. "Drink, my love. Sate your thirst. I will stop you before it could do irreparable damage."

Meaning, he would never let her turn into a vampire like him.

Her mouth moved toward the liquid, trickling down his neck. She lapped up the trail, moaning in ecstasy when he thrusted deep inside her. Then she clamped down on the spot, sucking on the dark liquid, moaning some more as it slid down her throat. The bold flavor filled her senses, making her suck even harder. As she feasted on his neck, Donnie pumped passionately, bringing the desire she felt to an even more intense plea-sure. It's as if drinking his blood electrified all her senses, bringing everything into a clearer picture. The world was brighter. The air in the room thicker. The desire between them stronger.

She stopped before he could warn her to, sensing she'd had enough.

"Harder, Donnie. I need you deeper."

He growled in satisfaction, doing as she bid. His thrusts were swallowing her whole, bringing her to a place she never wanted to leave.

Did he feel the same?

She turned her head, brushing her hair away. "Your turn."

HE FROZE IN PLACE, his cock embedded deep inside her.

Had she lost her mind?

It was one thing to allow her to drink his blood. He could stop her at any time, knowing when too much was past the point of no return.

But him?

He would lose himself in bloodlust, drinking until he had every last drop. That's how much he ached for her taste.

She placed her hand on the back of his head, pushing him downward. He couldn't even fight her. Her strength had improved to something he struggled to match. His lips kissed her neck, right where her vein was, but his mouth didn't open.

"It's okay. If you're worried you'll hurt me or won't be able to stop, you're being foolish. I won't have this conversation with you. Drink. Sate your thirst as I sated mine."

He couldn't resist her any longer.

His fangs elongated and sank into her delicate skin. The

blood seeped out of her and into his throat, sliding down as delicious as he knew it would be.

Her hips arched up, telling him to get back to what they were doing. He didn't think he'd be able to focus on two things at once, but he found himself thrusting again. Moving in tune to her body that guided them.

The taste of her blood was everything he'd imagined and more. Sweet and rosy and intoxicating. He could get drunk off her.

She still held his head in place, telling him she wasn't afraid he'd lose control. Yet, he felt on the edges of it. The barrier there, ready to be pushed aside.

Then, it was as if a light switch in his mind told him enough! Stop drinking! You can have more later!

He lifted his head and her hands fell back to his ass, holding on as he rocked in and out of her.

A trickle of blood fell down her neck and he licked it gone. His fangs were still displayed, but she didn't look fearful. No, the bliss in her eyes sent him into a deeper frenzy.

Their bodies connected as one, moving in tune to a sound only they heard.

He knew she was close by the way she murmured low for him to go deeper, faster. She always wanted more from him that way. He always gave her what she wanted. He would always give her what she wanted.

Then it hit her. She screamed his name as the pleasure spread across her face. He followed shortly after, loving the feeling that washed over him. Not that any other time wasn't amazing with her. But for the first time, he felt truly content. Nothing was hounding his senses. Not the need for blood. Not the need for something more. Something just out of his reach.

He cradled her in his arms as he turned them to their sides, brushing her back with light, smooth strokes.

"I've never felt more content. I want to feel like this for the rest of my life."

And he sensed he could have that. With her.

She cupped his cheek, smoothing up and through his hair. "Your life is forever."

Yes, he was immortal. He could never decide if that had been a blessing or a curse. Right now, he considered it a blessing. Because forever would never be enough with her.

"You're stronger. You can heal yourself." His fingers tickled the sides of her face. "The crinkles around your eyes are gone. Your skin is as smooth and flawless as mine. Even the scar you received after healing Kade has disappeared."

She pressed a hand to his chest, narrowing her eyes. "Excuse me, mister. Are you suggesting I had wrinkles on my face? I am *not* that old!"

Oh, she was adorable when she got upset.

"One or two, maybe. Small little wrinkles near your eyes. Now, gone."

She slapped him, causing him to laugh, yet wince. Because it hurt.

"Do you know what I'm saying, my love?"

"Other than I look older than I should, no," she pouted.

"As long as we're together. As long as our love thrives. I believe we'll live as long as we want. That *you* will live by my side...forever."

She frowned. "You're suggesting I have the same abilities as a vampire, but without the whole dead part and not having to feed on blood."

"Yes. I don't even think you need to drink my blood. I think you want it as much as I want yours because we're so connected."

Her expression said she was deep in thought. "When do you think the speed part of your abilities will hit me? Because I think that would be kind of cool."

He rolled her over, pressing his body into hers, swallowing her squeak of surprise. Like he always did.

"Never. That is my superpower. You can't have it."

She giggled until it turned into a low moan as he entered her once again.

Are you ready for forever, my love?

I was ready the moment I met you. I just didn't know it until now.

EPILOGUE

A week later

"Come in, come in."

Mona had a sweet smile on her face, but Donnie could tell it didn't reach her eyes. Hopefully, what they were about to tell her would change that.

They exchanged greetings with Mason and gathered in the living room. Donnie bowed his head at Peter when he entered the room. George wasn't around. Scatter and Bozo strolled in as well, taking a spot near Mona.

"I hear you two are leaving for a while. Be safe out there," Mason said. "If you need help, don't hesitate to call us."

"Of course. We appreciate that." Donnie gestured toward the furniture. "Why don't we have a seat."

He sat next to Stella on the couch, holding her hand. A part of him felt bereft when he wasn't touching her. He knew she felt the same. They'd been inseparable the last week. Stella had moved in with him.

"So? What did you two want to talk about?" Mona sat

next to Mason on the couch opposite them. Mason grabbed her hand as quickly as he'd grabbed Stella's.

Now that Donnie knew more, everything clicked into place. It made the closeness Mason had with Mona clearer.

They shared what he and Stella shared.

"First, before I tell you anything, can I hold your hands?" Stella asked. Donnie was forced to let hers go as she held out both of her hands.

Mona frowned but took her hands.

Stella closed her eyes, though didn't say anything. The room was silent for the longest time before Stella reopened her eyes and sat back, grabbing ahold of his hand once again. She squeezed it hard. Enough of an indication he knew what it meant. They'd decided together not to chat in their thoughts, not wanting to distract them from anything they were about to tell them.

Mason gripped Mona's hand once again, a slight fear in his eyes. He had nothing to fear. The news would be good news.

"You're starting to freak me out." Mona dug into her pocket and pulled out a piece of licorice, chewing on it vigorously. "Please tell me what's going on."

"Giselle did some research." Stella chuckled. "A lot of research. I think you're going to be happy with what she found. You're going to get the answers you've been seeking."

Relief hit Mona's face, but Mason still looked leery. No surprise there. Donnie would be wary in his shoes too until he heard everything.

"Have you ever figured out how Mason went from ghost to human? Or how your mom did the same with Bailey?" Stella asked.

Donnie was letting her lead this, so even though she wasn't jumping in with the news, he remained quiet. To see how she navigated everything. It would be a lot to take in.

"No. I don't understand any of it. Mason doesn't remember much about his past like Bailey does. And he remembers nothing about turning from a ghost to a human."

"Your mother was a very powerful witch," Stella said, as if they didn't already know that. "Your aunt was too, but she was nothing compared to your mother." Stella leaned closer. "Mona, your mother was a cosmic witch."

Mona flinched and Mason's brows popped up. "That can't be. No, it can't be."

"Giselle's research is spot on. It's true," Stella insisted.

"But Donnie and the boys..." Mona looked utterly confused.

"They can cloak their abilities, Mona," Donnie said. "Stella is proof of that. Your mother obviously had done the same, not even telling us her true powers. I don't know if she didn't trust us, or if she just never told anyone. I understand why she kept it to herself. I don't blame her. Mona, it makes sense. Only a witch so powerful could turn a ghost back into a living person."

Mona tore her gaze away from them and at Mason. "She saved you."

Mason caressed her cheek, a loving expression on his face. "I wish I could thank her for giving us a chance together. I love you, my sweet Mona."

Stella cleared her throat, bringing their attention back to them. "I don't think your aunt is one. Only your mother. It doesn't touch everyone in the family. I'm sure that created a lot of resentment and hatred toward your mother."

"She killed her," Mona whispered with the pain laced in each word. "Stole her powers."

Stella shook her head. "No, she would've killed you on the spot, Mona. Yes, I have no doubt she killed your mother, but she was unable to steal her powers. That's why she needed you. She wanted to take your powers. And you stopped her."

"How come I can't feel the evil rising in this house and everyone else can?"

That was a great question. Everyone could except her.

Stella sighed. "Your mother was trying to protect you. My mom did the same thing growing up. They both went about it in a different way. My mom made sure I had every knowledge of who I was and how to protect myself. Your mother thought you not knowing you were a witch would keep you safe." Stella paused, then forged on. "She bound your powers."

"I don't understand."

"When I held your hands in the beginning, I was seeing if she had done so. And she did. I can feel part of your powers are trapped. You have so much inside of you waiting to be unleashed." A wicked smile touched Stella's lips. "I can help unbind the rest of your powers. You will be unstoppable. Like me."

"Holy shit. There be two cosmic witches in our group," Peter exclaimed with awe.

Donnie forgot he was in the room with them. Then he grinned. "We'll be able to do so much good in the world with that much power on our side."

"Mason," Mona shrieked with giddiness, "I thought I was losing my mind when we handled that nasty warlock, but I wasn't. I heard you in my head. I know I did. Donnie and Stella have that connection ever since they professed their love for each other."

"But I love you, my sweet Mona. You love me. It should already—"

"No, Mason," Stella cut in. "Her powers are not fully available to her. Once I unbind them, you will have the same powerful connection with each other that I have with Donnie. Her mother was trying to protect her in the only way she knew how. It's the only reason I can think why she'd bind her powers. I don't know if she half-bound her powers, or if Mona is resisting the spell and that's why some of her powers work and some don't."

"The fireball came out of nowhere," Mason commented. "I'm leaning towards her mother fully bound them and Mona's resisting it." He caressed her cheek again. "Because you are a powerful, strong witch. Something I tell you all the time."

"I bet," Donnie added, "Mona started resisting the binding spell the moment she met you, Mason. Your love for each other, even though her powers were bound, broke part of the spell."

Mason nodded. "It makes sense. It is all starting to make so much sense."

"So I will unbind your powers, and I'll give you the spell to strip your aunt of her powers. You can take care of the rest."

Mona looked frightened by that prospect.

"You got this, Mona," Stella urged. "You don't need me. The one thing my mother taught me was to have confidence in my abilities. A fraction of doubt could mean life or death. So wipe away any kind of doubt you might have because you are stronger than that."

Mona stood up, determination in every point in her body. "Let's do this. I'm ready to get that bitch out of my house."

"Hear, hear," Peter cheered.

Stella rose to her feet as well. "I can't wait to see the amazing things you can do. That we can do together. I'm done hiding."

Donnie wrapped his arm around her, fearful of that prospect, but ready to stand by her side for whatever may come next.

"Yo, Jock! You have visitors."

Jock set down his spoon. His bowl of chili would have to wait. He grabbed ahold of the pole, sliding down until his feet hit the floor. Some guys liked taking the stairs when the alarm didn't go off, and some guys, like him, enjoyed the thrill of going from one level to the next in a second.

He walked past the firetrucks and outside the garage to see Donnie and Stella standing by their car. He'd heard they were leaving town. Max and Giselle were sticking around, putting down roots for the first time. He was happy for them.

Stella grabbed a hug, and Donnie shook his hand in greeting.

"What brings you two by?" Not that he didn't like the visit.

"We're leaving tonight. We want to get as far as we can before the sun rises." Stella made sense. Wouldn't want the sun to turn Donnie to dust.

He'd heard watching the psycho stalker vampire go up in dust was a sight to behold. He would've loved to witness it himself. Or any vampire for that matter. Except his friends. He'd never wish harm on them.

This whole new world he'd been introduced to was

fascinating as hell. His brother still balked at some things, wanting to pretend it wasn't real. But he didn't see it that way.

"Safe travels. When will you be back?"

Stella shared a look with Donnie. "We're not sure. There's quite a few vampires Donnie wants to find. Tell them it's safe to come out of hiding. That their master is dead."

Ah. So that's why they were leaving. He hadn't understood it when Breck told him Max and Giselle were staying but these two were leaving.

It meant they'd be back at some point. When their mission was complete.

Stella touched his arm. "We wanted to say thank you for everything you did. Meeting with Benny couldn't have been easy. I'm sorry we didn't tell you that sooner. We couldn't have solved this issue without you."

Did the dude scare him now? A little bit. Knowing he was a lycan and could change into a wolf in a moment's notice would scare anyone. What scared him the most was he had never thought someone he knew, someone he'd interacted with quite a bit, could be something more than just human.

Who else had he met that was something else?

That's what scared him. That's why he wanted to learn as much as he could. To be more prepared. To know who, or what, he was talking to.

"No problem. I'm glad I could help."

"If you need anything, let us know," Donnie said. "If Benny gives you problems, let us know that too."

Odd.

Had Donnie sensed his apprehension toward the guy?

Wouldn't surprise him. Donnie was in tune to a lot of things people didn't think he'd be aware of.

"I will. Don't worry about me. I can handle myself."

"I never doubted it." Donnie slapped him on the shoulder, chuckling. "Don't tell Holstrom, but you've got more guts than him."

Ah! He couldn't wait to rub it into his brother.

He grabbed another hug from Stella, shaking hands one more time with Donnie, and waved goodbye as they got into their car. He wished them safe travels.

And he also wished he wouldn't have to deal with Benny for a long, long time again. It had been more nerve-racking than he would ever admit. Sure, he'd played it off like nothing had affected him that night, but he'd been scared out of his mind. Obviously, his friends and the lycans hadn't noticed.

Why would they? He'd had a steady heartbeat. Because he walked into dangerous situations every day of his life. Being a firefighter was a tough job. Only the strong and brave could handle it.

He sat down to finish his chili, the spoon hitting his lips, the hot, savory flavor touching his tongue, when the alarm went off.

"Damn it!"

This time the spoon fell with a clank against the bowl.

He rushed with his fellow co-workers, donning his turnout gear and jumping on the truck. They raced through the night, lights and sirens blaring until they reached a house engulfed in flames.

Another day on the job tackling the flaming beast.

One truck started working on the front while another ventured to the back.

"There's someone inside." Ted jabbed a finger at the window on the third floor.

Sure enough, someone was plastered against the window, beating on it.

"Ladder!" Jock shouted, and was the first one up as soon as it was positioned to reach the window.

He climbed, motioning for the person to step back. He'd have to break the window to get them out. It had to be stuck or something, that the person hadn't opened it yet. Of course, he couldn't break it right away. The last thing he wanted was a back draft to occur. Getting this person out as safely as possible was his goal. The closer he got, the better he could inspect the situation.

The window was two more rungs away when the person disappeared. What the hell? Where did they go?

He saw it happening in slow motion. His mind triggered his mouth to move. Yet it didn't connect fast enough.

The chair the person grabbed hit the window with such force, it broke it with one hit.

The explosion hit instantaneously. The flames that burst outside should've killed him. But the force of the explosion threw him through the air away from the flames, saving him from that.

But then he was flying. And considering he wasn't a creature of any kind, it wasn't possible to do something like that without coming down with a crash. He had no time to prepare for the impact. Not that there was much he could do in that sense.

Instead of hitting the ground, crushing him like a bug, he hit the pool, causing a massive splash and knocking him out.

The last thing he remembered was the feeling of hitting a brick wall.

When he opened his eyes, his surroundings were not the same.

The room was cold and dark. The low beeping in the background, plus the junk hanging off his arm told him he was in the hospital.

Thank goodness for miracles. He hadn't died when he should be dead.

"Oh my god, Jock." Breck squeezed his hand, the relief plain and clear on his face. "You scared the living hell out of me. I never want to get that kind of call again. Got it?"

"Yeah," he croaked.

It hurt everywhere. His arm felt like it was in a brace as if he'd broken it. He didn't even have the courage to look at his body to see the full extent of damage.

"Lucy went to grab some food with Charly, but she's going to be damn glad to see you're awake. You were out for two days."

"Really?"

He didn't know why that surprised him. He'd flown three stories in the air, hit the water at too much speed, and that's not even taking into account the fire that scorched his skin as it burst out of the window.

"It'll grow back," Breck said when he reached up to touch his face. His eyebrows felt like they were gone. "But be careful touching your face. You did get burned in some places. Put your hands down."

"You're gonna be a nervous Nelly, aren't you? Getting on my case about everything while I recover."

"Yeah, well someone has to do it," Breck groaned.

"Does he not know how stubborn you can be? You're going to do what you always do."

Jock's head snapped to the left to a voice he hadn't heard in three years. His best friend, Carson, stood there as he remembered him. Cocky smile. The devil dancing in his eyes. The baggy shorts and black shirt with the hole near the bottom right hem.

"You think you're invisible and nothing can touch you. You were always cocky like that." He chuckled. "Like me." Carson nodded his head as if Jock had responded. He couldn't. Not yet. The words were stuck in his throat. "You know what's funny. You died. Like I did. Drowning. You had to follow in my footsteps."

What. The. Hell. Was. Going. On?

Jock looked away from him to his brother, grabbing his hand in a death drip. "Did I die, Breck? Am I dead?"

Breck stood up, shaking his head. "You're alive. You're fine." His brother squeezed his hand. "You might've been dead for a minute or two. They pulled you out of the pool, but you weren't breathing. That's why I'm telling you not to scare me like that again. I could've lost you."

Holy shit!

"Yeah, dude, I'm a ghost and you're stuck with me. We're going to have so much fun together. Just like old times."

———

Do you want to find out how Kade & Bailey met? Check out Third Time's the Charm!

FOR KADE & BAILEY'S STORY, CHECK OUT
THIRD TIME'S THE CHARM
A HAUNTING LOVE NOVEL, #1

He's not running this time...

Kade thought nothing could be worse than when his wife died in a car accident—especially because he'd been behind the wheel. To forget the pain, he moved on. Maybe too quickly. Now he's the prime suspect in the death of his second wife. But they have nothing on him because he didn't kill her.

Buying a house that needs more repairs than it's worth seems like a good escape. When he meets Bailey, despite everything telling him to look away, guard his heart, he can't help but fall under her charm. There's just one problem. She's a ghost. There can't be any harm in loving a ghost, right? Nothing can hurt her, not even him. Except there's another presence in the house. One that terrifies her.

Between contending with a pesky detective determined to peg him for murder, a ghost he's falling in love with, and the mysterious accidents that keep happening to him at work, Kade fears he might be joining Bailey on the other side sooner rather than later.

FOR BRECK & CHARLY'S STORY, CHECK OUT
THIRTEEN DAYS GONE
A HAUNTING LOVE NOVEL, #2

A ticking clock. A vision of her own demise.

Psychic Charly Yarrow's curse is about to turn deadly. Ever since she was young, her visions of past and future have haunted her—but never has she foreseen her last day on earth. In thirteen days, the killer will come for her.

Charly's only lifeline is stern Detective Breck Holstrom, though at first he doubts her unique abilities...until the evidence proves uncanny. Determined, he vows to unravel the cryptic clues in her vision to stop her fate.

Drawn together in a race against time with a serial killer's twisted game, Breck battles his skepticism while fighting an undeniable attraction. Charly wants to trust him to help her cheat death and solve the mystery shrouding her murder. But she knows better—her visions always come true. As the encroaching deadline creeps closer, Charly must risk trusting Breck with her life...and her heart.

Don't miss this nail-biting paranormal romantic suspense guaranteed to keep you guessing until the final chapter.

LET'S GET SPOOKY. BUT NOT TOO SPOOKY! JOIN MONA & MASON IN THE PARANORMAL CHRONICLES, VOLUME 1 FULL OF MYSTERY, HUMOR, A LITTLE BIT OF CREEPINESS, AND A BLACK CAT WITH ATTITUDE!

The Doll House

He's a ghost. She's not afraid.

Buying a house without seeing it first might not have been the best plan when Mona decided to run away from her problems. Doors slamming without notice, a dumb cat that won't leave her alone, and a handsome man who only appears when he touches her with a touch so cold, it numbs her to the bone. Yet she never wants him to let go. Life just got more complicated, but she's up for the challenge of solving how Mason became a ghost and helping him to move on, follow the light...or whatever a ghost is supposed to do. Only problem with that, the house has another plan. If she's not careful she could be soon joining Mason on his side.

Witch Way to Turn

A journal full of secrets...

Mona is determined to uncover the truth her mother kept from her, starting with meeting an aunt she never knew she had. But before her aunt will divulge any answers, she needs help vanquishing some nasty vampires. Mission accepted. Not that Mona knows how to kill a vampire, but it can't be too hard, right? A stake to the chest, chop the head off, sprinkle a little garlic and holy water. One of those things should do the trick. But there's more going on than meets the eye. Can she trust the woman she just met but shares blood with? In a world filled with more questions than she has answers, it's hard to know. But one thing Mona does know: she's not about to let anyone tell her what to do or hurt the man she loves.

A Simple Halloween

Nothing is ever what it seems...

It's that time of the year, and Mona gets to have fun with the spooktacular holiday, being a witch and all. She's embraced who she is, so why not enjoy it. A little trouble with some neighborhood teenage bullies gives her the perfect opportunity to stretch her witchy fingers. With some practice, those boys will learn not to pick on her anymore. But all of her devious plans at revenge come to a screeching halt when one of them knocks on her door asking for help finding his cat. Well, asking Mason, who accepts. Fine. They'll help the miscreant, but it doesn't mean she's happy about it. How hard can it be for a witch, former ghost, and some vampires to find a missing cat? Not hard at all because she has a few tricks—and treats—up her sleeve.

ABOUT THE AUTHOR

I'm a *USA Today* Bestselling Author that loves to write contemporary romance and romantic suspense novels, although I am partial to romantic suspense. I even dabble in paranormal. Honestly, I love anything that has to do with romance. As long as there's a happy ending, I'm a happy camper. And insta-love...yes, please! I love baseball (Go Twins!) and creating awesome crafts. I graduated with a Bachelor's Degree in Criminal Justice, working in that field for several years before I became a stay-at-home mom. I have a few more amazing stories in the works. If you would like to learn more about me and my books, head to my website by scanning the QR code. Thanks for reading!

Scan me

www.ingramcontent.com/pod-product-compliance
Lightning Source LLC
Chambersburg PA
CBHW021957010726
47494CB00003B/774